As she stood in front of the mirror fixing her hair, the doorbell rang. With one last swipe of the brush, she rushed to the door. Assuming what she hoped was a sexy pose, she threw the door open and squealed in embarrassment when she spied Taylor leaning against the doorjamb.

Within a matter of nanoseconds, she saw a series of emotions reflected in Taylor's face and eyes—surprise, amusement, a slight tinge of embarrassment—but the strongest was the momentary flash of lust. It was so strong that Sara took a step back.

"Payback is a bitch," Taylor said, as she moved away from the doorjamb. "Here, I brought this as a peace offering, but my timing seems to be off a tad." She held out a bottle of Shiraz, Sara's favorite wine.

Sara realized she was clutching the front of the low-cut dress. She struggled to think of something witty to say that would relieve the tension. Nothing came to her. When had talking to Taylor become so difficult? She realized Taylor was still holding the bottle of wine. Releasing the hold on her dress, she reached for it. As she did, she saw Taylor's eyes stray to where her hand had been holding the thin material together. In almost dream-like slowness, she watched Taylor's hand float up and gently smooth the silky fabric.

"You wrinkled the front." Taylor's voice sounded thick and far away. Her hand felt hot against Sara's chest. A wave of desire stronger than any she had ever experienced burned through her. She felt her body sway forward as Taylor's strong hand dropped to Sara's waist.

Visit

Bella Books

at

BellaBooks.com

or call our toll-free number

1-800-729-4992

Passionate Kisses

Megan Carter

Bella
BOOKS
2006

Bella Books, Inc.
P.O. Box 10543
Tallahassee, FL 32302

Printed in the United States of America on acid-free paper
First Edition

Editor: Christi Cassidy
Cover designer: Linda Callaghan

ISBN 1-59493-051-1

Martha
My sunshine

Acknowledgments

Martha—Thanks for keeping my head above water. You were beside me every step of the way. Thanks to Gaye Carleton, president of Mantra, Empowered Public Relations, for all her help with the details of dealing with the media. I would also like to thank Christi Cassidy for all her help and suggestions. She never fails to make the manuscript better.

About the Author

Megan Carter lives in Texas. She enjoys hanging out with friends at the coast and taking long, romantic road trips with her partner. Megan is the author of *On the Wings of Love* and *When Love Finds a Home*.

You may e-mail the author at mcarterbooks@aol.com.

Chapter One

Sara Stockton held her breath and slowly counted to ten. No one was going to ruin her day. She turned her attention to the beautifully landscaped yard with stone paths leading to a variety of sitting areas. The overall effect was too formal for Sara's personal taste, but it was pleasant to look at. It was a shame it was only for show. Her father paid a small fortune each month having the work done, and yet the only time they used the area was when they hosted a spring or fall gathering. She had been the one who insisted they sit out here this afternoon.

The back-to-back storm fronts pelting the San Antonio area over the past several days had finally moved on, allowing the early April day to arrive on a dazzling sunrise, soft balmy breezes and a brilliant robin's-egg blue sky. After an unusually long, cold and wet winter, the warmth of the afternoon was a welcome respite.

The mountain laurel in the neighbor's yard was in full bloom, filling the air with its wonderful perfumed scent. Sara inhaled deeply before slowly releasing her breath and studying the two people who were awaiting her response.

Her mother, Eloise, was immaculately groomed in a pair of white twill Capri pants and a gauzy, multi-colored orange floral crinkle shirt worn over an orange shell. Her carefully pedicured feet were showcased in delicate white sandals that looked like they were better suited for lounging than walking. At her throat lay a sterling silver and yellow gold box chain. Eloise held a degree in business administration, which she put to good use in running a socially active household for her husband.

The man, James Edwards, was Sara's fiancé. In his dark gray linen herringbone suit and silk tie of navy blue with a thin red pin-stripe and pristine white shirt, he looked as elegant as her mother did.

Sara glanced down at her own simple sage green slacks, white cotton shirt and sensible brown loafers and knew she was fighting a losing battle. Eloise and James had just informed her that another thirty names needed to be added to the already out-landishly long list of invitees. "I thought we agreed that no more names were going to be added," Sara said, as calmly as she could.

"That was before the Reverend Hendricks announced his endorsement of James's campaign," Eloise replied.

Sara looked at James. "Is this ever going to stop? The wedding is only two months away. We have to stop changing things."

He shrugged and buried his hands in his pockets. "I'm sorry. I know we talked about it, but these people could really help my campaign."

Sara tried not to show her impatience. James was running for the city council and with the elections less than a month away, the campaign consumed his every waking moment. "We agreed we were going to have a small wedding and it's already grown to over six hundred names." Her voice grew shrill. She stopped and swallowed. "James, I really wanted a small wedding."

"It's too late for that," her mother argued. "The church and the hall have been reserved. The invitations have been ordered and then there's the caterer and all those other things." She fanned her face with small, perfectly manicured hands. "I ordered plenty of extra invitations so don't try that excuse either."

"It isn't too late." Sara looked at the man she had known since preschool. He kept glancing away. "There's still plenty of time to go back to our original plan." She folded her arms across her stomach in defeat. "All right. I know it's too late for a small wedding, but can we at least stop making it larger?"

Her mother waved away her complaints before sipping her mint tea. "Sara, you can't continue with your hermit ways. James is going to be a politician. It's time you started thinking of others."

"Mother, this is *our* wedding we're talking about here. It's not a party for James's campaign or your social event of the year. I never wanted a large wedding. You both know how much I hate extravagant affairs. Besides, by the time the wedding occurs the election will be over." She turned to James. "Promise me that this is the last of the names. We've added seventy names since we booked the hall."

James smiled and nodded. "No more," he promised.

She held out her hand with the little finger extended. "Pinky swear."

He wrapped his pinky around hers in their old childhood sacred promise. "I pinky swear."

Sara hated elaborate gatherings and all of her life she had been surrounded by them. Her father, Lawrence Stockton, was a prominent lawyer in San Antonio. He specialized in corporate law and over the years, his name became well-known throughout the state, particularly around Austin, the state's capital. He had served on numerous political committees as well as several state-appointed boards. Many of Sara's childhood memories were of her parents' stately stone Alamo Heights home being overrun by hoards of workers preparing for one of Eloise's elaborate parties attended by elegantly dressed men and women. As children, "the Three Musketeers," as her father had named them—Sara, James, and their friend Taylor—would sit at the top of the massive staircase and gaze down at some of the most powerful people in Texas.

"I really didn't want a large wedding," she reiterated.

"You're a grown woman," her mother replied, in the stiff manner that told Sara her mind was made up. "It's time you began acting like it. Your husband's political future is more important than your little girl dreams. There's more to public office than just being elected."

Sara felt the sudden urge to stomp her foot and scream at the top of her lungs, but she realized it would only validate her mother's accusations. Her resolve started to slip as it always did whenever she was faced with adversity. Maybe they were right. Perhaps she was being selfish. "I'll try to stop whining," she replied, before turning to James. "Not one more name is going to be added to that list. I don't care if both of our grandmothers rise from the dead. No one else is invited to this wedding."

He smiled and nodded. "I promise." He stood suddenly. "I have to get back to the office." He leaned over and gave Sara a chaste peck on the cheek.

Sara watched him walk away. It sometimes still caught her by surprise that she and James were engaged. As his slim, well-toned body disappeared into the house, she experienced a moment of longing, not for James, but for the passion their relationship was missing. They were lovers and had been since right after they both left San Antonio for college. That separation had been hard for all of the Musketeers. At her father's insistence, Sara attended his alma mater, Yale, where she studied historic preservation and architecture. James attended UT-Austin before going on to Harvard for his law degree. Only Taylor stayed in San Antonio and attended Trinity University.

After graduating, they all eventually returned to the River City and again they became the Three Musketeers. Sara worked as a senior planner on the Historic Preservation and Design Staff for the City of San Antonio. James was with the law firm of White, White and Thurmont. If he was elected to the city council he would probably be made a partner in the firm. Taylor worked as a physical therapist, specializing in sports injuries. She and two other women had formed a partnership and opened a private office the

4

previous year. Taylor had been so busy with the new business that they had seen little of her recently.

Sara made a mental note to call Taylor. Maybe they could all get together for dinner later in the week. She smiled slightly. Taylor was the rebel of the group. She was a bundle of energy, always on the go. During their freshman year of high school, Taylor surprised her parents and most of the school by announcing she was a lesbian. Fearful of the backlash her announcement would cause, Sara and James rallied around her, ready to give her their full support, but Taylor was so well-liked by her teachers and the other students that the news barely made a ripple. It was during this time that James suddenly began to show a different sort of interest in Sara. They dated throughout high school. The sexual aspect of the relationship never moved beyond a couple of embarrassing attempts at necking in the backseat of James's Dodge Neon, until Sara was preparing to leave for college. They chose a night when James's parents were out of town. Sara told her folks she was spending the night with Taylor, which was such a common enough occurrence they never questioned it. Even now, Sara still blushed when she recalled the awkward fiasco of James being too nervous to perform and her having to pretend she enjoyed his fumbling.

Since then they had grown a little more comfortable with lovemaking. He would occasionally spend the night at her apartment. They had started talking about moving in together. Those plans were abandoned when he decided to run for city council. The decision had been a relief to Sara. She loved her small apartment and felt a sense of sadness in leaving it. Of course, she was certain she would grow to love the wonderful Victorian that James lived in. She loved older homes with their less-than-perfect hardwood floors and tall graceful ceilings, but still she suspected she would miss her apartment.

"Sara, you really must start thinking more of others." Her mother's voice pulled her back.

"I think I'm being reasonable," Sara argued. "I agreed to a

church wedding when I would have been much happier with a small, private ceremony."

Her mother sighed loudly. "I simply do not understand why you are so reserved. Your father is outgoing and I certainly have no problem relating to people."

"Maybe there was a mix-up at the hospital and I'm really the child of some gypsy family."

Eloise laughed suddenly as she reached over and squeezed Sara's hand. "You can't get off that easy. You look just like your father." She leaned back and picked up her tea. "I'm sorry things aren't turning out exactly as you planned, but you do need to think about James. Sometimes, little things can make such a difference in a relationship."

Sara wanted to say that she didn't consider six hundred strangers attending her wedding a little matter but held her tongue. Her mother honestly thought she was helping them. Eloise Ricker Stockton had devoted her life to helping her husband and only child. Even though there were times when she could drive Sara crazy, she still loved her mother. In her heart, she knew Eloise only wanted the best for her. "Don't you ever want to do something just for yourself?"

Eloise looked up, surprised. "What do you mean? I do things for myself everyday."

"When was the last time you did something for yourself?" Sara asked.

"Just this morning. I went to see Felix and had a complete facial and manicure."

Sara suppressed her sigh. Sometimes she felt as though she and her mother were from two different worlds. Maybe she did look at things wrong. After all, what was so horribly wrong with a large wedding if it made James and her parents happy? It would all soon be over and she could get back to her quiet, settled life.

Chapter Two

When Sara arrived at her apartment, Mr. Tibbs, her three-year-old mammoth black and white cat, was waiting for her just inside the doorway. His condemning glare served as a reminder that she was late in providing his evening treat and cleaning his litter box.

"I'm not that late," she replied.

In response, he flicked a tattered ear.

"All right, I'm going." She headed to the bathroom where the box sat in the corner.

Sara had found the severely mauled kitten beside her apartment complex. It appeared to have been attacked by a dog. She rushed it to the vet's office and waited for hours while the kitten was in surgery. At the end of the day, the vet, an older woman with kind blue eyes, warned her that there wasn't much chance he would survive. Sara wouldn't give up. She returned each afternoon after work to sit and talk to the kitten. When he was finally well enough to leave the vet's, she took him home and catered to his every whim. The only problem was that the cat seemed to hate her. James insisted it was because she hadn't yet named him. So, as soon as the kitten was fully recuperated, Sara invited James and Taylor over to help her select the perfect name. After a wonderful meal of salmon, for both human and feline guests, the naming party grew serious. Sara refused to consider any of the normal cutesy cat names. She insisted it be regal and dignified. As the group settled down on the floor to play with the guest of honor, they soon discovered that it wasn't just Sara the kitten had issues with. Whenever they tried to pick him up or cuddle him, the kitten didn't hesitate to show his displeasure with a sharp hiss or a sudden swat of his paw. James declared the cat to be an independent soul. That was when Taylor came up with the name, Mr. Tibbs. She pointed out that the kitten showed the same prickly spirit as the assertive homicide detective played by Sidney Poitier in Norman Jewison's Oscar-winning film, *In the Heat of the Night*. And so, the cat was named.

As time went by, a mutual peace gradually developed between owner and pet. She fed him and kept his litter box clean and he became ruler of the household.

After cleaning the litter box, Sara emptied a small package of salmon treats into his bowl. The vet warned her to stop feeding him so much, but these small treats were the only way she could get back into his good graces.

She stood in the doorway watching him slowly eat the contents of the bowl. He never seemed to get in a hurry for anything. "You are so spoiled," she said, as he delicately licked his lips. She couldn't resist running her hand down his shiny back before rushing away. Even with her back to him, she could almost feel his glare of disapproval. "This is ridiculous," she said, as she reached for the phone to call Taylor. It had been a while since they had spent any time together and she wanted to see if she was available for dinner tomorrow night. James had a standing Friday night poker game. "My life is being ruled by a cat."

Taylor answered on the third ring. "I was just getting ready to call you," she said when Sara spoke.

Sara wasn't surprised. They often seemed to have the same ideas simultaneously.

"What's up?" Sara asked.

"I was just wondering how the wedding plans are progressing. Is the wedding party still a measly twelve people or has Eloise expanded that again?"

Originally, Taylor had been her only attendant and James's cousin was to be his best man. Eloise had nagged until there was an even dozen now.

"I haven't heard from you or James for a while. I guess you've been too busy." Taylor's tone was teasing, suggestive.

"Nothing's going on."

"I'm so sorry," Taylor said, and laughed.

"Stop it."

"You sound grumpy."

"I'm not grumpy."

"Umm, denial. That's a sure sign something is wrong."

"James is adding thirty more names to the invitation list."

Taylor waited.

"I don't want a big wedding," Sara continued. "I've tried to get over it, but whenever I think about all those people, I start to panic."

"Why?"

"Because I don't know them. This is a private matter. I don't want to share it with strangers." Sara could hear a muffled tapping and knew Taylor was drumming her fingers. The woman was never still.

"That's understandable. What does James say?"

"He says he needs to suck up to these people for his campaign."

Taylor made a buzzing sound as if Sara had answered the question incorrectly. "James would never utter the words *suck up*, so what did he really say?"

"He said—oh, damn, I don't know what he said exactly, but he keeps adding people to the list, and of course, Mom agrees with him."

"You know it's only going to get more extravagant, so you might as well prepare yourself."

"What do you mean?"

"If James wins the election, he'll be a public figure. I'm sure Eloise will make certain that all the local television stations and the newspaper will be there to cover the event. She's going to make this an *extravaganza*." She drew out the word in a smoky Marlene Dietrich voice.

"No, she won't," Sara said with a touch of panic. "She knows I want it simple."

"Sure, that's why there's now over six hundred people invited. I know Eloise and the word *small* is not in her social vocabulary."

"Then I'll just have to set my foot down and insist."

Taylor chuckled. "Sara, please. You can't even control your cat."

Sara glanced over in time to see Mr. Tibbs flick his tail at her as he strode out of the room.

Taylor continued talking. "I'll bet you twenty bucks that if James wins, Eloise starts contacting the media as soon as the elections are over." They had always been competitive and wagers between them were common. It was something that James found irritating.

"I'll take that bet," Sara said, trying to sound more confident than she felt.

"No. Forget it. That's too easy. I prefer a challenge," Taylor said, and quickly changed the subject. "I've been seeing someone. We spent the weekend in a wonderful little cottage on Lake Travis."

From the dreamy sound of Taylor's voice as she described the romantic weekend, Sara knew the woman was special. She pushed away the pinprick of jealousy and told herself that her relationship with James would become more romantic once they were married. "Who is she and why am I just now hearing about her?"

"Her name is Debbie Greene. She's a rep for one of the clinic's suppliers. We've been dating for about two months. I haven't mentioned her because . . ." She hesitated. "Well, you know my track record with relationships isn't very good. I didn't want to mention another one until I was sure."

"You sound like it's pretty serious."

"I think it is."

"What happened to your golden rule about not dating anyone you work with?" Sara asked.

Taylor faltered slightly before answering. "We don't exactly work together. I don't have anything to do with ordering supplies for the clinic, so we don't have any contact professionally."

"But you met her at the clinic."

"No, I didn't. I mean, I had seen her and been introduced to her, but we'd never really talked. We actually met at Ta Molly's, that Mexican restaurant down the street from the clinic. She came in while I was eating and stopped by to say hello. I asked her to join me. We started talking and before we realized it, we'd been sitting there for almost three hours."

"Does she live here in San Antonio?"

"No," Taylor replied, with a touch of sadness in her voice. "She lives in Houston. We've been taking turns flying back and forth."

Sara suddenly felt better. "That's too bad. Long-distance relationships are hard to maintain." When Taylor didn't answer right away, she felt guilty for her selfishness. Why shouldn't Taylor find someone? "But you're right, Houston isn't far from here. It's not like it's really a long-distance relationship."

"Yeah." Taylor seemed to cheer up some. "Maybe we can all go to dinner or something sometime when she's in town. I really want you guys to meet her."

It took Sara a moment to respond. If Taylor wanted them to meet this woman, she must truly be special to her. The only woman she had ever introduced them to was Wanda, and they had lived together for a couple of years. "That would be great. I know James would love to see you and meet Debbie."

11

"Does it ever seem strange to you, that you and James are getting married?" Taylor asked suddenly.

"Strange how?"

"I don't know. It's just that we were all so close and I always thought—" She stopped.

"What?"

"Oh, it's nothing. I guess I'm a little jealous that it isn't me, that's all."

"Jealous. Why would you be jealous? You never showed any interest in James."

Taylor gave a shallow laugh. Sara recognized the laugh as Taylor's attempt to hide something. Before she could pursue it, Taylor cut in. "Hey, Sara, I've got to go. Debbie is trying to dial in. I'll talk to you later."

Sara sat holding the phone for several moments. It wasn't like Taylor to hang up so abruptly. Sometimes their phone conversations could go on for hours. Sara hadn't even had a chance to invite her to dinner. After hanging up, she made herself a sandwich and ate it in front of the television. She tried to concentrate on the gardening show, but her mind kept drifting back to Taylor and the new woman in her life. Would she be anything like Wanda, who was tall and athletic? Taylor had been devastated when that relationship ended. In the two years since the split-up, she rarely mentioned Wanda. Sara wasn't completely sure why it had ended. Since then Taylor occasionally dated other women, but to Sara's knowledge, none of them had lasted more than a few weeks.

Her thoughts turned to Taylor's admission that she was jealous of her impending marriage to James. Why would Taylor be jealous of her marrying James? Maybe she'd had a crush on James, at some point when they were much younger. That didn't explain why she would be jealous now. Taylor was a lesbian. She wasn't interested in men. When the answer finally came, it stopped her cold. She struggled to recall exactly what Taylor had said. As she replayed the conversation, she realized that James had never been mentioned. Did that mean that Taylor was jealous of him? *No.* She pushed the thought away. Taylor had never shown any interest in her, not in that way. Maybe she was afraid the marriage would eventually push her out. There was no way that would never happen. She and James both cared too much for Taylor to lose her friendship. True, they hadn't been seeing her as often as they would like, but there were several reasons besides the wedding. Most of James's time was consumed with the campaign and would be until after the elections that were scheduled for the first weekend in May. If he won the election, things would only grow more hectic. The city charter dictated that the newly elected council members take office on the first day of June, which was three days before their wedding date. Sara had wanted to postpone the wedding until October, but James was adamant that the date not change. The only thing he would agree to changing was to postpone their honeymoon, since they were both so busy. She had been working longer hours than normal in preparing a presentation for the proposed restoration work on the old Stinson School building.

The possibility that Taylor could have a crush on her left her with a strange feeling that she was unable to identify. It was an odd mixture of happiness and fear. When she couldn't immediately place it into a familiar category, she pushed it away. She was obviously reading much more into Taylor's statement than was intended.

The show she had been trying to watch went off and another one started. Rather than wasting time pretending to watch it, Sara turned the television off and began to straighten up the apartment. She ended up vacuuming the living room and bedrooms and then mopped the kitchen floor. By the time she fell into bed, she was too exhausted to do anything but sleep.

Chapter Three

The following afternoon Sara was at her desk preparing her recommendations for the restoration of the roof of the Peter Jolly home. The city had recently purchased the historic home to prevent it from being demolished. She was so engrossed in the project that when her phone rang she let her assistant, Gracie, answer it.

Gracie stuck her curly head through the doorway. "It's James."

Sara slowly returned from a world of precise measurements and tedious details. "Thanks," she said, as she reached for the phone. James seldom called her at work.

"I have to fly to Dallas tonight to see a client," he announced, when she answered.

"When will you be back?"

"Not until late Sunday evening. I've been helping this company with a merger. An agreement has finally been reached. They've invited me to stay over for some golfing."

A small wave of relief ran through Sara. She was usually free on

Friday night because of his poker game, but they always spent Saturday evening either with her parents or with his, and it was usually his. She liked Mr. and Mrs. Edwards, but unlike James with his outgoing personality, they were withdrawn and preferred watching television to talking.

"I'll call you when I get back on Sunday," James assured her.

"All right. Have a safe trip." As she hung up the phone, she realized they never ended their calls with any of the silly little declarations of love that she'd heard other couples use. Her dad still kissed her mother good-bye and told her he loved her each morning before leaving for the office. "Don't start making comparisons," she warned herself. James was a good, kind man. He would make a great husband. He might never spew romantic platitudes, but he would always be steady and dependable. So what if he wasn't the greatest lover or the most romantic? They already shared the most important things in a relationship—friendship and trust. Sex wasn't all it was cracked up to be anyway, she decided.

Sometimes she found herself wondering if maybe there should be more. James was the only person she had ever dated—well, unless she was to count Shawn Davidson, back in the seventh grade. For reasons she couldn't begin to fathom now, she had agreed to go with him to a pool party for Taylor's twelfth birthday. He had followed her into the house and trapped her against the hallway wall. He was trying to show her his newest talent—french kissing. Her face still burned when she remembered the humiliating result—she hurled all over the front of his shirt. When Shawn started screaming at her, Taylor and James suddenly appeared. After threatening his life if he ever told anyone, Taylor sent him home before taking Sara upstairs to her room and running a bath. Sara spent so much time at the Jenkins's household that a large portion of her wardrobe was already there. By the time she stepped out of the bath wearing Taylor's robe, the hallway had been cleaned and fresh clothes were laid out for her. They never mentioned the incident, and apparently neither had Shawn Davidson.

As the afternoon wore on, Sara found herself thinking more

and more of Taylor. She finally called her office, but Taylor had already left the clinic for the day. Sara called her house and left a message that she would call later to see if Taylor was interested in going out to dinner. With that taken care of, she went back to work on the roof project and worked until she had a preliminary recommendation. She would have to wait until Monday to run it past her boss, but she felt good about the work she had accomplished.

It wasn't until she stepped into the empty outer office that she realized how late it had gotten. The large black and white clock on the outer office wall indicated it was almost seven. She had been so engrossed in working that she had failed to hear the others leaving. She smiled as she walked back to her office. Gracie hadn't told her good-bye, which meant she had probably slipped out early. These kids now—she stopped herself and wondered when she had started thinking of herself as being older. She was only twenty-eight, but sometimes she felt so much older than most of the interns and assistants who worked for her. In truth, Gracie was actually a few months older than she was. Sara gathered up her belongings and a folder containing details on the Main Street Project. Rosa Saenz, the Historic Preservation Officer and Sara's immediate supervisor, had asked her to review the project and give the staff a briefing at the weekly Tuesday morning huddle. Sara planned to read the information over the weekend. As she headed for the door, she realized Taylor hadn't called back, but that wasn't unusual for her. If you told her you'd call back later, she'd wait for you to call.

As Sara drove through downtown traffic, she decided to go directly to Taylor's house, since Taylor lived closer to downtown than Sara did. The three of them often appeared on one or the other's doorstep without notice. If Taylor wasn't home or had other plans, Sara would simply go on home.

Taylor lived in the area known locally as Baja King William. Sara's apartment was much farther out toward Huebner. She pulled her gray Ford Ranger into the driveway and parked. By jumping up, she could see the roof of Taylor's red Jeep Liberty through the garage windows. She hurried up the walkway. Maybe they could go to a movie after dinner. She punched the doorbell playfully. When Taylor didn't answer right away, she did what they always did to each other and held the bell down. It occurred to her that they were probably getting too old to keep doing this, but for now, it was fun. She heard Taylor's steps approaching. When the door swung open, Sara started to step inside but stopped when she saw that Taylor was wearing her robe.

"Didn't you get my message?" Sara asked.

Taylor looked toward her phone and hesitated. "Uh, no. I didn't check my messages when I got home."

"I called to see if you wanted to go to dinner." Before Sara could finish, she heard a noise from deeper inside the house. She stopped and cringed. "You've got company. I'm so sorry."

Taylor shrugged and blushed. "Debbie decided to fly in this afternoon."

"Oh. Well, I just stopped by on my way home. Since, you know, you're on my way home and all, I didn't call." She felt like a fool. She should have waited for Taylor to call her back, but she had never needed to before. Taylor was nearly always available to go out on a moment's notice. They stood for another long, awkward moment.

"I would introduce you, but—"

Visions of a strange woman appearing in a bathrobe to stand beside Taylor snapped Sara out of her stupor. "No. Really, it's all right. Call me when . . . um . . . when you're free." She turned and rushed back to her truck. She hadn't been this embarrassed since the Shawn Davidson fiasco. As she drove away, she realized she was crying. She wiped the tears from her eyes, feeling like a fool. Why had she driven over to Taylor's without calling? They were too old to be acting like kids. What would Debbie think about her just showing up like that? Actually, she didn't really care what Debbie thought, but she didn't want Taylor to be angry with her. Taylor wasn't angry, she reminded herself. *She was embarrassed.* Sara reached for her cell phone to call James, but then remembered he was with a client. A deep sense of loneliness settled over her. She wasn't accustomed to being without both James and Taylor at the same time. Knowing she was being silly, she forced herself to take a deep breath. She was a grown woman; surely, she could get through a weekend without someone there holding her hand.

By the time she made her way back to the interstate, she had developed a plan for the weekend. It began with her stopping at the video store to rent a couple of movies she had been wanting to watch. From there, she went to her favorite Mexican restaurant and ordered takeout. As soon as she got home, she gave Mr. Tibbs his evening snack and settled down with her puffy tacos in front of the television. After watching one of the movies, she looked through the newspaper, noticed the new exhibit at the Witte Museum that she wanted to see and made plans to go the following morning. She tidied up her mess before returning to the living room. Even though it was after midnight, she was still wide awake. She thought about trying to call James again, but he was probably already asleep. She decided to watch the second movie instead.

Chapter Four

By Sunday afternoon, Sara's apartment and truck was spotless. Mr. Tibbs was so out of sorts with all of the activity that he had hidden himself beneath the bed in the back bedroom. Even the offering of his favorite salmon treats wouldn't lure him out. It was after six when Sara's phone finally rang. She grabbed it up, knowing it would be James.

"I hope you aren't mad at me," Taylor said.

Sara faltered a moment at the sound of Taylor's voice. "Why would I be mad at you? If anyone should be upset, it's you. I shouldn't have assumed you'd be alone." She felt a flush run up her neck as she recalled Taylor standing in the doorway in her robe. It had been blatantly obvious what she had interrupted.

"Hey, in your shoes I would have done the same thing. We've never been much for social protocol."

"Maybe we should change that. I mean, we're grown now. Maybe it's time we started acting like we are."

"No, thank you. I'm not ready to grow up that much yet. I like being able to barge in on you and James any time I want," Taylor replied.

"You've never barged in on us."

"That's because with James there's never anything to interrupt."

Sara gasped. "Taylor Jenkins, I don't believe you said that about my future husband."

"Oh, please. I've known James since he was in preschool. I was the one who explained wet dreams to him."

Sara giggled but felt she should defend him. "Well, we weren't all as worldly as you were."

"I'm glad you aren't upset with me," Taylor said, catching Sara off-guard with the sudden change in conversation.

"Of course I'm not angry with you. I was embarrassed for inter-rupting your . . . um."

"Wild sex."

Sara rolled her eyes. "You always did exaggerate."

"Who's exaggerating? I'm so sore I can barely get out of bed."

"Taylor!"

"What? I'm only telling you the truth. She's a wild woman."

A series of clicks saved Sara from having to respond. "That's probably James trying to call in. I'll talk to you later."

"See, you can't wait to hear his voice. You two probably have kinky telephone sex—"

Sara pushed the flash button before Taylor could finish. She smiled when James's voice came through the receiver. She couldn't imagine him having telephone sex. She tried to listen as he told her all about his weekend, but her mind kept drifting to other things. "Are you coming over?" she asked when he finally stopped talking.

"No. I'm exhausted and I know you like to go in early on Mondays. Let's have dinner tomorrow night and you can tell me how your new project is going." He said good night, but she stopped him before he could hang up.

"James, have you ever had telephone sex?" The silence that fol-lowed let her know he was as surprised by her question as she was in asking it.

He cleared his throat. "No. I can't say that I have."

"Did you ever want to?"

Another silence followed. "Sara, why are you asking me these questions? Do you need . . . I mean, I know it has been a while. Should I come over?"

"Damn, James, you sound like I'm looking for stud service." She heard his sharp intake of breath. "I'm sorry. I'm just a little cranky. I'll see you tomorrow."

He stayed on the phone for a moment longer. "I apologize for being away all weekend. I know everything has been hectic lately with the campaign and all, but it'll get better soon."

Sara sat staring at the phone for several minutes after he hung up. How did he expect things to get better? If he was elected, he would be even busier. If he wasn't elected, he would start planning his next campaign. She knew their sex life was lacking, but with no prior experience to use as a gauge, she didn't know if it was her or him that was the problem. Maybe it was both of them, she decided. She considered asking her mother, but this wasn't something she could talk to her about. She smiled at the thought of approaching Eloise with questions about her sex life. She went to take a shower.

Her parents were in their early fifties and both were in excellent health. There was no reason why they shouldn't still have an active sex life. She wrinkled her nose at the thought and decided she would wait and talk to Taylor about it. As she stepped into the shower, she found herself wondering if Taylor and Debbie indulged in telephone sex. What exactly did phone sex involve? The possibilities that came to mind caused an odd tingling to begin deep in her stomach. She blamed it on the tacos she had eaten for dinner and adjusted the water temperature to a cooler setting.

When James called the following evening and suggested he bring over takeout, she knew he planned to spend the night. He never suggested they cook on those nights. She found herself feeling slightly angry that he had automatically assumed he could spend the night. Since barging in on Taylor, she had spent a lot of time thinking about ways to spice up her nights with James. Any change would have to be initiated by her. She began by setting the table with her grandmother's china and putting out several candles. After lighting them, she dimmed the lamps and smiled at the pleasing atmosphere. Then she loaded the CD player with a medley of her favorite music and programmed it to select songs at random. With everything ready, she went to her bedroom and changed her jeans and sweatshirt for a long, flowing sea-green silk, low-cut dress that she had purchased years before but never worn. She liked it because the color complemented her auburn hair and hazel eyes, and the low-cut, slightly gathered bodice flattered her small breasts. As she stood in front of the mirror fixing her hair, the doorbell rang. With one last swipe of the brush, she rushed to the door. Assuming what she hoped was a sexy pose, she threw the door open and squealed in embarrassment when she spied Taylor leaning against the doorjamb.

Within a matter of nanoseconds, she saw a series of emotions reflected in Taylor's face and eyes—surprise, amusement, a slight tinge of embarrassment—but the strongest was the momentary flash of lust. It was so strong that Sara took a step back.

"Payback is a bitch," Taylor said, as she moved away from the doorjamb. "Here, I brought this as a peace offering, but my timing seems to be off a tad." She held out a bottle of Shiraz, Sara's favorite wine.

Sara realized she was clutching the front of the low-cut dress. She struggled to think of something witty to say that would relieve the tension. Nothing came to her. When had talking to Taylor become so difficult? She realized Taylor was still holding the bottle of wine. Releasing the hold on her dress, she reached for it. As she did, she saw Taylor's eyes stray to where her hand had been holding the thin material together. In almost dream-like slowness, she watched Taylor's hand float up and gently smooth the silky fabric.

"You wrinkled the front." Taylor's voice sounded thick and far away. Her hand felt hot against Sara's chest. A wave of desire stronger than any she had ever experienced burned through her. She felt her body sway forward as Taylor's strong hand dropped to Sara's waist.

"Hey, I didn't know this was going to be a party."

Sara nearly screamed as James suddenly appeared behind Taylor. Once more she was stunned mute.

"It's not a party, yet," Taylor replied, as she casually turned to James. "You caught me playing Cupid." She motioned to the bottle of wine that Sara was clutching to her breast.

James's face colored slightly when he noticed Sara's apparel. "I picked up salads. I'm sure there's enough for everyone," he said lamely. From his perfectly pressed navy pleated chinos, Alden cordovan bluchers and a pale blue button-down stripe seersucker shirt, James radiated the image of a rising young lawyer.

Taylor chuckled and slapped him on the arm. "James, you dunce, does it look like she wants company?"

Sara had the sudden wish that James would leave and Taylor would stay. Confused, she shook her head to clear it.

"See," Taylor said, misinterpreting Sara's shaking. "She wants me to leave."

Before Sara could find her voice, Taylor had disappeared down the sidewalk, leaving the other two staring after her. It was several seconds before James cleared his throat to catch Sara's attention. "I suppose we should go inside."

Sara stepped back into the apartment and silently closed the door behind him. They stood in awkward silence and he looked everywhere except at her. She finally regained her composure enough to take the large carryout bag from him and head toward the kitchen. The candlelight and soft music suddenly irritated her. After setting aside the bag and wine, she flipped on the overhead light and blew out the candles. With an almost savage jab, she turned off the music.

"That was nice, you didn't have to turn it off," James said.

She looked down at the dress. "Would you please set out the food? I'll be back in a minute." She went to the bedroom and changed back into her jeans and sweatshirt. As she returned to the kitchen, she could have sworn she saw a look of relief pass over his face. She turned to the table and felt the sting of tears when she saw that he had removed the china plates and was serving the salads in their carryout containers.

"I didn't see any need in dirtying dishes," he said, as he removed forks from the silverware drawer.

"That's fine," she replied flatly. "How was your trip?" He had already told her all about it, but she knew he'd be happy to repeat everything again. She didn't feel like talking. As he droned on about Dallas and the merger, she found her thoughts turning back to the way Taylor's hand had felt against her chest and then at her waist. What would have happened if James hadn't appeared when he had? She stopped short. "Nothing would have happened."

"I'm sorry?"

She looked up to find James watching her.

"I didn't hear what you said," he stated.

She realized that she had spoken aloud. "It was nothing," she said, pushing a piece of lettuce around in the container.

"Is there something wrong with the salad? I could go get something else, if you'd rather not have salad."

She put the fork down and leaned back in her chair. "The salad is fine. I'm not very hungry."

He put his fork down and reached out to take her hand. "Taylor spoiled your plans for tonight, didn't she?"

She was on the verge of denying it when tears began to stream down her face.

James wasn't like most men who fell apart anytime a woman cried. He stood and pulled her up. As he hugged her gently, he ran a hand over her hair and held her until the tears stopped. "You're tired," he said, as he led her to the living room. "We'll have lots of nights together. I know you're under a lot of pressure with the wedding and having to deal with your mother. I'm going home, so you can rest. I'll call you tomorrow at work to see how you're doing." He kissed her cheek. "Call me if you need to talk during the night. I'll be there."

As he walked away, Sara realized that with James, she had a wonderful friend, but he would never be a great lover.

24

Chapter Five

When Sara arrived at work the following morning, she felt irritable and out of sorts. A mishmash of disjointed dreams had invaded her sleep, leaving her feeling confused and exhausted. Each time she tried to recall the dreams they would scamper just out of reach. When Gracie stepped in to remind her of the Tuesday morning huddle, Sara groaned in frustration.

"I forgot to read through the Main Street Project," she admitted.

Gracie's surprise was reflected in her dark chocolate-colored eyes. "I'll go tell them you're stuck on the phone. I read the file before I gave it to you. It won't take but a minute to glance through the materials. It's basically a summary of the houses located along that one section of Main Street and explains that the owners are willing to assume the expense of the building renovations as long as the city agrees to keep the local park maintained and install additional streetlights."

Sara took a deep breath. "Thanks. Try to buy me ten minutes."
Gracie nodded.

"I owe you," Sara called out.

"You'd better believe you do," Gracie replied, before she pulled the door closed.

Sara glanced through the folder and found that Gracie had hit the high spots. The project appeared to be a win-win situation for both the city and the property owners. She felt comfortable in recommending it for further study and as a possible item for the next fiscal budget. Due to Gracie's help, she was less than ten minutes late for the huddle. She found it hard to concentrate on the other reports. Her mind kept drifting back to her body's reaction to Taylor's touch. She might be limited in sexual experience, but she knew what she had felt yesterday. The disturbing part was that James never made her feel that way. Simply remembering Taylor's touch made her body react. She squirmed in her chair at the memory of Taylor's hand on her waist. There was something exciting about the sense of strength and gentleness she had felt in the touch.

Oscar DeLeon, another senior planner, nudged her.

Sara snapped out of her reverie to find the entire staff of fourteen staring at her.

"I'm sorry," she stammered. "I was thinking about . . ." She blushed as a wave of laughter ran around the room.

Rosa shook her head and smiled. "We understand. With the elections coming up, and the wedding looming on the horizon, I know it's hard to concentrate on something as mundane as a briefing on the advisability of the Main Street Project."

Sara smiled sheepishly. "Actually, the project looks good." She quickly filled them in on the particulars and gave her recommendations.

Rosa nodded. "Any comments, suggestions, complaints, yada yada?" she asked the room. When no one responded, she made a notation on the yellow legal pad in front of her. "All right, we'll try to place it in next year's budget. If no one else has anything, that's it for now."

The group began to drift away. Sara cringed when Rosa motioned for her to follow her to her office. As they walked down the hallway, she gave herself several mental kicks for not reading the folder over the weekend. It wasn't as though she had been pressed for time. She had simply forgotten about it. That wasn't like her. She couldn't even use the wedding as an excuse. Truthfully, her mother and James had taken care of almost all of the arrangements. James had even arranged the appointment with the dressmaker. When they reached Rosa's office, she waved Sara into a chair in front of her desk.

"How are the plans with the wedding coming along?"

"Good. It would be better if I could convince my mother and James to stop inviting people. Everything is pretty much set. There's still the final fitting for the dresses. Which reminds me. You were going to check the vacation schedule to see if I could take off the week before and after the wedding."

Rosa nodded. "Don't worry about it. Go ahead and take the time. I don't think two weeks will create any adverse results to any of your projects." She leaned back in her chair. "Speaking of which, how's your workload?"

Sara swallowed. "It's fine. I'm sorry about zoning out in the meeting. I'm—"

Rosa held up her hand. "Hold on. I'm not getting ready to chew you out," she said, and smiled. "I received a call from Tom Wallace. You probably remember him. He's with the Texas State Historical Commission."

Sara nodded. "I worked with him on the Steadman excavation and restoration last year."

"That's why he called. He remembered being impressed with your work." She pulled a folder from the side drawer and placed it on the desk in front of her. "They have a rather unusual situation and they're asking for our help. Have you ever heard of the Brodie brothers?"

She searched her memory. "I vaguely remember reading something about them. They were ranchers, I believe."

"They may have been more than ranchers. Bo and Dudley

27

Brodie were also suspected of being members of the Williams gang."

"Williams?" She frowned. It took a moment for the old rumor to surface. "Isn't that the group who stole that mule train of Confederate gold?"

"Yes, it's believed they're the ones." She pushed the folder over to Sara. "Dudley Brodie's great-great-granddaughter, who is now sixty-five, is the sole owner of what remains of the ranch down near Wilford Springs. Originally, the homestead consisted of six thousand acres. Currently, only a little over eighteen hundred acres and the house remain. Ms. Brodie contacted the state historical commission and showed some interest in donating everything to the state upon her and her partner's death. Apparently, she's the last of the descendents."

Sara opened the folder. Attached to the inside cover was a photocopy of an Atascosa County map with a segment in the northeast corner outlined in red. Stuck to the bottom of that was a sticky note with what appeared to be directions. "Sounds like a generous thing for her to do."

"Yes, but she has a few stipulations."

Sara glanced up. "What kind of stipulations?"

"The land can never be sold, mined, or drilled, and it's to be set aside as a wildlife refuge. She wants the homestead preserved."

"That's going to involve some money. With state funding being reduced each year, I'd think the state would be hesitant to take such a project on." Once the state accepted property that had provisos attached to it, the state was legally bound to uphold the stipulations of the agreement. "I'm assuming the county historical commission isn't in any position to take on such a project."

"No. They've already turned it down. They don't have the necessary funds," Rosa replied.

Sara sensed there was more to the story. "Is she offering any sort of financial endowment?"

"No, but she has hinted at certain family documents. She won't give up the documents unless they agree to take the homestead and keep up its maintenance."

"What sort of documents?"

"According to Tom, she's not giving them many specifics. Apparently, she has hinted at family diaries. It's those hints that have Tom in a tizzy."

"If they're that important, then he should jump on it."

"He has, but the individual they sent out to interview Ms. Brodie pissed her off royally and now she has withdrawn the offer and absolutely refuses to talk to anyone from the commission."

Sara placed the folder back on Rosa's desk. "Then it's settled."

Rosa shook her head. "Not exactly. The state boys aren't ready to give up on it and Tom was hoping we might assist them."

"We can't go poking around in Atascosa County."

"No, but Tom wants to appoint you to a special committee that would report directly to him. It shouldn't take more than a week. In fact, he seems to think you can convince Ms. Brodie to reconsider her offer, with just a couple of visits. Unfortunately, since we're already short-handed, I can't release you from your current projects."

A frown creased Sara's forehead. She didn't mind being assigned to a special committee. Those kinds of things looked good on a résumé and this wasn't the kind of project that took up much time. No extensive travel would be involved since Atascosa was a neighboring county. Either the woman would donate the land or she wouldn't. If she did, someone from the state commission would step in and handle the paperwork. "I don't see why this is such a big deal. I understand from a historical point of view the benefit of preserving the ranch, and the documents would be a nice addition to the state library, but since there's already an extensive volume of data for that area and time period, I don't see how the commission could justify the expense of maintaining the homestead."

"Think about it," Rosa said with a slight smile.

Sara leaned back in her chair and examined what she knew. "The state stands to gain an eighteen-hundred-acre wildlife refuge. If they designate it as a state park they're allowed to collect entrance fees, but I can't imagine that area drawing enough interest to make it a financial success. It'll simply join the long list of locations the state has to maintain. Unless there's something I don't know, the diaries of a couple of ranchers, who may or may not have been outlaws—" She stopped suddenly and looked at Rosa. "Now I remember. The Confederate gold was never recovered."

"Bingo."

"And Tom thinks these diaries will lead them to it. The state gets the land and a nice bonus."

"Give the woman a cigar," Rosa said and smiled.

"That's the silliest thing I've ever heard," Sara scoffed. "You know as well as I do that most of these lost Confederate gold stories stem from tall tales told by old men to impress their grandkids. Is there a single shred of evidence to support this rumor?"

"Tom mentioned an Army report and a newspaper clipping reporting the robbery, but according to him the researcher drew a blank after that. That's what he wants you to find out."

Sara suppressed a groan. This was quickly becoming a major project, or goose chase. "Would you think I was whining if I asked whether I have to do this?"

"Think of it as an adventure. Heck, I wish he had asked me. I would love to go searching for lost gold and get paid for doing it."

"You're serious, aren't you?"

"You bet I am." Rosa stood to indicate the meeting was wrapping up. "Tom's number is in the folder. Give him a call and see how he wants to handle this."

Sara picked up the folder and started to leave.

"Aren't you even curious?" Rosa asked.

"About what?"

"How much gold there was?"

"No, I'm not interested, because there is no gold. You're sending me on a wild goose chase."

"According to Tom Wallace, close to three hundred thousand dollars in double eagles were taken."

Sara didn't bother to suppress her groan this time. "Yeah, and for the last one hundred and forty years the Brodie heirs have just been sitting around waiting for the final descendent to die off so that they could give it back to the government." She stopped suddenly and turned around. "Wait a minute. If the Williams gang was supposed to have stolen the gold, why would the Brodies have the loot?"

Rosa pointed a finger at her and smiled. "See, you are curious."

Sara struggled not to roll her eyes as she left Rosa's office. She had read dozens of stories of lost Confederate gold, and from a historical viewpoint only a couple of them warranted more than a passing glance. The only positive thing from this assignment would be the few brownie points she could rack up. She would love to receive an appointment to the Texas Historical Commission someday. If she managed to convince this woman to turn over the documents, it might provide her résumé a little extra clout.

As soon as she got back to her office, she called Tom Wallace and discovered that all he really wanted was someone who could sweet-talk and coddle a little old lady until she handed over the diary and land.

"If you can pull this off, it could go a long way toward advancing your career," he told her.

"Tom, I'll take the job, but only because Ms. Brodie has already shown an interest in donating her land. I have to be honest with you up front. I don't believe there's any gold or ever has been."

Silence fell between them. She realized she probably shouldn't have mentioned the gold since he hadn't mentioned it to her. She bit her tongue and let the silence hang. It was a trick her father had taught her when she was a kid. Very few people were comfortable with silence. Most would rush in to fill it and Tom was no exception.

"No one really believes there is, but the diaries of these two early ranchers could shed a lot of insight into this particular area. To my knowledge, there's no concrete evidence to connect the Brodies to the Williams gang."

"Good. I'm glad we agree on that. I wouldn't feel comfortable pretending to look for lost gold."

He laughed a little too loudly to be convincing. "All you need to do is convince Ms. Brodie that it would be in everyone's best interest if she were to donate the land and homestead to the state without stipulations being attached." He stopped and cleared his throat. "If she has written documents from her family, we would certainly be happy to see that they are placed in the state library."

She could hear him fidgeting with something near the phone.

"If she does have documents, you should call me immediately. I'll personally drive down and take possession of them. I'm sure they'd be in a fragile state and we wouldn't want to risk damaging them further by inept handling."

Sara flinched. "Tom, I'm not exactly an amateur in the preservation of historic documents."

"Of course not. I apologize if that's how it sounded. I was very impressed with your work on the Steadman restoration. That's why I asked for you personally."

After she hung up, she sat staring at the folder. She was starting to get a bad feeling in her gut. Money made people crazy. She didn't want to be mixed up in anything where large sums of money were involved. Rosa had said the stolen gold was estimated to be nearly three hundred thousand dollars. She wondered what that would equate to in today's market.

"Christ," she whispered as she jumped up. "Now they have me thinking about gold." She put the folder in her desk. She had a meeting on the Stinson School renovations starting in ten minutes. She would read the information in the folder later.

Chapter Six

Sara eased her Ford Ranger onto the ribbed gravel road and quickly discovered it was impossible to go faster than twenty-five miles per hour. She held her breath in fear that something vital would be jarred from the truck's engine. That anyone was able to travel in and out on this road on a regular basis amazed her. She had called Amanda Brodie to make an appointment. It had taken some convincing on Sara's part, but the woman finally agreed to meet with her. After giving Sara directions, they agreed that Sara would be out around eleven Thursday morning. It was now ten minutes beyond that time. The trip had taken longer than Sara had anticipated. She reached for her cell phone but was still unable to get a signal. As she tossed it back onto the seat in frustration, she saw the first landmark on her list, a windmill on the left side of the road. From there she was supposed to drive another four miles to a fork in the road. Sara tried to speed up, but the truck's rear end began to dance about like a windsock in a brisk wind.

After reaching the fork in the road, she took the left fork and drove another mile. Just as Amanda Brodie had described, she rounded a curve and the homestead spread out before her. She was surprised by how well the place had been maintained. The house sported a coat of brilliant white paint with kelly green trim. All of the outer buildings were painted a deep barn red. Several cows drank from a large stock pond in the pasture beside the barn. In addition to the cattle, Sara spotted half a dozen horses in the pasture.

As she pulled up to the house, a large tan dog of indeterminate heritage came charging toward the truck. Terrified of dogs, Sara stayed in the truck until a tall woman came out onto the porch and called the dog back to the house. Slowly, Sara slipped out of the truck, but she made sure she didn't lock the door. If the dog headed back toward her, she wanted to be able to get back inside quickly.

"Come on up. Roscoe won't bother you none." The ramrod-straight woman, dressed in a western shirt with the sleeves rolled up nearly to her elbows, faded jeans and a battered pair of boots that might have once been black, patted the dog's head.

"Ms. Brodie?"

"Yeah, but call me Mandy." She removed a battered Stetson hat and ran a hand through short, steel-gray hair.

"I'm Sara Stockton." She held out her hand.

Amanda Brodie's handshake was firm. Sara could feel the calluses on the palm of the woman's hand. Her face was a weathered map of her life, from the tiny shallow squint lines to the deeper lines that reflected harsher times or deeper pains.

"Have a seat," Mandy motioned toward the half-dozen rockers that sat on the wide front porch. "I find that as I get older, my old bones appreciate sunshine more."

Sara smiled. "It's a beautiful day. Spring is my favorite time of year."

"Don't see much of it here in South Texas," Mandy said, as she settled herself in a rocking chair in the sun.

"No," Sara agreed. "It seems like we go directly out of winter into summer."

"So, they sent you here to talk me out of my family's documents, did they?"

Sara blinked in surprise. "Ms. Brodie, I assure you I'm not here to talk you out of anything. I was led to believe that you were interested in donating certain items to the state historical commission. If that's not the case, then I apologize and I won't bother you further." Sara stood.

Mandy waved her hands to motion Sara back down into the rocker. "You sort of lean toward the touchy side, don't you? Well, that's okay. I tend to do the same myself. You can call me Mandy. That Ms. Brodie business makes me nervous."

Sara sat back down. "All right, Mandy. Why don't you tell me what you'd like to do?"

Amanda Brodie rocked slightly as she studied Sara. Her bright blue eyes seemed to sparkle. "I think I'd like to have a glass of sweet tea. What about you?"

Sara hid a smile. Amanda Brodie wasn't going to make this easy. "I think a glass of sweet tea would be wonderful," she said.

"Have you eaten lunch yet?"

"No," Sara admitted.

"Well, come on and we'll go see what we can rustle up."

Sara followed her inside into a large, cheerfully decorated living room. There were literally dozens of framed photos hanging on one wall. Mandy noticed her looking at them.

"All those"—she waved a hand toward the photos—"are kids that Arcy taught over the years."

"Arcy?"

Mandy stopped, turned back toward her and smiled. When she did, her entire face seemed to soften. "Arcy is my girl. I think you young folks call it a domestic partner now." She lowered her voice and leaned toward Sara. "Arcy doesn't take kindly to being called a domestic partner. Says it makes her feel like a maid. That's what we used to call maids in my day. Domestics. Of course, we never had one. My mom and I were the domestics in our house. Dad worked the range. I used to beg him to let me come with him. Lord, how I hated housework."

"She still does," a voice called out.

Sara looked up to see a short, slightly plump woman drying her hands on the blue-and-green-checkered apron she was wearing.

"Ah, there you are," Mandy said. "Sara, this is Arcy Anderson. This is Sara Stockton. She's with the historical commission."

Sara shook Arcy's hand. Where Mandy's grip was sure and confident, Arcy's felt more protective and nurturing. Sara could easily imagine that hand wiping away a child's tears.

"We decided we were hungry. Is there any of that peach cobbler left?" Mandy turned to Sara. "A neighbor woman made the cobbler. It's good, but not nearly as good as Arcy's cobbler."

Arcy looked at Mandy and shook her head. "You've already had your ration of peach cobbler for the day. I have fresh strawberries in the refrigerator. You can have a bowl of those, if you're still hungry."

Mandy gave a slight nod toward Sara.

Arcy wasn't falling for her maneuvering. "I know what you're trying to do," she said. "You think that because we have company you're going to be able to wrangle an extra helping of cobbler, but that dog won't hunt with me, old woman."

"Ah, fiddle-faddle, what do you know about hunting anyway? This young lady and I would really enjoy a bowl of cobbler. Wouldn't we, Sara?"

Caught off-guard, Sara glanced between the two women. She was still reeling over discovering they were lesbians.

Mandy stopped and turned back toward her. "Well, do you want that cobbler or not?"

Sara saw the look of disapproval in Arcy's eye. "Actually, if you have enough, I think I'd prefer some of those fresh strawberries."

Arcy nodded her approval and beamed at Sara. "There's more than enough. You come on in to the kitchen."

Mandy, on the other hand, settled her fists on her hips and glared at them. "You two are about as much fun as a big wrinkle in starched underwear," she grumbled.

"Stop being a butt. I just want you here with me for as long as possible," Arcy declared, as she rushed out of the room.

Sara heard the catch in her voice.

Mandy looked after her and sighed as she rubbed her neck. "I had a heart attack a few months back. Doctor said it was a mild one and that I'd be fine if I took it easy, but she's been worried sick. She's been trying to feed me brussels sprouts and tofu ever since." She turned to Sara. "What the heck is tofu anyway? I looked it up in a dictionary but couldn't find it."

Sara smiled. "I think it's made from bean curd."

Mandy grunted as she glanced toward the kitchen where Arcy had disappeared.

"I'm sure she only does it because she cares for you," Sara said.

Mandy rubbed her neck again. "Well, I know that. But I still don't want to eat brussels sprouts." She turned to Sara. "You got someone special in your life?"

"I'm engaged." She held up her hand with the engagement ring. "The wedding is in June."

"Do you love him so much it hurts?"

Sara hesitated. The bluntness of the question surprised her. "He's a good man," she replied.

Mandy's blue eyes peered at her closely. "There are a lot of good men in this world. The question is do you love this one?"

Before Sara could answer, Arcy called them into the kitchen. Sara didn't waste any time going. Mandy's questions made her uncomfortable. Despite its large size, the kitchen felt warm and homey. A long wooden table dominated the center of the room. The gleaming marble countertops and modern appliances were a nice contrast to the antique kitchen utensils displayed on a length of shelving that ran most of the way around the room.

"Have a seat," Arcy said, as she waved Sara to the table where a deep dish of peach cobbler sat alongside a stoneware bowl filled with fresh strawberries.

As soon as she sat, Arcy placed a small bowl and spoon before her. "Just help yourself. Would like some tea or coffee?"

"Tea would be great," Sara said, more from politeness than actual desire. She dipped out a small serving of the strawberries.

Mandy took a place at the end of the table and looked at the peach cobbler with longing before sighing and reaching for the bowl of fresh berries.

Sara saw the look of relief that passed over Arcy's face as she headed for the refrigerator to get the tea.

After they had finished eating the three women sat on the front porch with Roscoe lying at Mandy's feet. They talked about everything from the weather to politics. Sara knew she should bring the subject back around to the land and documents, but somehow it seemed wrong. After a couple of hours, she thanked them for their hospitality and started back to her truck. Mandy walked with her.

"The next time you come out, I'll show you the ranch," she said.

"I'd like that." Sara smiled when she realized she genuinely meant it.

As she cranked the truck, Arcy rushed out and pushed a paper bag through the opened window.

"I guess that's the last of the peach cobbler," Mandy said regretfully.

"I saved you some," Arcy said, as she patted Mandy's arm. "When our peaches ripen, I'll make you a small one."

Mandy's face brightened like a child's at Christmas.

As Sara drove away, she found herself looking in her rearview mirror for one last glimpse of the couple. She felt certain that she and James would never have that sort of relationship. The thought left her feeling sad.

When she arrived back at her apartment, she ate a bowl of the peach cobbler for dinner. Mandy was right. It was good. She kept thinking about Mandy's question. Would she ever love James so much it hurt? She tried to imagine her life without him but couldn't. He and Taylor had been in her life for almost as long as she could remember. Her thoughts turned to Taylor and a spark of something flashed through her. She tried to analyze the feeling. It was very similar to what she had felt when Taylor's hand was on her waist. As she kept probing her feelings about Taylor, the odd tingling sensation began to tease her lower stomach. She squirmed around on the couch and tried to get comfortable. As she did so, she became increasingly aware of the pressure her jeans were placing against her groin. She found herself squeezing her legs tightly together and slowly releasing them as the pleasant sensations intensified. Her body began to ease into a more prone position. The phone rang. Sara was so startled by the sudden noise, she dropped the bowl she had been holding, but luckily there was no more cobbler left in the dish. She snatched the phone up.

"Are you all right?" James asked when she answered.

"Sure, why?"

"I don't know. You sound funny. A little out of breath maybe."

"Um . . . I was exercising," she lied.

That seemed to satisfy him. "I was just calling to see if you wanted me to come by tonight and bring dinner?"

"I just finished eating," she said, as she leaned over to pick up the bowl she had dropped. "Besides, I need to go in early tomorrow." She quickly gave him an overview of the Brodie case.

"You're looking for the stolen gold?" he teased.

"No, I'm following up on a citizen who wishes to donate land and historic buildings to the state. Tom Wallace is looking for buried treasure."

"Do you think there is any?"

The question caught her by surprise. It was such an unusual question from someone as down to earth as James was. "No, actually I don't. It doesn't make sense that the family would have held on to it for all these years. Plus, there's no logical reason for the Brodies to even have it. If the Williams gang stole it, I think they took it with them."

"What happened to them?"

"Who?"

"The Williams gang. Were they ever captured? Did they die of old age or with their boots on?"

Sara chuckled at his use of the western slang. "We don't know a lot about them. There were usually two, but sometimes four, members in the gang, Emmett and Cletus Williams and the two unidentified men. According to the report Tom gave me, there was some speculation then that the other two were the Brodie brothers. The gang was active from around eighteen fifty-eight until eighteen sixty-five when they supposedly stole the Confederate shipment. From the newspaper accounts of the robberies they pulled, the Williams brothers usually worked alone. I suspect they were the ringleaders and occasionally worked with these other two whenever they had jobs they couldn't handle alone." She could almost see him concentrating, already trying to solve the puzzle. She went on with her story. "During the robbery of the gold shipment, one of the soldiers swore he wounded Cletus during the brief shootout that occurred, but there was no way to ever verify his story. After they stole the gold neither of the Williams brothers was ever heard from again. That's all we know."

"That's it? That's all you know."

"That's all."

"Where did they come from? Who were their parents? Where did they live?"

Sara chuckled. "James, it doesn't work that way. There's a reason these old stories survive. If we had all those answers, the mystery would have been solved years ago. The legends live on because we don't have any of those answers."

"Well, yes. I can see where that would help."

She could hear the disappointment in his voice. "Once you become governor," she teased, "you can help arrange for more funding for historical research and we can find answers to these questions."

He gave a small grunt. "Let's see how I do as a city councilman first."

"Stop that. You'll make a wonderful politician."

"Do you really think so?"

Sara heard the doubt in his voice and she realized that she had been so wrapped up in the wedding and her work that she hadn't noticed how nervous he was. "Yes, I really do."

"Thank you."

"What's going on, James?"

"Nothing. I'm just tired. I need to get some sleep. We'll talk tomorrow."

As she hung up, Sara couldn't help but notice that he hadn't seemed disappointed that she had begged off from his spending the night.

Chapter Seven

After talking to James, Sara went to bed early but couldn't sleep. She lay staring at the ceiling, unable to get Mandy and Arcy out of her mind. The visit had accomplished nothing as far as the land or documents were concerned. When she returned to the office, there had been two messages from Tom Wallace wanting an update. He hadn't been happy when she told him that she would need to make another trip back out to the ranch.

A glance at the bedside clock indicated it was only a little after nine. She wanted to talk to someone about her day, and without stopping to think, she reached for the phone and called Taylor. When the call was finally answered, she was surprised to hear that Taylor sounded a little tipsy. "Have you been drinking?" she asked. Taylor rarely drank enough to get drunk.

"No. I was sleeping."

"Oh, I'm sorry I woke you. I didn't think you would be asleep yet. You're usually a night owl."

"Yeah. I think I may be coming down with a cold or something. What's up?"

"I was just—nothing." Sara stopped. "Call me when you feel better."

"Yeah, sure."

Sara stared at the phone for several seconds. Was Taylor truly sick or was she simply avoiding her because of what had happened the last time they were together? Feeling worse than before, Sara got out of bed and walked into the kitchen to get a glass of milk. Mr. Tibbs appeared at her heels. "You never miss the sound of the refrigerator door opening do you?" Again ignoring the vet's advice, she poured a small amount of milk into his dish. For her efforts, she received a glare of disapproval at such a meager serving. "You're an ungrateful beast, Mr. Tibbs."

He flicked his tail as if to dismiss her before turning his attention to the milk.

She walked to the living room window and stared out. In the far distance, she could see the faint glow of downtown. A sense of loneliness settled over her as she thought about Mandy and Arcy. Would they already be asleep, or would they be sitting on their front porch rocking beneath the stars? Trying to see the stars, she pressed her face closer to the window, but the glare of the apartment's security lights was too strong. After making her way back to the bedroom, she crawled into bed with a new mystery she had been saving for a rainy weekend. It was after two before she finally fell asleep.

The following day Sara had to drag herself to work.

"You look tired," Gracie said, as she brought in the morning mail. Gracie had been Sara's assistant for nearly three years. She was good at her job and they had a good working relationship.

"I started a new book last night and couldn't put it down." Sara settled on a small lie. "I'm going to leave early today to go look over that project on Baker. They called this morning to let me know it was finished. I want to see how it turned out."

"That's where they were restoring that old garage that was built in the early nineteen hundreds?" Gracie asked.

"Yes. It was originally a diner but it was eventually converted into one of the first gas stations here. The new owners wanted to restore the building. They even installed replicas of the original gas pumps."

"How's the gold mining working out?" Gracie asked, as she adjusted the several gold bracelets on her wrist.

Sara looked up. "How did you know about that?"

"Oh, please, Rosa's about to have a stroke. She just knows you're going to be the one to discover the lost treasure."

"Rosa's dreaming. If there ever was any gold, it disappeared a long time ago. I mean, think about it. They could have left the country decades ago and taken the money with them. No one would have been the wiser. Why wouldn't they spend it?"

"Maybe they were afraid the law was watching them."

"That makes sense for the Brodie brothers and even their kids, but not their grandkids. How many people even remember the robbery? Besides, most criminals aren't that rational. If the gold ever existed, it was spent long ago."

"But wouldn't someone get suspicious if all these old coins started showing up?" Gracie argued.

"There's always some way to get around the law if you really want to."

Gracie looked at her closely. "It sounds like there's a story behind that statement."

"Gracie, please. I'm too chicken even to try to sneak candy into the theater. I'd never make a good criminal."

"That's probably just your way of throwing me off the trail. Where do you think they buried the loot?"

Sara looked at her in exasperation. "Don't you have something to research? If not, I'm sure I can find something."

"See how you are," Gracie grumbled, as she scurried back to her desk.

As soon as she was alone, Sara dialed Taylor's personal number at the clinic. The receptionist answered. Sara had met her several times. When the receptionist heard Sara's voice, she didn't hesitate to tell her that Taylor had left early to go to Houston and wouldn't be back until Monday. Sara thanked her and told her not to leave a message; she would call Taylor when she returned. After hanging up, she sat staring at the phone. She considered calling Taylor's cell phone but stopped when she realized that Taylor hadn't been sick after all. She was avoiding her. Sara made up her mind that as soon as Taylor returned she was going over to see her. They needed to talk about whatever it was that was wrong between them.

It was time she stopped thinking about the reaction she'd had to Taylor's touch. Whatever it had been was a fluke. She had known Taylor for most of her life. If she'd had any sexual attraction to her, it would have made itself known long ago. This was probably nothing more than pre-wedding jitters.

Gracie poked her head back in. "Your mother is on line one."

"Hello, Mom," Sara said, as she picked up the phone.

"Can you and James come to dinner Saturday night? We need to finalize the guest list."

"Mom, the guest list is finalized. I thought we agreed to that the other day."

"Yes, but I received a call from your cousin Tina and she reminded me that Michael Canton—he's a third cousin on your father's side—is working as an aide for State Senator Jackson in Austin. We really should invite him and his family. He might prove to be a valuable source for James."

Sara rubbed her temple. "Have I ever met this third cousin?"

"Well, no, but it's time we changed all that."

While her mother was talking Sara opened her Internet browser and typed in Jackson's name. "Mom, Senator Jackson is a Republican. He's not going to help James."

"Of course he will. Family ties outweigh political parties."

"No, they don't. Besides, I told you the other day. Not one more name is going to be added."

"He's family—"

45

"No."

"We'll discuss it when you come to dinner. I have to go." She hung up before Sara could argue.

Sara disconnected and called James's cell phone. When the voice mail kicked in immediately, she suspected her mother's speed dial had been faster than her own number-punching. She left a message telling him they had been invited to have dinner with her parents on Saturday.

Chapter Eight

Sara's cell rang when she was on her way home from the service station restoration on Baker Street. The owner and architect had done a fabulous job of maintaining the integrity of the building's original design. The caller was Amber Lee, a former classmate of Sara's.

"Hey, girlfriend."

"Hi, Amber."

"Stef and I are going to the Boardwalk Bistro for dinner. Do you want to join us? I'm sorry it's such short notice, but we just decided a few minutes ago ourselves."

"Sure. James plays poker on Friday nights. What time?"

"Sevenish."

Sara glanced at her watch. It was already twenty after six. There wasn't time for her to go home and change. She would have to turn around and head back downtown. If it had only been Amber she was meeting, she would have had plenty of time to go on home, because Amber was always late. Stef on the other hand would arrive five minutes early. "I'll meet you guys there."

"Ciao," Amber called.

Sara dropped the phone back into her purse. Amber Lee and Stephanie Foster were friends from high school. She had never run around with them much because neither James nor Taylor cared for the duo. Sara still got together with them on rare occasions.

It was five minutes after seven when Sara walked into the restaurant. Stephanie waved at her from across the room. "I haven't seen you in ages," Stef gushed, as she stood and gave Sara a hearty hug.

"No. I guess it was at your sister's wedding, and that was, what, almost six months ago."

Stef gave a small snort. "The planning took longer than the marriage."

"What do you mean?" She pulled out the chair across from Stef and sat down.

"She has already filed for a divorce."

Sara looked up in surprise. "What?"

"Yeah, she caught her old man cheating on her."

"After only six months?"

"Yeah, can you believe it? Course, it don't surprise me none. I always say my troubles began the day I married Derek."

Sara agreed that Derek was a loser, but she kept her opinions to herself.

Twenty minutes later, Amber sailed in and temporarily stopped the conversation with a frenzied account of the horrific traffic she had encountered. She stopped her monologue long enough for the waiter to take her drink order and she was off again on a one-sided discussion of road rage.

Sara glanced at Stef and smiled. It was like being back in high school. They sat and listened while Amber held court. She now remembered why she didn't get together with them very often.

As soon as the waiter returned to take their orders, Stef waited until Amber began to order and used the opportunity to comment on Sara's upcoming wedding. "You only have two more months of freedom, Sara, you should make the most of it."

"We should all go to Vegas," Amber clattered, as the waiter left.

"Derek would never let me go to Vegas." Stef sighed.

"Oh, yeah, well, Charlie wouldn't be too happy about me going either," Amber admitted. "He almost had a cow when I went to Corpus to visit my sister when her baby was born."

"James isn't like that," Sara explained. "He wouldn't mind if I went somewhere for a few days."

"Is he having an affair?" Stef asked bluntly.

"No! James would never have an affair."

The two married women turned and gave each other a knowing smile.

Sara stared at the two in surprise. "Are you suggesting that Charlie or Derek would have an affair?" she asked.

Amber shrugged. "Charlie did, but he promised he wouldn't ever do it again."

"And like a noodle, she believes him," Stef scoffed.

"He promised."

"Yeah, and how many times has Derek promised, but he always meets some bimbo and bam. Back in the sack he goes."

"Well, my Charlie isn't like Derek."

"You're right," Stef admitted. "Charlie is much smarter. Derek is too stupid to remember to take the hotel receipts out of his pockets, or the dimwit uses the credit card." She looked at Sara with disbelief in her eyes. "Like, I'm not going to notice a charge for the Marriott when I'm paying the bills."

Amber reached across the table and touched Sara's arm. "You forgive James the first time, but if he does it again, you kick his ass out and make him pay. Don't be a doormat, like Stef."

Sara tensed, waiting for Stef to explode, but Stef simply tore into a new piece of bread. "You two aren't exactly making me feel any better about this," Sara admitted.

Clearly surprised, they both looked at her. "Marrying Charlie is the best thing I've ever done," Amber declared. "If I had it all to do over again, I'd still marry him. I wouldn't let him join the gym—that's where he met that woman," she explained.

Stef shook her head. "Not me. I'd go on to college and make something of myself the way Sara did." She leaned toward the center of the table and lowered her voice. "Sometimes, I think Taylor had the right idea. I think we'd all be better off without men in our lives."

"Oh-h-h," Amber said with a shudder. "Don't be gross."

"What's gross about it?" Sara asked without thinking.

Amber's eyes nearly popped out of their sockets. "Are you kidding me? Just the idea of touching another woman like that is . . . is . . . oh-h-h."

Sara fought the urge to roll her eyes.

"It was all I could ever do to just be in the same room with Taylor."

Sara's hackles came up. "Amber, Taylor is a dear friend of mine, so be careful what you say."

"Oh, get off it, Sara, you're no more a lezzy lover than I am. The whole thing is disgusting."

"Amber," Stef cautioned, as she kept her eyes on Sara.

But Amber was on a roll. "And now, they want to get married. Why, for God's sake? The president is right. They're trying to destroy the sanctity of marriage."

"They want equal rights that marriage would provide them," Sara said.

"What equal rights? They should be thankful decent folks don't run them out of town."

Sara stood. "I suppose you think you're one of those decent folks. Why shouldn't two people who truly love each other be together? And if you two are examples of the sanctity of marriage, I for one don't want anything to do with it or you." Sara pulled money from her purse and threw it on the table before stalking out.

Stef called to her to come back, but she wasn't going to give

Amber the satisfaction of seeing the tears in her eyes. They had no right to talk about Taylor that way.

Sara took her time in driving back to her apartment. Once again, she found herself alone. She could call James. He would leave his card game and come over; however, James wasn't the person she wanted to see. She wanted to see and talk to Taylor, who was now in Houston with another woman. She tried to tell herself that she felt a closer bond to Taylor because they were both female, but deep inside a small kernel of doubt was starting to grow.

"I'm getting married to a wonderful man in two months," she reminded herself aloud. For the rest of the evening, she kept repeating the mantra.

Chapter Nine

The following evening, James arrived a little after seven. "Sorry I'm late. I had a late meeting with a client and it lasted longer than I had anticipated," he said, as he helped her with her jacket. It had rained earlier in the day, and the damp evening air was cool.

"Mom is going to start pressuring me to add more names to the invitation list," she said, as she locked the apartment door.

"That would be your third cousin, who works as an aide for Senator Jackson," he said, as they made their way to his car.

She chuckled. "So she did call you."

"Yes. I reminded her that Senator Jackson had already endorsed my opponent."

"What did she say?"

He stopped and turned to her with his hand on his hip. In his best Eloise Stockton impersonation, he said, "James, you'll simply have to change his mind. How are you ever going to make it in politics if you don't put yourself out there and meet people? You'll simply have to charm Senator Jackson into changing his mind."

He sounded so much like her mother that Sara began to laugh. She slipped her arm into his. As kids the three of them had gone everywhere like this, arm-in-arm, with James in the center. "You were always our center," she said, as she kissed his cheek.

"What do you mean?"

"The Three Musketeers. Taylor was the bravest . . ."

"You were the smartest," he interjected.

"And you were our centering point. Whenever we went off the deep end or had a problem we ran to you."

He smiled. "It's strange you should mention that," he said, as he opened the car door for her. He waited until he had gone around and gotten into the car before continuing. "I received a call from Taylor, Thursday night. She was drunk."

"She told me she thought she was coming down with something."

He shook his head. "The only thing she was coming down with was a bottle of Jack Daniels. It's the second time in the last few weeks that I've heard her drunk."

"My God, James, what's going on with her? She's never been much of a drinker." It hurt Sara that Taylor was talking to James rather than her.

"I guess it's this woman she's seeing in Houston, but something's strange." He waited for an oncoming car before pulling the car out of the parking lot. "She was pretty loaded and she wasn't making a lot of sense, but she just kept saying, 'I love her. Why can't I tell her?'" He flipped on the defroster fan. "She must have said it half a dozen times. When I asked her if she was talking about Debbie, she burst into tears."

A sharp queasiness oozed through Sara's stomach. Some truth was trying to make itself known, but she refused to let it surface. "Maybe this woman is involved with someone else or something."

James shook his head. "No, Taylor would never allow herself to become involved with someone who was already taken. You know her. She has too much integrity for that."

"That's true," Sara mumbled, as she stared through the windshield. "Taylor wouldn't put herself in the position of being the other woman."

They rode in silence for several minutes. James began to fidget. She knew he was trying to find a way to ask her something. Waiting for him to do so created a nervous fluttering in her chest. She kept taking deep breaths to try to relieve the pressure. She jumped when he finally spoke, but he didn't seem to notice.

"Sara, do you ever wonder . . . what I mean is . . ." He stopped.

She tolerated the silence as long as she could. "Wonder what?"

"We've been friends for so long. Do you think we could be getting married for the wrong reasons?" He blurted the last part out.

She stared at him.

"I've upset you," he said and reached for her hand. "I'm sorry. Of course we're not. We've dated since we were old enough to date. Marriage is the next logical step."

Sara listened to him, unsure whether he was trying to convince her or himself. "Are you having second thoughts?" she asked.

"No! Of course not." He peered at her. "Are you?"

"No. I guess I might be getting a slight case of the pre-wedding jitters. Everyone says it's a natural reaction."

"I suppose men get something similar," he said.

"I'm sure they do."

"Yes. That makes perfect sense. With the tension of the upcoming election and then the wedding, it's a wonder we haven't both been committed to a psych ward."

"We probably could have made things easier on ourselves if we had timed everything a little better," she agreed.

"Should we delay the wedding?"

They glanced at each other. "I don't think we can," Sara said eventually. "So many arrangements have been made—the church, the hall, invitations have been ordered." Again, silence. "Do you want to delay the wedding?"

James seemed to be struggling with something, but before he could verbalize it, his cell phone rang. He looked at her apologetically as he answered it.

Sara deduced from the one-sided conversation that the caller was his campaign manager. By the time he was finally off the phone, they were pulling into her parents' driveway. She started to open the car door, but his hand on hers stopped her.

"Sara, you know how much I care for you, so please don't let my momentary bout of cold feet worry you. We will have a wonderful wedding. You are my dearest friend." He gave her hand a squeeze.

As she stared into his pale blue eyes, the kernel of truth grew a bit more. They got out of the car and made their way up the driveway. It was Saturday night and here they were, James dressed in his neat, blue button-down shirt and khaki Dockers and her in a light sweater and slacks. "James," she whispered. "When did we become our parents?"

He started to say something but stopped when Sara's father met them at the door. "We were starting to get worried," her father said.

Sara hugged him and removed her jacket. "I'm sorry, I should have called."

"I'm afraid it's my fault," James said. "My meeting ran over and then Sara and I were talking on the way over and I guess we sort of lost track of time."

Her father waved off the explanation as he led them into the den. "Don't worry. Eloise is still in the kitchen. She's attempting some new duck recipe tonight and the last time I checked, things weren't going very well."

Sara cringed. "Should I go check on her?"

"No. Give her a few more minutes." Her father held up a pitcher of martinis. "Anyone care to join me?"

They both nodded.

"How is the political race going, James?" he asked, as he passed out the drinks.

James shook his head and sighed. "I'm not sure I'm cut out for this," he admitted.

Sara looked up in surprise. She had never heard James allude to being disappointed with politics. "What's wrong?" she asked.

James stared into his drink. "I'm just not sure this is what I want to do."

Lawrence Stockton cleared his throat and sat in his recliner. "Did something happen?"

"Not really." James hesitated as he stared into his drink for a moment. "A few weeks ago, someone who I previously held in high esteem suggested my political career would have a greater chance of eventually rising above the local level if I were to vote certain ways after I'm elected." He leaned back and sipped his martini. "I'm not even elected yet. What will it be like if win?"

"What did you tell them?" Sara asked.

James looked at her and frowned. "I told them I'd vote as the majority of my constituents wished."

Sara's father rubbed a finger along the bridge of his nose. "That probably didn't make you very popular," Lawrence replied.

"No, sir, it didn't. The following week, those negative ads about my age and inexperience started popping up and my approval rating has steadily dropped."

"I've been noticing that," the older man admitted. "I wouldn't worry about the ads. I think you have a decent chance of defeating Hume and Broderick, but you knew going into this that David Brooks was going to be a tough opponent. The important thing is that you do what you feel is right."

James nodded.

Sara remained silent, feeling guilty that she had been so wrapped up in her own work that she hadn't taken an active role in James's campaign.

The tension dissipated as a slightly flustered Eloise appeared with a tray of cheese and crackers. Grateful for the interruption, Sara rushed to help her.

"I was just coming in to see if you needed help," Sara said.

"No. I think I have everything under control. Dinner will be another twenty minutes or so. I hope everyone's hungry. I've prepared roast duck with an apple-and-sesame-seed stuffing," Eloise said and smiled brightly. "Can you believe it? I've never tried to cook duck before."

Sara could sense her mother's nervousness.

"It sounds delicious," James said. "How is it prepared?"

Eloise sat beside him and began going over the recipe while her husband poured her a drink. Sara stared at the three of them. What would her parents say if she or James suddenly blurted out that they didn't want to get married? *Stop being silly*, she scolded herself. *We're both just nervous.* Marriage was a big step. It was natural that they both should be concerned. In fact, it was probably a good sign that they were nervous. Surely that was an indication that they understood the seriousness of their decision. Feeling somewhat better, she turned her attention to her mother, who was still discussing the recipe with James.

An hour later, they were sitting at the dining room table.

"That was a wonderful meal, Mrs. Stockton. The duck was excellent, and the stuffing complemented it perfectly," James replied, as he stood and began gathering plates from the table.

"Thank you, James. It really wasn't difficult to make at all. Although, I'll have to admit I was a little nervous because it was a new recipe."

Sara's father retrieved the platter containing the leftover duck and quickly headed toward the kitchen, but not before Sara saw him smile. "Eloise, it was delicious," Lawrence assured her.

"Yes, Mom, it was wonderful," Sara agreed, as she picked up the bowl of stuffing and followed them into the kitchen.

Chapter Ten

After leaving her parents, Sara and James returned to her apartment. There was a new awkwardness between them that she couldn't remember ever existing before. As she was changing into her usual sleepwear, an oversized T-shirt, it occurred to her that ever since they had decided to get married, they had slowly stopped talking. She broached the subject after they went to bed.

"James, what's happening between us?"

He lay on his back staring at the ceiling, while she lay beside him, their arms and legs barely touching.

"I don't know, but I don't like it." He sighed.

It took her a moment to form her next statement. "I think our decision to get married may have been a mistake."

"I think you're right."

Even though she admitted it first, his agreement still shocked her. She forced herself to take a slow steady breath. "What are we going to do?"

He sat up and turned on the bedside lamp before facing her. "As I told you before, you're my best friend. I don't think I could ever find a woman I'd respect or love as much as I do you." He gave a small chuckle. "Don't tell Taylor, she'd probably beat me up."

Sara grinned as she sat up and propped herself against the headboard.

They sat staring at each other for several seconds before he spoke. "Did you ever wonder why the three of us were such good friends?"

A nervous spasm ran through Sara's body. On some level she knew they were about to tread into dangerous territory. If they continued with the conversation, things might be said that couldn't be taken back. She cleared her throat nervously. "Not until recently," she admitted.

"What conclusions did you come to?"

She tried to speak but her throat seemed too dry. All she could manage was a shrug. She could see James was struggling as well. His hands shook when he reached up to brush back a lock of honey-blond hair from his forehead.

"I think that old adage about birds of a feather might apply."

"Why do you say that?" Her voice was little more than a whisper.

"That client in Dallas I was telling you about. The one I've been helping with the merger." He waited for her to acknowledge that she remembered.

All she could manage was a nod. All the pieces were falling into place—all those years of never dating anyone but James, the lack of passion and excitement in their lovemaking, the feeling of Taylor's hand on her waist, the deep sense of loneliness that consumed her sometimes—it was all beginning to make sense. Sara wasn't ready to face the truth. She wanted to put a hand over his mouth to stop him from saying what she knew he was about to say.

"His name is Clint and . . . and . . ." Tears filled his eyes. "I don't want to hurt you," he whispered.

Sara moved over to him and put his head on her shoulder. There was nothing sexual in the contact. She was merely comforting a dear friend. "Don't cry. It's going to be all right." She lost track of time as she sat rocking him. Slowly he told her the story of meeting Clint and falling in love with him.

"I didn't mean for it to happen," he said, as he sat up and grabbed a handful of tissues from the box on the bedside table. "We kept trying to avoid each other, but we had to keep meeting because of the merger. It just happened." He dried his eyes and blew his nose.

"Was this the first time?" she asked.

He looked away and shook his head. "No. I first started noticing I was attracted to boys in junior high. I didn't understand it until after Taylor came out. I wanted to be as brave as she was, but I couldn't. My parents aren't as understanding as Taylor's and I already knew I wanted to be in politics." He tossed the used tissues back onto the bedside table. "What about you?"

Too dumbfounded to speak she could only stare. She watched his eyes grow round as he realized his mistake. His hand flew to his mouth.

"I'm sorry," he said, as he reached out a hand to her. "I thought . . ." He stopped.

Sara pinched the comforter between her fingers. "I don't know what's going on with me," she finally admitted. It took her a while but she finally managed to tell him about the incident with Taylor.

"Have you talked to her about it?"

"No. I think she's avoiding me. Besides, I can't say anything now. She's seeing someone."

"What are you going to do?"

She looked at him. "I don't know. I guess it's time I took a serious look at Sara Stockton and try to discover who she really is."

"I'll help you in any way I can."

She nodded. "What are we going to do about the wedding?"

He took a deep breath and slowly released it. "I wanted to talk to you and our parents first. My original plan was to tell you before we went to your folks tonight, and then tell them after dinner, but of course, I chickened out." He looked up. "I'm going to withdraw my name from the city council race tomorrow."

"What!" She stared at him in disbelief. "Why? You've practically won it already."

"I don't want to hide anymore. I've spent too much time hiding from myself. If I try to stay in politics I'll have to keep hiding who I am. Besides, after the past few days, I'm not sure I have the stomach to be a politician. I'm too . . ." He struggled for the word.

"Honest," she said. There still might be some hope for him in the political arena. "There have been openly gay politicians in Texas, and you can't let the actions of a few greedy people get to you. Ultimately, you have the final decision on how you conduct yourself." Even as she said the words, she knew she was oversimplifying the situation. Sometimes honesty and hard work weren't enough. The good guy didn't always win.

He shook his head. "I don't think I'd have the courage to face all the uproar it would cause. Besides, I'd lose my job. The firm wouldn't keep me on if they knew I was gay."

James was probably right about the law firm. From the few interactions she'd had with the partners, they all seemed extremely conservative. "What does Clint think?"

James smiled. "He thinks I should paint a big rainbow flag on my office door and throw caution to the wind. I have to keep reminding him that being out is easier for him since he owns his own company."

"Your parents aren't going to handle it very well either," Sara said with a grimace.

He shuddered. "I was putting off telling them until tomorrow morning. Dad's going to have a coronary and Mom will spend the rest of her life praying the rosary."

Sara experienced a clear vision of Mrs. Edwards and began to laugh.

"What?" James asked.

"Your mother," she gasped as she laughed harder. Soon they

were both laughing hysterically. On some level, Sara realized they were laughing because they were both scared and relieved. When they finally fell over onto the bed exhausted, James took her hand.

"I'm sorry if this is going to make things difficult for you," he said.

"Don't worry about me. I'm a big girl. I can take care of myself."

"When do you want to tell your parents?"

Sara thought about it for a moment. "Let's tell my parents tomorrow morning. Then your folks afterward." She squeezed his hand. "I'll go with you to talk to your parents if you'd like."

"No, thanks. I think it would be better if I went alone."

She was embarrassed by the feeling of relief that rushed through her. She didn't envy him having to face his parents. "James, I don't think you should take your name out of the election yet. Why not give the people a chance? You might be surprised."

He was silent for a while. "I'll think about it."

From the tone of his voice, she knew his mind was already made up. "What about the law firm?"

He cleared his throat. "I submitted my resignation yesterday afternoon. I let them think it was because I needed to concentrate on the election."

"You're going to move to Dallas, aren't you?" A deep sense of sadness filled her when he nodded.

"I'm going into private practice," he said.

"When?"

"I'm not sure. There are a few things I want to do first."

They sat in silence for a moment. "We'll need to cancel all the arrangements." Sara rubbed her forehead. "Luckily, the invitations haven't been mailed yet. We'll lose the deposit on the church and hall." A knot began to form in the pit of her stomach. "And there's the caterer, photographer, band and florist." Beads of sweat formed along her hairline as she thought of the five hundred dollars she had spent on her gown. Then there were the expenses incurred by the rest of the wedding party. So much time and money had been wasted. Her heart began to pound as her breathing grew more shallow.

"It's all right." James put an arm across her shoulders and held her. "Calm down. Take a deep breath." The calm gentleness of his voice eased the tension gripping her. "Everything is going to be all right," he assured her. "I'll take care of canceling everything. I caused this and I'll take care of it."

Sara glanced at him. "Everything."

He nodded.

"The cake, my dress, the band—"

"Everything," he promised. He continued to hold her until she relaxed and began to breathe normally.

After a long stretch of silence, Sara removed the engagement ring from her hand and held it out to him.

"You can keep it."

She shook her head. "I wouldn't feel right about keeping it. Can you return it?"

He took the ring from her. "If you won't keep it, I think I will. Who knows, maybe someday they'll legalize gay marriage and I'll be prepared."

Sara grimaced. "It's bad form to use the same engagement ring twice. Besides, I doubt it will fit Clint." She wondered what sort of man Clint was. He must be something special if James was willing to toss away both his political and professional career.

He slipped the ring onto his pinky. It barely went to his first knuckle. "You may have a point there."

They continued to talk deep into the night. Mostly they remembered good times they had shared with Taylor as they were growing up. Once he tried to get her to talk about her feelings, but she wasn't ready. She needed to sort them out for herself first. All of her life she had been the follower. It was time for her to look deep within herself and try to find her own answers.

Chapter Eleven

The following morning, Sara met James for coffee before calling her parents to tell them that she and James needed to talk to them. After leaving the coffee shop, Sara glanced into the rearview mirror to see James's car following her and was filled with a sense of sadness. She knew how much the decision to call off the wedding was going to hurt her parents, as they both cared deeply for James. They would be worried about her as well.

As she pulled into her parents' driveway, she took a deep breath before stepping out of the car to wait for James.

After parking on the street, he came over to join her. "It'll be all right," he whispered, as he took her arm. They had agreed that James would be the one to break the news. He had jokingly insisted he would need the practice.

Her father opened the door as they started up the sidewalk. Sara saw him notice the separate vehicles and was touched by the flash of sadness that crossed his face.

Sara took another deep breath but continued to cling to James's arm.

"Your mother is in the den," her father said, as they entered the house.

Sara clasped both men's hands as they went to join her mother. She felt as though she was in a dream. Nothing felt real.

Lawrence Stockton stood by his wife's chair as Sara and James sat together on the sofa. She clung to James's hand and watched her parents' faces change from concern to confusion as James told his story. As soon as he admitted that he had known he was gay since childhood, Eloise reached up to grab her husband's hand. It seemed to Sara that they were both watching her closely. When James finished his story, silence filled the room. Sara tried to think of something to say, but nothing seemed appropriate.

Ironically, her father was the first to speak. "Are you okay?" he asked his daughter.

Sara nodded. "I'm fine, Dad." She hesitated, wondering if she should mention her own doubts, but the look of panic still on her mother's face stopped her.

When silence again filled the room, James stood. "I guess I'd best be going. I need to go talk to my parents."

"I'll walk you out," Sara said.

"James," Lawrence said, stepping forward. "I'm sorry things didn't work out between you and Sara, but I appreciate your coming here and telling us why." He extended his hand. When James took it, her father pulled him into his arms and gave him a fatherly hug. "You'll always be welcome here, son. If you need *anything*, you call me."

James's voice was thick with emotion when he spoke. "Thank you, sir. I appreciate that."

Eloise stepped forward and hugged him. "If you think it would help, I could call your mom later this afternoon," she said.

"I appreciate the offer, but I doubt she'll be taking calls," he said.

James turned suddenly and gave Sara a fierce hug.

"Don't see me out," he pleaded.

"Call me when you can," she whispered.

He nodded before rushing from the room.

Tears slid down Sara's face as she embraced first her father and then her mother. She couldn't remember a time when she had been more proud of them.

Sara walked through the outer office deliberately ignoring the sideways glances and whispers that followed her. After talking to his parents, James issued a statement to the press announcing his decision to withdraw from the campaign. He called to warn her that the story would make the evening news on the local television stations. As Sara watched the news, she was filled with a sense of pride. Impeccably dressed, James stood confident before the small group of local reporters who had gathered in front of his home. When asked why he was withdrawing, he cited personal reasons for his decision. Before they could bombard him with questions, he quickly announced his endorsement of David Brock, sent a dazzling smile toward the cameras and with a quick wave disappeared into the house.

Sara's phone had started ringing long before the evening news came on. Reporters called to ask her why James had resigned. After the story broke, friends and people she hadn't seen or heard from since high school began calling. Everybody wanted the *real scoop*. She finally got tired and unplugged the phones.

This morning's news programs had given her another surprise with their announcement that the wedding had been called off. The reporter claimed to have a source who had informed him the arrangements for the church and hall had been canceled. She realized her mother must have spoken to the priest after mass the previous day.

Half a dozen enterprising reporters had been waiting for her when she came out of her apartment building. She made a short statement that the decision to cancel the wedding had been a mutual one, and that she and James were still friends. When ques-

66

tioned about his decision to withdraw from the race, she referred them back to James.

Before Sara had time to say good morning, Gracie told her Rosa was waiting to see her.

"Are you okay?" Gracie asked, as she followed Sara into her office.

Sara slid her purse into the bottom desk drawer before placing her briefcase on the floor beside her desk. "I'm fine." She forced a smile before leaving to go to Rosa's office.

When she entered Rosa's office, she was touched by the genuine look of concern on her face.

"Close the door, please," Rosa said, as she came around her desk and motioned for Sara to take a seat. Rosa sat in the other side chair. "Are you all right?" She pointed to a newspaper on the side table.

Sara turned to look at the smiling image of James beneath a blaring banner announcing his decision to withdraw from both the campaign and his engagement. "Yes. I'm fine. James and I agreed that this was the best course of action."

Rosa nodded slowly. "If you need to take a few days off, let me know and I'll arrange it."

"That's not necessary."

"A couple of reporters called and left messages on my voice mail," Rosa informed her. "I won't be returning their calls."

"I'm sorry about that. This will all be old news in a couple days and everything will be back to normal."

"I suspect it will. Are you sure you don't want to take a few days off?"

Sara met her gaze. "Not unless you think my being here will cause a problem."

Rosa stood. "No. This is your personal business. It has nothing to do with the office."

Sara wasn't sure if it was her imagination or if Rosa had added a little extra stress to her last statement. Maybe it was Rosa's way of telling her to make sure it stayed that way.

"How's it going with the Brodie woman?" Rosa asked.

"I visited her and we spent a little time talking. Since Tom said she had been unhappy with the last person who went out there, I didn't press the donation issue. I'll give her a few days before I call again." Sara stood.

"Sounds good." Rosa was moving toward the door. "I'll be around all day if you need anything." She patted Sara's shoulder. "If you change your mind about the time off, just let me know."

Sara forced a smile and nodded. "Thanks." All she really needed was for everything to get back to normal. The thought of James moving to Dallas saddened her because they wouldn't be able to spend as much time together as they normally did, but she obviously couldn't tell people that canceling the wedding was a relief.

She went back to her desk and buried herself in work—or at least she tried. First, Tom Wallace called. Somehow, he had heard the news of her wedding being canceled. He tried to be polite, but it was obvious that he was more concerned about her progress with Amanda Brodie.

"I don't want to pressure her," Sara said. "I'll call her this afternoon and broach the subject of the land then."

"At this point, we're much more interested in the documents. You should concentrate on getting them first," he said.

Sara gritted her teeth. "And of course, I'll discuss the documents." She couldn't believe a man as intelligent as Tom would be so easily consumed by the rumor of gold.

"You need to get this wrapped up."

"Tom, I believe Rosa explained to you that I'm still carrying a full workload here. The Brodie homestead has been standing for several decades, so I think it'll still be there for a few more days."

"I didn't realize you had such a problem with authority. Perhaps I made a mistake in choosing you."

His comment hit a raw nerve. "You're free to replace me any-time you like—after all, I work for the City of San Antonio, not you." She mentally pinched herself. The historical restoration field was like a small community; pissing off someone she could easily find herself working for someday wasn't a smart move. To her surprise, he backed off.

"I'm sorry. It's just that this is such an important acquisition I'd hate to lose it due to neglect."

"I'm not neglecting it. Amanda Brodie is a tough old bird. She's not going to be pushed into anything. The harder she's pushed the more stubborn she'll get."

"Well, yes. Just keep me informed."

"I'll call you as soon as I've talked to her." She wasn't sure he was completely happy with her comment, but what else could she do? She wasn't going to waste time calling him with updates that didn't exist, and she didn't intend to pressure Mandy into donating her property.

Before she could get back into the project timeline she was working on, Eloise called, and Sara spent another ten minutes reassuring her mother that she was all right. After hanging up she called Gracie into her office.

"Pick up my calls, please. I don't want to talk to anyone unless they're calling about a project."

"No one," Gracie reiterated, her face a serious mask of concern.

"Well, I suppose I'd reconsider if the President of the United States called, or even the Queen of England."

Gracie relaxed suddenly and smiled. "Sorry, I guess I was being a little overly dramatic."

Sara smiled. "Have you spent the morning fielding phone calls from people with inquiring minds?"

Her assistant nodded.

"Feel free to tell anyone who asks that I'm fine. Canceling the wedding really was a mutual decision between James and me. We're still friends and always will be."

"What about the gold? Is that why James isn't running for city council anymore? Is he going to help you hunt the gold?"

She was so thunderstruck by the absurdity of the questions that it took her a moment to react. Before she could, she saw the look of suspicion cross Gracie's face. "Where in the name of God do you get these ideas?" Sara shook her head. "Gracie, there is no gold. There's land and a homestead. That's it." It was clear that the woman didn't believe her.

"The newspaper article said they stole the gold."

"Who did they say stole the gold?"

"The Williams gang."

"Exactly, and what does the Williams gang have to do with the Brodies?"

"They were part of the gang."

"That is undocumented speculation. I don't know of a single piece of evidence that ties these four men together. Now, if you know something I don't, I'll be glad to give it consideration, but otherwise the story about gold being on Brodie property is a rumor."

Gracie waved her hands in frustration. "Okay, so there's nothing but a lot of people suspecting they were guilty. There were newspaper reports about the million dollars being stolen. I saw copies of them in the folder Tom Wallace gave you. That's not a rumor."

Sara bit her tongue as she went to her desk and retrieved the folder. From it she removed the photocopy of the newspaper article Gracie was referring to and handed it to her. "Glance through it again. Nowhere in there does it mention an amount."

"Yes, it does." Gracie took the paper and began to scan through the information. After reaching the end, she shook her head in confusion. "Wait a minute. I know it's here."

"No, it isn't. I've read that article twice and the amount isn't mentioned."

"Then why would Lucie say it was a million dollars?"

Sara shook her head. Lucie was one of the interns. "How did Lucie hear about this?"

"She said Terrance told her."

"Okay, look, it doesn't matter where it started. My point is, it's all a rumor."

"But the robbery was real," Gracie proteste
mation about it on the Internet. The articles all
Brodie brothers as being involved."

"As *possibly* being involved," Sara corrected. "I've alre
you there is no evidence to prove they were members o
Williams gang."

"My grandmother always said that if you walk into a room filled
with smoke, you could bet there was a fire somewhere, whether
you could see the flames or not," Gracie added emphatically.

Sara leaned back in frustration; as she did, she noticed the clock
on her desk. The morning was nearly gone and she hadn't finished
anything she had intended to. "I'm sorry, but I need to get back to
work." She hesitated. She didn't like to curb her staff, but rumors
were dangerous. "I'm going to have to ask you not to talk about
the Brodie case to anyone. I don't want the media getting wind of
this. Fortune hunters would be all over those poor women. You
remember the damage caused at the site on Durango Street, when
that idiot told a reporter that he had found a treasure map in his
recently deceased grandfather's personal belongings that indicated
there was Spanish gold buried somewhere on the grounds." The
entire thing proved to be a hoax, but before they could prove it
was, treasure hunters had already ripped out most of the walls in
the old house. They even tore down the tool shed so that they
could dig under it. Sara took the article back, put it in the folder
and placed it on her desk. "If anyone on the staff mentions this
again, please tell them it's a rumor and remind them they shouldn't
be engaging in idle chit-chat."

Gracie looked away and nodded.

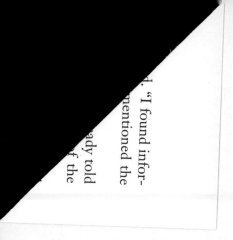

Chapter Twelve

After Gracie left, Sara sat staring at the timeline in front of her. After several minutes, she reached for the folder on Amanda Brodie and dialed her number. Arcy answered on the second ring. "Arcy, it's Sara Stockton, how are you today?"

"Sara." The warmth that flowed through the phone made her smile. "We were just talking about you this morning."

Sara tensed. They shared the same local television stations as San Antonio. She wondered if they subscribed to the San Antonio newspaper. She finally relaxed when she realized she hadn't mentioned James's name to them. "Really," she replied, as calmly as she could. She didn't want her personal life to be drawn into this project.

"Yes, Mandy was going to call you and invite you out for a tour of the ranch."

Relieved, Sara's shoulders relaxed. "That's why I'm calling. I have a free afternoon and I was wondering if it would be all right to stop by to see you and Mandy?"

Arcy made a soft poofing noise. "You don't need to call before you come. One of us is always around here. Come on out anytime you want."

"Thanks. I could be there in about an hour."

"Well, come on. I made a meatloaf last night. When you get here, we'll have meatloaf sandwiches."

"Sounds delicious."

After hanging up, Sara sent Rosa an e-mail to let her know where she would be in case anyone was looking for her. Gracie wasn't at her desk when Sara left, so she wrote her a note and put it on her desk.

After getting out of the downtown traffic, the remainder of the drive to the ranch was pleasant. Sara rolled her window down to enjoy the warm spring air. The wildflowers—bluebonnets, pink-capped Indian paintbrushes, yellow buttercups, pink evening primroses and large clusters of Indian blankets that looked like yellow and red woven tapestries—lined the roadway.

The washboard gravel road had not improved since her previous visit. Once again, she was forced to reduce the speed of her pickup to prevent it from dancing off the road. As soon as she pulled into the driveway, Roscoe ran to meet her. She moved slowly to give him time to remember her. "Hey, Roscoe," she called as she held out her hand for him to sniff.

"Hurry up, woman. I'm starving."

Sara looked up to find Mandy standing at the corner of the porch, a wide smile lighting her suntanned face. Arcy appeared in the doorway, again drying her hands on her apron. Sara realized that in the short time she had known them she had developed a fondness for the two women. As Arcy came alongside Mandy, the taller woman automatically placed her arm around her lover's shoulders. The genuine display of affection brought a smile to Sara's face. Along with it came a fleeting stab of pain. Would anyone ever love her with the same intensity as these two loved each other? A mental image of Taylor flashed but she pushed it away. "I'm sorry if I kept you from your lunch," she said, as she came up the steps to the wide porch.

"I just took the bread out of the oven," Arcy said. "Your timing is perfect." She came forward and gave Sara a hearty hug.

"You bake bread?" Sara asked mainly to hide her surprise at the sudden display of affection.

"Oh, yes," Arcy took her by the arm and led her inside to the kitchen. Mandy followed. "I don't care for that stuff they call bread at the store," Arcy explained. "I'd much prefer to bake my own, and it's much healthier without all those preservatives."

"I keep telling her it's those preservatives that keep me so young-looking, but she won't listen," Mandy said. "She's right about the taste, though. You just wait until you taste it," she bragged. "You won't ever want to eat that store stuff again."

"With that kind of glowing recommendation, I can hardly wait."

They headed inside where the kitchen table was set for three.

After Sara had consumed a hearty meatloaf sandwich, she leaned back. "Gosh, that was good, but I shouldn't have eaten so much."

Mandy jumped up. "Come on, we'll walk it off of you in no time."

"I won't be able to join you," Arcy said with a look of genuine regret. "Father Donovan called earlier and asked if I could bake a pineapple upside-down cake for the church raffle tomorrow."

Mandy's ears perked up. "A cake raffle. I didn't know there was a cake raffle. What time will it be?"

Arcy made a shooing motion with her hands. "You don't need to be thinking about a cake raffle. Go show Sara the ranch, and take Roscoe with you. He needs the exercise."

On the way out the door, Mandy grabbed her battered old Stetson and settled it on her head. "Come on, Roscoe," she said with a sharp whistle as they started down the steps.

Sara was miserably full. The bread had been wonderful, but now she was sorry she had been such a glutton.

"I'll show you the barn first. The old corncrib is behind the barn. I use it as a toolshed now," Mandy said.

Sara found that the log structures were typical of buildings from their era. The only thing that set them apart was their excellent condition. "These were very well built and maintained."

"This was all built by Bo and Dudley Brodie. Dudley was my great-great-grandfather. Bo never married and didn't have children, so when Bo died all the property passed on to Dudley's only child, William Jefferson. He . . ." She hesitated. "He wasn't much of a rancher and neither was his son, Robert E. Brodie. By the time the ranch finally came to my father, Sam, and his brother, Andrew, it was in sad shape. Uncle Andrew wasn't interested in ranching. He had other dreams to pursue. After his wife left him and their son, Virgil, Uncle Andrew moved into an old line shack over on the south end of the property. Virgil lived here with us. Dad would go out to check on my uncle occasionally and take him supplies. I only remember seeing him once or twice. He wore his hair and beard long." She chuckled. "In truth, he scared the bajeebers out of me. One day Dad went over to see him and he was gone." She stopped. "No one ever knew what happened to him. He just disappeared."

The historian in Sara was on the verge of probing for more facts when Mandy started talking again.

"Dad spent most of his life restoring the place to its original condition. The only thing that has changed is the outhouse. It blew away in a storm back in 'forty-two. I was just a baby, so I don't remember ever seeing it. Mom insisted the storm was God's way of telling Dad it was time to install indoor plumbing. I've been toying with the idea of rebuilding it just for the sake of authenticity."

Sara laughed. "I don't think I would have made a very good pioneer. The thought of using an outhouse really doesn't appeal to me."

"Sometimes, I wonder how any of them made it," Mandy replied. "Living out here isn't easy, even with today's modern conveniences. I can't imagine how it must have been then."

"What made you think about donating everything to the state?"

Mandy gazed at her through eyes squinted against the sun. "I wondered how long it was going to take you to get around to that."

"You knew that's why I came," Sara reminded her.

Mandy nodded and seemed to give the question some consideration before answering. "I'm the last of the Brodies. Like I said, I had a cousin, Virgil, but he was killed in Korea. Arcy has a couple nieces and an older brother. They don't have any interest in living on the place. After I had my heart attack, it got me to thinking. Arcy and I may not have many years left. If I don't make some kind of arrangements, the old place will sit here and rot until the county finally takes it for taxes." She started back toward the house. "I figured if I gave it to the state historical commission, they'd keep the place up."

"You had the right thought, but unfortunately, budget cuts don't allow the state historical people to take on much of anything new anymore. It takes every cent they have and then some just to maintain the properties they already have."

"Are you saying they don't want the place?"

"No." Sara cursed herself for allowing Tom Wallace to put her in this position. "I'm simply saying there has been more interest shown in the documents you mentioned."

Mandy stopped at looked back at her. "Are you serious? There's eighteen-hundred acres that I was going to just hand over."

"It's my understanding that you were attaching some stipulations that included the maintenance of the property as well as a wildlife sanctuary," Sara said evenly. "Unfortunately, those things cost money and the state simply can't afford to take these items on at this time."

Mandy started walking again. "I see. I thought they would just let the land sit fallow."

"Even then that's a big chunk of nonproductive land. Until some decision could be made on how best to use the property, the house would remain empty. Anytime you have vacant buildings vandals will be an issue. I'm sure you already know how expensive it can be to properly maintain buildings as old as these."

A weary sigh escaped Mandy. "So, they only want Bo's diary." She looked around at the homestead. "Strange, isn't it? Years of sweat and blood were poured into building all this and now it's worth less than a handful of paper."

Sara placed a hand on Mandy's arm. "That's not what I meant. This place is wonderful and I know the state historical commission would love to accept it if they had the funds to care for it. They don't want to make a commitment to you that they won't be able to fulfill." Sara knew there weren't many people who could afford to buy a piece of property as large as this one. At some point, it would probably end up being subdivided into several smaller sections.

"We're almost twenty miles away from the nearest town," Mandy said, as if she had read Sara's thoughts. "Not many people want to live so far out anymore."

Sara didn't know what to say.

Roscoe, who had been loitering along several feet behind them, suddenly growled and shot past them toward the house.

They looked up and saw the Channel 12 news truck coming up the driveway.

"They must be lost," Mandy said.

A sense of dread filled Sara as the truck came to a halt in front of the house. *God*, she prayed, *please let her be right*. But as the crew piled out and a heavy man with a camera began to pan the area, she knew they were exactly where they wanted to be. They had gotten a whiff of the gold and she was afraid she knew where they had gotten their information.

Chapter Thirteen

The news crew waited until Mandy called Roscoe back and had a hand on his collar before they rushed toward them.

For the briefest moment, Sara considered telling Mandy to let the dog loose on them. She quickly suppressed the foolish thought.

"Are you Sara Stockton?" the reporter asked. Without waiting for her to answer, he rushed on. "Is it true that James Edwards dropped out of the city council race to help you search for the millions of dollars of Confederate gold?"

"No, he did not." Sara fumed. "There's no gold. That's a rumor—"

"Sonny, I'm an old woman and my grip isn't what it used to be," Mandy began. "I'm not sure how long I'll be able to hang on to this dog."

The reporter glanced down at Roscoe and took a small step back. "You would be Amanda Brodie," he said.

Mandy looked down at Roscoe. "And this is Roscoe. I never

thought he would grow to be so large. Look at those teeth." As if by some silent command, Roscoe snarled. "He's usually not so aggressive toward guests." She looked at each man. "It's almost as if he knows you're trespassing."

The cameraman and reporter glanced at the dog. "Ma'am, we only want to—"

Mandy and Roscoe lurched a step forward. "Whoa," she said with a small chuckle. "You boys should leave. I'm really not going to be able to hold him much longer." She looked the reporter in the eye.

Again, she and the dog moved forward. Roscoe looked so fierce that even Sara took a step back.

The men started backing toward the news van. "The public has a right to know if your ancestors stole money and hid it out here," he challenged.

Mandy let go of Roscoe's collar. "Uh-oh, my grip gave out."

The dog lowered his head slightly and began walking toward the news crew with a menacing growl. As the men continued to retreat, Roscoe stayed with them. It didn't take but a couple of seconds before they scurried into the van. As soon as the van pulled onto the road, Roscoe turned and trotted back to Mandy.

"Good boy," Mandy praised him as she scratched his head.

"I'm so sorry about that," Sara said.

"Is that why you're here?" Mandy asked. The look of disappointment on her face made Sara long to get her hands around Tom Wallace's neck.

"No. Not directly, anyway. Can we please go inside and talk? I'll tell you what I know about this."

Mandy continued to stare at her until Arcy's voice floated from the house. "Mandy, I think you'd better come here."

"Come on." There was neither welcome nor condemnation in her voice. "What's wrong?" Mandy asked, as they approached the porch.

"Moon called. He's our nearest neighbor," she said to Sara before turning back to Mandy. "He said a reporter stopped by their house asking about you." She put a hand on Mandy's arm. "I saw that news truck as it was leaving. What's going on, Mandy?"

"That's what Sara is about to tell us." Mandy took off her hat and slapped it against her leg before heading into the house.

They sat in the living room with its comfortable, overstuffed chairs and the wall filled with framed photos of Arcy's former students. Sara told them how she had come to be involved. When she mentioned the diaries and Tom's belief that they might lead to the lost Confederate gold, Mandy laughed aloud. Arcy politely hid her smile behind her hand.

"So they sent you out here thinking I'd tell you where all this gold was hidden," Mandy said.

"They thought the documents might tell them something."

"What do you think?" Mandy crossed her ankle over her opposite knee with an ease that belied her age.

Sara looked her in the eye. "I believe that if there ever was any gold it disappeared a long time ago. There's no concrete evidence that Bo and Dudley Brodie ever had any connection to the Williams gang. The rumored amount of nearly a million dollars is completely ridiculous."

"You're right about that. It was only two hundred thousand," Mandy replied.

Sara waved her hand. "See, even the rumors aren't consistent. By the time this new wave of interest gets done with the story, it'll probably be something totally different."

Mandy stretched her long legs out in front of her and folded her hands across her stomach. "That's what I'm trying to tell you. It's not a rumor. They stole two hundred thousand in gold double eagle coins."

Sara rubbed a hand over her face. "I'm afraid someone within my own office may have leaked the news to the media." She started to say she would investigate the leak when Mandy's words registered. "Did you say the rumors are true?" she asked, not certain she had heard correctly.

Mandy nodded. "Yes. Bo and Dudley helped Emmett and Cletus Williams steal the gold."

"Mandy, dear, do you think it's wise to go into this?" Arcy asked.

Sara turned to Arcy expecting to see her smiling, but she was staring anxiously at Mandy.

"It's been a hundred and forty years and too many people have been hurt," Mandy replied. "If the television people start in on us, we won't be able to handle it by ourselves. Maybe Sara can help us." She ran a thumbnail along the crease in her jeans. "It's time to get everything out into the open." She turned to Sara. "I'm going to tell you the entire story as my father told it to me."

"Wait!" Sara held up her hand and shook her head. She sensed them watching her as she walked to the window and stared out toward the open fields to give herself a moment to think. Once she had full knowledge of the story, it would be difficult, if not impossible, for her to avoid being pulled into the frenzy that was certain to ensue. She turned to face the women. "Before you say anything else, I have to tell you that I can't lie to my superiors. I'm out here in an official capacity, and I'm compelled to be honest."

"I understand," Mandy said.

"I want to make sure you *both*"—she looked at Arcy—"fully understand what your lives will be like if you tell people that gold really existed. People will swarm out here. You won't be able to keep them off your property. They'll be worse than locusts. They'll destroy anything that gets in their way of searching." She saw the panic in Arcy's eyes and waved her hands before starting for the door. "I'm sorry, but I don't want to hear this."

"Well, hell's bells!" Mandy thundered, as she leapt to her feet so quickly that the other two women stared at her with open mouths. "I've been carrying this damn secret around for thirty-five years and now that I want to tell it, no one wants to listen!"

The tension in the room made Sara's nerves vibrate. This was what she got for trying to brown-nose with the state historical commission. She could have said her own workload was too heavy and Rosa would have understood. No less than eight projects were on her desk at this very moment. None of them was getting the attention they deserved because she was out here chasing Tom

81

Wallace's greed. She knew with unqualified certainty that this entire thing was going to blow up in her face.

"Dear, please sit down. It hurts my neck to have to stare up at you," Arcy said calmly. "I'm sure Sara is only thinking about our best interest. Maybe we should listen."

Sara nodded and silently thanked Arcy for her calm demeanor as she and Mandy sat back down. "As a historian, I want to hear the story," Sara admitted. "The problem is that if I hear it, I'll feel compelled to tell Tom Wallace." She thought about how he had been pestering her for information. "He most definitely wants the story." She hesitated, not wanting to project her own personal opinions onto the others. "Tom has a strong interest in the gold. Not for himself," she added quickly. "I've worked with him before and he seems like an honest, dedicated archaeologist. You have to understand that a discovery of this magnitude would be the highlight of his career." She leaned toward Mandy and clasped her hands together. "I know he would do everything in his power to protect you and your property, but it's an impossible task. If Channel Twelve goes ahead with their story—" She stopped and leaned back as brutal reality finally broke through. "It might already be too late. People are starting to talk about the gold. There's something about gold that brings out the worst in people."

"Lord, don't I know it," Mandy said sadly.

Arcy spoke up. "I'm no expert on these matters, but it seems to me that the more your people know, the faster they'll find the gold, and the faster it's found the less trouble we'll have."

Sara started to nod at the logic but stopped when the impact of what Arcy had said hit her. "What do you mean by 'the faster they'll find the gold'? Don't you know where it is?"

"I think you should listen to Mandy's story." She turned and added, "Dear, start at the beginning. I know it will spoil your big surprise but it's less confusing."

Mandy's lips thinned with displeasure. "It's my story, I reckon I can tell it as I see fit."

Arcy nodded. "Of course you can, dear."

"I may as well start at the beginning," she grumbled. "My great-great-grandfather Dudley Brodie's parents died when he was eight and Bo was thirteen. After they died Bo pretty much raised Dudley."

Arcy gently cleared her throat.

"Don't rush me. I'm getting to that part," Mandy griped. "Bo's real name was Bonnie Jean."

"Bo Brodie was a woman?" Sara asked, shocked.

Mandy's good nature returned. Her announcement had received the proper response. "Yes, and it's her diary that I wanted to donate. I thought it was about time people realized that women of the Old West did more than birth babies and scrub floors. Bo left a chronicle of the eleven robberies she and Dudley were involved in."

"Including the Confederate gold?" Sara asked. She kicked herself for leaving the project folder on her desk. She should be adding this information to it. No, that was silly. Writing it down would just get her further involved.

"That was the last robbery they pulled," Mandy said.

"This is going to take a while. So, why don't I get us all a glass of iced tea before you get too deeply engrossed in your story," Arcy said. She patted Mandy's shoulder as she made her way to the kitchen.

Chapter Fourteen

As soon as the small group was settled with their tea, Mandy resumed her story.

"Like I was saying, after their parents died Bo took over raising Dudley and this would have been around eighteen forty-three. They didn't have any other family and their nearest neighbor was a day's ride away. Life was a struggle. Bo soon found that her father's old clothing was better suited for traipsing through the woods, while they were gathering wild berries or hunting game and such. Late one afternoon they were out a good ways from their cabin when they heard what sounded like shots. Since they didn't have close neighbors they decided to investigate. That's when they first met Emmett and Cletus Williams. A posse had cornered the brothers in a box canyon." Mandy sipped her tea and chuckled. "You can bet they were surprised when those two kids showed up out of nowhere from behind them. According to Bo's diary, Cletus had been wounded in the side. She and Dudley led them out of the canyon and took them back to the cabin where the brothers stayed until Cletus was able to get around."

Sara interrupted. "I'm sorry, but where were the kids living then?"

"Up near Amarillo," Mandy replied. "Bo never says exactly where, but she mentions that it took them nearly three days to reach Amarillo by wagon."

Satisfied, Sara nodded, wishing she had a tape recorder.

"During the time that Emmett and Cletus are at the ranch they bonded with the kids. Let me throw in here that Bo estimates Emmett to be in his late twenties or early thirties and Cletus to be in his mid- to late-twenties. She never mentions anything about their backgrounds. It seems both men were always rather tight-lipped about that. I've always figured their father was someone whose name might be recognized. Or maybe they already had a lot to hide from." She shook her head. "I'm straying. When the brothers left, they gave the kids some money and it was agreed that they could return whenever they needed to. Over the next few years that's exactly what happened. Then around eighteen-fifty, the brothers show up, but this time it's to ask for a different kind of help. They wanted to rob an Army payroll courier coming out of San Antonio and headed to the new forts that were being built in the western section of the state. Bo doesn't mention the locations, but she does say the actual holdup occurred in Uvalde County. I've done a little research, and in eighteen-fifty there were four military installations out that direction—Fort Lincoln in Medina County, Fort Inge in Uvalde County, and Fort Duncan and Camp Eagle Pass, which were both in present-day Maverick County."

Sara nodded. The forts were among many that had been built during the latter part of the eighteen-forties and early eighteen-fifties in an attempt to protect settlers from Indian raids. Many of the facilities had been decommissioned during or soon after the Civil War ended.

"The payroll was being transported by a small detachment of six troopers. Emmett's plan was to use Bo as a damsel in distress, a decoy, and Dudley would be an extra gun. In her diary, Bo tells how hard she and Dudley were struggling to survive, and I think that living alone with almost no contact from the outside world had an effect on them." Mandy shifted into a more comfortable position before continuing with her story. "At one point in the route, the patrol would have to enter a large grove of trees. Within the grove, a blind curve wound around an enormous outcropping of rock. Emmett's plan was simple. They would wait for the Army to come to them. The men took turns being the lookout. When the lookout spotted the Army patrol, he was supposed to race back to warn the others. Then, the buggy they had hidden in the brush in case some traveler other that the patrol came along was to be pulled onto the road and tipped over. Dressed as a woman, Bo would lie down near the overturned buggy to make it look like it had turned over with her. The gang thought that the patrol would rush to her aid and while they were distracted, the three men would step in and take over. That might have worked except a hellacious storm blew in. While they were sitting in camp trying to take shelter from the storm, the soldiers rode right into their camp looking for shelter also. The outlaws reacted quicker and were able to take the soldiers by surprise. They relieved them of the payroll without a single shot being fired. Then as soon as the storm let up some, they took off with the patrol's horses and made a clean getaway. Bo was still dressed in her men's traveling clothes and the troopers were none the wiser. Thus the legend of the four-man Williams gang was born. The gang netted nearly twenty thousand dollars for their troubles."

Sara knew a little of the history of the Williams gang and saw where Bo could have managed to hide her identity to the public, but once the Brodies settled in Atascosa, how had she continued that charade? She decided to keep quiet until Mandy had finished her story.

Mandy continued, "Bo assumed her male persona completely after that. She was determined never to be broke again. She guarded every penny of her money religiously. She was able to convince Dudley to set some of his money aside as well. Emmett was smart enough to know they couldn't hit the same area twice. He picked their targets carefully and made certain it was monetarily worth their effort. The four of them would travel in pairs to the site of their next holdup. They averaged pulling one heist a year together. Emmett and Cletus would occasionally do a smaller job alone. This continued until the Civil War broke out and all three men went off to fight."

"They joined the Army?" Sara asked in surprise.

Mandy nodded. "Yes, for a while. They were in Hood's Texas Brigade. Again, I did some research and found service records for them. They saw action at Eltham's Landing, Gaines' Mill, Second Manassas and Sharpsburg. Bo hated the place back near Amarillo, so prior to the men leaving, Bo and Dudley used some of their ill-gotten gains to buy a little over six thousand acres of land here. At that time, it was covered in scrub oak and not much good for anything, but it was far enough from any settlements that they weren't likely to draw much attention. They built a small cabin for Bo to live in while Dudley was away. The original cabin is now part of the master bedroom." Mandy turned and pointed toward the right side of the house.

Sara was so engrossed in the story that she barely noticed when Arcy refilled her tea glass.

"Bo lived here and managed to clear a small section of the land where she planted vegetables to eat. She was able to hunt for fresh meat. The war didn't hit Texas as hard as it did most of the southern states, and by being way out here no one bothered her. By early sixty-four, Dudley, Emmett and Cletus realized they were fighting a losing battle and decided it was time to take care of themselves. They deserted and headed back for Texas and Bo. By now, they were all broke except Bo, who had buried her carefully hoarded stash in an old coffee tin in her vegetable garden. After picking up Bo, they drifted over toward Houston and pulled a couple of small jobs that put a few dollars in their pockets, but everyone was having hard times. Bo mentions Emmett saying there wasn't a decent place left to rob. That's when they headed toward El Paso. Bo left her stash buried beneath the garden plot knowing it was safer there than it was with her. I think that on some level, she didn't trust Emmett or Cletus. The group was casing a bank in El Paso when Emmett ran into an old buddy of his. After a few drinks to the glorious Cause and her fine boys—" Mandy stopped and explained, "Emmett apparently found some way to explain his presence there rather than on some battlefield." She glanced at Arcy and smiled. "Don't worry, I'm not going to stray too far from the story."

"You're doing fine, dear," Arcy replied.

The look of love that passed between them caused a stab of jealousy in Sara. She envied their relationship. She wanted someone to love and who would love her with the same intensity that these two had for each other. Mandy began her story again, and Sara pushed away her longing and listened.

"As they continued to drink, Emmett's friend mentioned that he had been scheduled to help escort a mule train that was carrying an important shipment to Galveston, but he had been reassigned because of a fight he'd been involved in. Well, you can imagine how curious Emmett got over this shipment. After a few more rounds, he learned that it was a gold shipment that was being taken to Galveston, where it would be used to purchase ammunition and supplies from the blockade-runners. The new supplies were to be used in a final attempt to save the South. By the next morning, Emmett and the gang had a plan to follow the pack train from a distance and when the time was right they would attack it during the night."

"How many mules and men were involved in this train?" Sara asked.

"Four mules carried the gold and two additional mules were used for supplies. The patrol consisted of eight men."

Sara knew it was rude to interrupt but there were too many questions bouncing around in her head to keep still. "So, it was simply a matter of luck that they just happened to bump into the right person at the right time?" she asked skeptically.

Mandy took a deep breath. "I'm not sure *luck* would be the correct word for what happened."

Sara kept quiet and sat back to listen.

"They followed the mule train for over a week. Late one evening it started raining and the patrol stopped in a grove of trees." She looked at Sara. "Bo said it gave her an eerie feeling because her first criminal escapade had started in a grove very similar to this one. The four waited until dark and used the rain to help cover their approach to the camp. The young guard on duty had fallen asleep. They quickly overpowered him and made their way right up to the sleeping men. When the four rushed in and yelled for everyone to reach for the sky, one soldier suddenly opened fire. His action encouraged others to grab for their weapons. That's when all hell broke loose. Two of the soldiers were killed immediately and two others were wounded before the patrol surrendered. The four outlaws loaded the gold onto the mules and rode away with all the horses and mules in tow." She held up her hand. "Bo mentions the isolation of the spot, so I'm guessing that because the patrol was burdened with two wounded men and no horses, it would have taken them a few days to reach a town to notify the authorities. By then the rain would have wiped out all the tracks, allowing the gold and outlaws to seemingly vanish off the face of the earth."

Chapter Fifteen

After taking a short break, the women returned to the living room and the conversation immediately resumed where it had ended.

"In the newspaper article I read, one of the soldiers said he thought he had wounded Cletus," Sara said.

"It wasn't Cletus," Mandy explained. "It was Emmett. He died a couple of days later and they buried him somewhere along the trail. The gang realized they would need a safe place to hide the gold and to lay low for a while. They started making the long journey back here. They knew they wouldn't be able to spend any of the money anytime soon. It was eighteen sixty-five and there weren't many people walking about with money in their pocket, much less twenty-dollar gold coins." She stopped and tugged on her ear. "As I said, Bo didn't mention exactly where the robbery took place, and even the newspaper article I found only says that the gold was stolen while en route from El Paso to San Antonio."

"How long did it take them to make the trip back here?" Sara asked.

"It's hard to say. Bo would sometimes go several days without making an entry. Then there were times when she would lose track of what the actual date was. After studying her diary, my best guess would be six-to six-and-a-half weeks," Mandy replied.

Sara gave a small whistle. "That must have been hell."

"They traveled mostly at night to lessen the chance of meeting people on the road, and there were a few times when they had to swing over to avoid towns."

"Did your research include looking for Army records documenting the gold shipment?"

Mandy sipped her tea before answering. "No. I didn't know who to contact. It's possible something might still be out there."

"The South was on the verge of collapsing," Sara thought aloud. "Everything would have been chaotic. I can do some checking, but it's not likely I'll find much."

After a short pause in conversation, Mandy continued with her story. "When the trio arrived here, they buried the gold behind the cabin and agreed they would leave it there until after the war ended and the country was back to business as usual. They all knew the war couldn't last much longer. A few days later, they began to run out of supplies. Here they were sitting on two hundred thousand dollars and they were, in essence, broke. Cletus insisted they dig up enough gold to buy supplies. Dudley agreed and decided that since they were going to be spending some of the money they might as well spend a little more to buy some cattle. Then they could at least work at ranching until they were free to dig up the rest of the gold. Bo argued that spending one single coin could bring the authorities down on them. She was so convinced that spending the gold would be the end of them that she broke down and dug up her secret stash. They agreed that Cletus and Dudley would take the paper money and the bulk of the smaller gold coins from Bo's stash and ride into San Antonio. There they would buy supplies and a few head of cattle. That is exactly what they did.

Things might have gone much smoother if Dudley hadn't insisted they stop for a quick drink. As they entered the bar, a deputy marshal recognized Cletus from a wanted poster. When he started to approach them, Cletus ran and managed to escape. They took Dudley in for questioning. He kept telling them that he had met up with Cletus on the way in to town. He later told Bo that he didn't think they ever believed him, but since they had no evidence to tie him to any of the robberies they had to let him go."

"I thought the gang simply disappeared after they stole the gold," Sara said.

"Either the deputy didn't write out a report or the report has been lost or thrown away," Mandy replied.

"It makes you wonder, doesn't it?" Arcy asked. "Think of all the information that has been lost over the years. I once heard that the basements of the White House and Library of Congress are literally crammed with thousands of boxes filled with documents that haven't been touched in decades."

Sara nodded. "I've heard that also. Wouldn't you love to be let loose in there for a few years?"

Mandy cleared her throat. "Now who's wandering off the subject?"

"Well, at least we know how the Brodies and the Williams brothers were finally associated," Sara said, in an attempt to bring them back to the diary. "I was beginning to wonder about that."

"Yeah, but that's all about to change," Mandy said. "After Dudley was released he picked up the cattle and supplies, which the sheriff had temporarily impounded, and headed home. It was slow going and not being a cowhand, he had problems getting used to moving the cattle. He didn't arrive at the cabin until the following day, right about suppertime. When he arrived, he knew something was wrong immediately. The front door to the cabin was open and there was no smoke coming from the chimney. He found Bo lying on the floor, shot in the back. Cletus and the gold were gone. Luckily, the bullet had passed through Bo's right side without striking anything vital. Dudley stayed and nursed her until he was sure she was going to be all right and then he went after

Cletus. It was almost two weeks later before he returned. Bo described him as looking like death itself and he was covered in dried mud from head to foot, even though it hadn't rained since before he left. He came back with a scalp wound and a bullet in his thigh. Besides his horse, he had Cletus's horse and the two pack mules Cletus had used to carry off the gold, but there was no gold. It was Bo's turn to act as a nurse.

"When Dudley recovered he told her he dumped the gold into the river. He said he did it because the gold was nothing but trouble and had almost gotten her killed. Bo didn't believe him. Over the next several months, they built the barn and outbuildings. Bo continued to press Dudley about where the gold was buried. Finally, in a moment of weakness he admitted that he had buried the gold, rather than dump it in the river, but he still refused to tell her where it was buried. Bo began searching for it. At first, it was just a day here and there, and then she would disappear for weeks. It became an obsession. Her diary entries became even more sporadic at this point, and they're all about the gold—where she had dug, where she planned to dig—and then one night Dudley woke up to find his sister standing over him with a pistol barrel pressed against his forehead. She told him if he didn't take her to where the gold was buried, she'd kill him. He finally agreed and they set out." Mandy stopped and leaned forward to make her point. "Everything that happened from the moment Dudley woke up to find Bo with a gun pointed at him has been handed down verbally."

Sara nodded as a lump of dread formed in her throat.

"Dudley agreed to take Bo to where the gold was buried come morning, but Bo insisted they leave right then. She made him saddle their horses and gather the mules. She intended to bring the money back. It wasn't until the sun came up that Bo realized Dudley had been leading her in circles. He tried to tell her that the gold was cursed, that it had brought them nothing but bad luck and death. Besides the two soldiers who had died during the holdup, the gold had gotten Emmett killed and turned Cletus against them. He reached out his arm to her and Bo must have thought he was trying to grab the gun. She jerked away and in the process, the gun went off. The bullet singed the neck of the horse Bo was riding. The horse reared in panic and pitched her off. The mules bolted and trampled her. She was dead before Dudley could get to her. He brought her back and buried her up on the hill behind the house, and according to family legend he moved the gold to where each time he was tempted to use it, he could see the spot where it was buried and Bo's grave at the same time."

Sara's mouth dropped. "The gold is buried around here?"

"If what's been passed down is correct, it is," Mandy said, with a slight smile.

Sara sat in silence for a moment. "Did Dudley kill Cletus?"

Mandy shrugged. "I think so. I doubt Cletus would have simply handed over the gold and rode away."

"So for all these years the gold has been buried out there and no one has bothered looking for it?" Sara asked.

"Oh, I wish," Mandy replied sadly. "That gold almost destroyed the Brodies." She picked up the story line again. "Dudley eventually married and had a son, William Jefferson Brodie, and a daughter, Rachel. She died when she was two. On his deathbed, Dudley gave Bo's diary to William and told him what had happened to her, but he died without ever telling where he buried the gold." She stopped again. "Let me back up some. After Bo died, Dudley drifted up to San Angelo and got a job on a ranch there. That's where he met his wife, Sophie. They were married the year after Bo died. Then he moved his new wife back here."

"So that would have been around eighteen sixty-six," Sara clarified.

"That's right," Mandy said. "Over the next several years, Dudley added on to the house until it was the size it is now, purchased more land and slowly built up his cattle herd. Sophie kept meticulous records. I have them. Every cent spent or earned is accounted for, so I'm positive he never touched the gold."

"What year did Dudley die?" Sara asked.

She squinted her eyes in thought. "He died October third in the year nineteen hundred."

Sara kept silently repeating everything Mandy told her in an

94

attempt to commit it to memory. She cursed herself again for not asking for a notebook to take notes. This time it was Arcy who seemed to read her thoughts.

"Mandy has all of this typed out on the computer," Arcy said. "She even transcribed Bo's diary. We'll run you off a copy of everything whenever you need it."

Sara smiled her relief. "Thank you. William was how old at that point?"

Mandy closed her eyes for a moment. "Let me see. William would have been thirty-three." She opened her eyes. "He was already married and had kids by the time Dudley died." She shook her head. "I can't imagine what possessed Dudley to talk about the gold. Maybe he needed to get it all off his conscience before he died, but all he accomplished was sparking another wave of gold fever. After hearing his father's story, William became obsessed with finding the gold. He stopped working the ranch and spent every waking moment poring over Bo's diary and digging up half the ranch."

"Are you sure he never found it?" Sara asked.

"Yeah, he died nine years later. It was in February and cold. He was in the back pasture when a rainstorm blew in, but he was so positive he was digging in the right spot that he wouldn't stop. He caught pneumonia and died two weeks later." As if anticipating Sara's question, she added. "He was forty-two."

"That's so young," Sara said sadly. "Seems like a lot of suffering for gold that no one has touched."

"That's not the end of it," Arcy said, from her chair in the corner.

Sara glanced over and saw that at some point in the story, Arcy had begun to sew. It looked as though she was doing some kind of embroidery work. "Others have been hurt?" Sara asked.

Mandy nodded. "William and his wife, Zelda, had three children, Alice, June, and Robert. The two girls had already married and moved away from here by the time William died. Robert was only sixteen at the time and he and his mom, who lived for another twenty-five or so years, continued to live here at the ranch until Robert got married in his early twenties. The story goes that Zelda didn't like his wife and went to live with June. Robert was my grandfather. He wasn't as obsessed as his father was, but the ranch suffered the most under his management. He started selling off pieces of the property. He and his wife, Betty, had two sons, Andrew and Samuel, my father. Andrew was more like my grandfather Robert Brodie." She looked at Sara. "I think I mentioned Andrew to you earlier."

Sara tried to remember. There had been so many names thrown at her in the last few minutes. "Was he the man who lived in the line shack?"

"Yes. When he was a boy, he would help his dad look for the gold. My father refused to have anything to do with it. Andrew was older and he married Katie Beldon. They had a son named Virgil. When Virgil was four, Katie ran off with an insurance salesman. After that, Andrew sort of went off the deep end and moved up to the old line shack. He left Virgil here with Dad. That was in 'thirty-eight. A few months later, Dad married Mom and she pretty much claimed Virgil as her own. Dad had a job working on a neighboring ranch. The automobile had made this place a lot less remote. By the time my father took over the ranch, the house was barely livable, the cattle had been sold off and the barn was starting to fall in. He taught himself to notch logs in the same style that Dudley and Bo had done in the original construction, and an old man in town taught him how to make the proper mud and straw mixture for the chinking. Slowly he and Mom whipped the old place back into shape. Virgil and I grew up here." She took a deep breath and glanced at Arcy. "Virgil was killed in Korea. Mom died in 'ninety-four and Dad followed her four years later. He gave me Bo's diary on my thirtieth birthday. I think he wanted to see how I was going to react to it all."

"Did you have any interest in looking for the gold?" Sara asked.

"No. Never had any interest in it. By then, I'd already found all the gold I'd ever need," she said, as she turned to Arcy and smiled.

Chapter Sixteen

Sara was satisfied she had done all she possibly could for Mandy by the time she finally drove her truck onto the main highway headed toward San Antonio. The story Mandy had told was amazing. Sara found herself torn between wanting to protect the women and snatching out her cell phone to call Tom Wallace to tell him the gold existed. If the television media continued probing, it was only a matter of time before they came up with enough to run something on the news. As soon as they did, treasure hunters would invade the ranch. Even if the state expedited the acquisition and declared the place a historical landmark, which they wouldn't, nothing within the government worked that fast, it wouldn't stop people from sneaking onto the property in search of the gold.

They had all agreed that if the media came back, Mandy would refer them to Tom Wallace and that for the time being she wouldn't tell her story to anyone else.

Sara would call Tom Wallace tomorrow morning to let him know Mandy was no longer interested in donating the land or the diary. As far as Sara was concerned, she no longer had any official involvement with the Brodie properties. Unofficially, she had accepted their invitation to Sunday dinner. As she drove, she realized that one of the biggest bonuses of the day was that she hadn't thought of James or Taylor all afternoon.

The traffic into the city was sparse and gave her plenty of time to think. She recalled James's question on why they had all been friends. Had they all sensed a common bond in their sexuality even then? Could a woman be a lesbian and not know it? she wondered. Was that why she had only dated James all those years? Because on some subconscious level she had known he was safe? But they had made love. True, it hadn't happened very often and was never very satisfying, but the act itself had occurred. Neither of them had avoided it. Yet, James was gay. If he had made love to her even though he knew he was gay, wasn't it possible that she could make love to him while not knowing she was? *How stupid can you get?* She hit the heel of her hand against her forehead. It wasn't like there was a gay and lesbian switch in people's bodies that flipped on and set up barriers the minute a member of the opposite sex appeared. She giggled as she envisioned a steel door closing off her vagina each time a man got near her.

The questions made her head spin. She rolled down her window and let the cool air blow over her. With it came more questions. Was she a lesbian? She had definitely experienced a reaction to Taylor's touch last week. She paused and mentally pictured a calendar. Had it only been a week ago that Taylor had come over? So much had happened in such a short time. Did Taylor sense something in her that attracted her? *Oh, God*, Sara thought, *what if she isn't attracted to me and I imagined the entire episode.* She recalled the look of hunger on Taylor's face. Sara might not have much experience, but she knew lust when she saw it and Taylor Jenkins's face had definitely reflected lust.

What am I going to do about it? Sara asked herself. Should she confront Taylor? What if she convinced herself she was gay when she really wasn't. Maybe her experience with James had been less than expected because *he* was gay. Maybe it was James and not her at all. Even if that was the case, it still didn't explain her reaction to Taylor. She reached for her cell phone to call Taylor but stopped. This was not a conversation to be held over the phone. She needed to talk to Taylor face-to-face. Even the thought made her stomach tingle. It's just a nervous reaction, she told herself.

Rather than drive home, she took the exit to Taylor's house. It was Monday, so she wasn't likely to barge in on her and Debbie. To be sure, Sara parked on the street in front of Taylor's and called. Taylor answered on the second ring.

"If you're free, I thought I'd drop by to see you for a few minutes," Sara said. Was it her imagination or did Taylor hesitate. "If you're busy, I understand."

"No, I'm just packing away a few things. Come on. I'll probably be done by the time you get here anyway."

"I wouldn't bet on it."

"Why? Where are you?"

"I'm parked in front of your house."

Taylor laughed suddenly. "You're such a goose. Come on in."

After hanging up, Sara pulled her truck into the driveway. Taylor was waiting for her at the door when she started up the walkway.

"Why did you call rather than just come on in?" Taylor asked, as she gave Sara a hug.

Sara's heart pounded as Taylor's arms held her. Why did Taylor hugging her now affect her so? she wondered. Over the years they had exchanged literally hundreds, maybe even thousands of hugs and she had never given it a second thought. So why was it so different now?

"Are you all right?" Taylor asked, as she stepped back and looked at her.

"Sure. It's just been a long week."

Taylor's hand went to her shoulder. "Sara, it's only Monday. Come on in and sit down. Then you can tell me what's going on."

They went into Taylor's comfortable living room. There was no one style to describe her decorating scheme. It was simply Taylor. Somehow, it worked for her. There were half a dozen boxes sitting on the floor. Upon seeing them a moment of panic hit Sara. "Are you moving?"

"No." Taylor stared at the boxes a moment. "I'm just packing some of the clutter away for a while."

Sara sat in her usual spot on the end of the couch. "You don't have clutter."

Taylor sat at that opposite end of the couch and tucked her bare feet beneath her. "I heard someone at work say that James dropped out of the race for city council. What happened?"

"You haven't talked to him?" Sara asked, surprised. She was positive he had told her he would call Taylor.

"No. Why?"

Sara wasn't sure where to start. "We've called off the wedding."

Taylor stared at her in stunned silence for a long moment. "My God, what happened? Are you all right?" She slid over closer to Sara and took her hand.

Sara tried to ignore the warmth of Taylor's skin as she spoke. "I'm fine. We both agreed it was best. It was a mistake from the very beginning."

Taylor peered at her closely. "Why would you say that?"

"Because James is gay and has known he was for years."

An emotional curtain settled around Taylor. "Is he sure? I mean—"

"He has been seeing a man in Dallas for a while now."

"I see." Taylor released her hand and moved back to her corner of the couch. "You seem pretty calm about this."

Sara shrugged. "I think that on some level, I've always known he was gay." Should she tell Taylor about her own personal doubts?

"Is that the reason he dropped out of the campaign?"

She nodded. How could she ask the questions that had been plaguing her all the way from the ranch?

"Who else knows why he dropped out?" Taylor was busy making small pleats on the tail of the cotton shirt she was wearing.

"He told my parents and then his."

"Ouch. Telling his parents must have been tough. How did your parents handle it?"

"They were wonderful. They really care for James and you," she added.

Taylor stared at her with a probing look that Sara couldn't read.

Sara's voice trembled as she spoke. "I wonder if they would have handled it as well if it had been me coming out to them." She couldn't meet Taylor's gaze.

"Why would you think about that?"

"We've all been such close friends for so long. Maybe that's why. Maybe we didn't realize it but there was a mutual bond that pulled us together."

Taylor gave a harsh laugh. "Hell, Sara. Joe Denton was gay and so was Sheila Brooks," she said, naming two of their former classmates. "I couldn't stand either one of them. You're not gay just because James and I are."

Sara tried to find a way to explain how she felt when Taylor had touched her, but it all sounded too Harlequin.

"If that has been bothering you then forget about it."

"You don't think I'm gay?"

Taylor hesitated a moment too long. "Of course not. Why should I?"

"Because sometimes when I'm around you—" The look on Taylor's face stopped Sara cold. Had it been anger or pain?

"You what?" Taylor asked in a strangled voice.

"I . . . I . . ." She took a deep breath. "I experience these feelings that I've never felt before," she blurted.

Taylor went to fiddle with the thermostat on the wall. A moment later, Sara heard the air conditioner start to hum. Rather than returning to her seat on the couch, Taylor continued to stand by the thermostat. Finally, she shoved her hands deep into the pockets of her jeans. "Have you ever had these feelings for anyone else?" she asked at last.

"No. That's why I don't understand them."

"Sara, you aren't a lesbian."

Sara stood and crossed the room to stand in front of her. "How can you be sure of that?"

Taylor raised her head and gazed at her. "God wouldn't be that cruel to me."

"I don't understand."

"Debbie is moving to San Antonio. She found another job here." Taylor's glance darted toward the boxes on the floor. "She'll be moving in with me at the end of the month."

Sara felt a sense of loss like none she had ever experienced. She couldn't let Taylor see how upset she was. She tried to swallow her pain as she spoke. "Why is God being cruel to you?"

Taylor raised a trembling hand and touched Sara's cheek. "Because, I've been in love with you most of my life." She leaned forward and softly kissed Sara's lips.

Chapter Seventeen

Her world stood still. How many times had Sara heard that expression and scoffed at it? When Taylor's lips met hers, she instantly understood it. Her breath caught as Taylor's hand slipped into her hair. The warm gentle kiss was unlike any she had ever experienced. As it deepened and Taylor's tongue began a gentle probe, Sara welcomed it completely. Her body hummed with desire as Taylor's free hand slipped down her back and pulled their bodies closer together.

Suddenly Taylor pulled away and stumbled back, almost falling over the boxes. "I'm sorry," she whispered hoarsely.

"Don't be." Sara reached for her.

"Please, don't," Taylor cried. "I shouldn't have kissed you. I have no right."

Sara started to argue before she realized what Taylor was saying. She wasn't worried about whether or not Sara was a lesbian. She was talking about Debbie. Taylor was in a relationship with Debbie. "It's my fault," Sara said. As the silence between them grew, she turned. "I should go."

Taylor didn't stop her.

Sara drove home with her mind in a swirl. So much had happened within the last forty-eight hours that she could no longer process her emotions. Thankfully, the press was no longer camped out at her front door. James's withdrawal from the campaign was no doubt already old news. Mr. Tibbs met her at the door, announcing his disapproval of her coming home later than usual. "Not tonight, okay, buddy?" she said. She started to the bedroom but stopped. It wasn't the cat's fault that she'd had a crappy day. A blinking red light indicated she had a phone message. That would probably be Taylor. In no mood to talk to anyone, she turned off both phones. Then she fed Mr. Tibbs his small packet of treats and cleaned the litter box before stepping into the shower. As the water pounded down on her, she forced herself not to dwell on James, the Brodies, work and most of all, Taylor. The pain and stress of the day slowly flowed from her body, to be replaced by complete exhaustion. By the time she stepped out of the shower, she barely had the energy to towel herself dry before dropping into bed. As she drifted off to sleep, she made a promise to herself that she was going to forget about Taylor's kiss. Taylor had Debbie, James had Clint, and she had her work.

When the alarm sounded the next morning, Sara awoke rested and ready to face another day. She refused to let herself dwell on anything other than getting to work. By doing so, she was at her desk an hour earlier than usual. The blinking light on the phone notified her that she had messages waiting. She reached to check them but stopped. If she started going through phone calls and e-mails, she wouldn't get anything else accomplished, and she was determined to remove at least one thing from her to-do list. She would wait and check them later.

By the time the outer office began to come alive, she had already completed the timeline she had been struggling with the previous day and was reading the outline for a new project Rosa had left on her desk. She decided not to call Tom until after she checked with Mandy one last time to see if any other media people had tried to contact her.

"Where have you been?"

Startled by the sudden noise, Sara looked up to find a frazzled-looking Rosa glaring at her.

"Right here," Sara replied. Rosa's abruptness surprised her. "Why?"

"We've been trying to reach you all night."

"I was at home." She rubbed her forehead as she remembered turning the phones off. "I was so tired, I turned off the phones. What's wrong? Please don't tell me another work crew hit a water or utility line."

"Mandy Brodie's in the hospital."

Sara flew from her chair. "No! Was it another heart attack? I was just out there yesterday afternoon. Which hospital is she in?"

Rosa held up her hand. "Come on, I'm headed out to the ranch now."

Sara snatched her purse from her desk. "What's going on?" she asked. She had to run to keep up. She noticed Rosa had a newspaper folded beneath her arm.

"Wait until we're in the car," Rosa replied harshly.

Confused by both Rosa's startling news and her unexpected behavior, Sara practically had to bite her tongue to stop the questions. Her confusion grew as Rosa approached a city-owned car rather than her personal vehicle. It was too much for Sara. No one in the department used a city-owned car anymore. Cutbacks had stopped that luxury ages ago. "Rosa, what the heck is going on? How is Mandy?"

"The doctor says she'll be fine. He kept her overnight to watch her, but she was getting ready to go home when I left the ranch earlier."

"You were at the ranch? Why?"

Rosa ignored her questions until they were safely in the car and headed out. Only then did she hand Sara the morning paper. "I'm assuming you haven't seen this."

Sara opened it to a glaring three-inch headline announcing:

BURIED GOLD IN ATASCOSA COUNTY. "No. I was so concerned about the television crew, I forgot the newspaper would be after the same story. They must have shown up after I left."

"The television networks have the story as well, right along with the radio stations." She glanced at Sara, "I can't believe you haven't heard any of this. It made the Channel Twelve evening news and by this morning it was everywhere. I called your home phone and cell. Arcy tried to call you. Tom Wallace tried to call you."

Sara held up her hand. She got the point. "I wasn't feeling well when I got home last night. I turned off the phones, took a hot shower and crashed. My cell phone was in my purse in the hall closet. I forgot to take it out." She felt a tinge of irritation at having to explain her actions.

"And you didn't check any of those things this morning?" Rosa snapped.

Sara's anger flared. "I was in a hurry to get to the office to try and make up some of the time I've been missing because of this *special assignment*." She spat the last two words out.

"Did it ever occur to you to give me a heads-up, after that television news crew arrived yesterday?"

Sara took a deep breath. In truth, it hadn't. She wasn't reporting to Rosa on this assignment. "They didn't seem to have any information and they didn't get anything from Mandy. I thought we'd have a few days before things went crazy. Will you please tell me what happened?"

Rosa sped onto the interstate before replying. "Arcy said that last night around eight-thirty Roscoe started racing around the house barking. At first they thought it might be a coyote or even a panther."

"A panther?" Sara interrupted.

"Yeah, apparently they spot one out there occasionally."

Sara shuddered.

"Anyway, they went out on the porch to see what was going on and they saw lights out by the barn. Mandy grabbed a shotgun and Arcy called the county sheriff's office and some guy named Moon."

"Moon is their neighbor."

"That's right. Arcy told me. I'd forgotten."

Sara noticed the dark circles beneath Rosa's eyes. "Were you at the ranch all night?"

"No. I stayed at the hospital with Arcy. Tom and a couple of county deputies stayed at the ranch."

"What happened after Mandy got the shotgun?" Sara could almost see the tall sturdy woman standing on the porch with the gun.

"The lights turned out to be treasure hunters searching the barn."

"Oh, please. How stupid could they be?" Sara snapped. "It's not like Mandy would just leave the gold lying around." She stopped and turned to Rosa. "Wait a minute. You said the news broke at ten o'clock. Why were these guys out there at eight-thirty?"

Rosa shook her head and gave a disgusted snort. "It was Gracie's husband, Jason, and his goofy brother."

Sara grabbed the armrest for support. "Gracie," she whispered. "Jason seems like a nice guy. I've met him a few times at department parties. Why would they do this?"

"It's my own damn fault. She and I have been talking about the project and I kept acting silly about the gold. I didn't think anyone was taking me seriously."

"Gracie and I talked about it. I told her the gold was probably just a rumor."

"I think she wanted to believe. She read the folder I gave you. Then she mentioned it to Jason. He in turn told his brother, who thinks he's Indiana Jones. The two brothers have a few beers too many and decide to go treasure hunting. When Mandy confronts them with the shotgun, they practically pee their pants and try to run. As soon as they start to run, Roscoe charges in and grabs Jason's pant leg. The guy is a little drunk and petrified. He kicks the dog off him. That's when Mandy cut loose with the shotgun."

"Oh, God, no."

Rosa held up her hand. "Jason's all right. The shotgun shells were loaded with rock salt. He'll have a few painful reminders for a while, but no real damage."

"What happened to his brother?"

Rosa snorted. "Mr. He-Man fainted when the shotgun went off. By that time, Moon was there and hogtied both of them. That's how Sheriff Vargas found them."

"What happened to Mandy? Why is she in the hospital?"

"After the sheriff arrived and found Jason peppered with rock salt, he called an ambulance just to be sure. When it arrived, Arcy insisted they check Mandy out as well. Of course, her blood pressure was elevated and her heartbeat was higher than the tech felt comfortable with. They took her in for observation. When Arcy couldn't contact you, she went through the office voice mail options and finally reached me. She was desperate to find you. When I couldn't reach you, I called Tom Wallace. He's at the ranch now. He tried to talk to them during the night, but neither of them wants to talk to anyone but you."

"What's going to happen? There's no way we can protect their property."

"I'm recommending they stay somewhere else until it's safe for them to return. I shudder to think what could have happened. By now, the story of that gold is all over most of South Texas and in a few days it could spread even farther. The next time it may not be a couple of intoxicated idiots poking around in the barn."

"We have to find the gold," Sara replied without thinking.

Rosa looked at her in surprise. "What do you mean, 'find the gold'? Don't tell me you've got gold fever now." She released her foot from the accelerator and darted glances at Sara. "Do you know something I don't?"

"No. Of course not." Sara cursed her carelessness.

"Sara, if there's something to this, you'd better start spilling it right now. I don't want the office to be pulled into this mess. Did they tell you something about the gold you're not telling me?"

Sara leaned her head back and began repeating the highlights of the story Mandy had told her yesterday. When she finished, Rosa looked more drawn that before.

"Well, isn't that just fucking Grade-A wonderful?" Rosa spat the words out.

Sara blinked in surprise.

"I am *not* taking this on. Tom can handle it. You're off this project as of right now. I don't want you talking to those women or anyone else about this project." She turned to Sara. "Is that clear?"

Sara frowned. "Wait a minute. You can't tell me who I can or can't talk to."

"I can if the department is in jeopardy."

"Well, it isn't."

"Bull. The press is going to be all over you. I don't understand why they haven't found you already. As soon as you tell them the truth, every half-wit with a shovel is going to descend on that property and the owners are going to sue us for . . . for . . ." She waved her hand. "Who knows what? On the other hand, if you lie to the media and then the truth comes out, the media will have a field day picking the department apart for every little thing we do. We won't be able to straighten a nail without them being right there watching over our shoulder, waiting for us to screw up, so they can crucify us."

"Rosa, you're going off the deep end. You're exhausted. I think we need to get everyone who's involved into one room and decide as a group the best way to handle this."

Rosa released a long sigh. "Maybe you're right. I'm just sick about what happened last night. I feel like it's my fault. Gracie was so upset, she resigned."

"She resigned!" Sara yelled. "She can't afford to resign. They're struggling financially already." She stopped when she saw she was only making matters worse. After a moment, she reached over and patted Rosa's hand on the steering wheel. "It'll all work out eventually."

They rode in silence for several minutes before Rosa spoke. "How are you doing with the other thing?"

Taylor's kiss jumped to the front of Sara's mind, but she pushed it away. That wasn't what Rosa was asking. She was asking about the broken engagement. "I'm fine. It was a mutual decision and we're both going to be fine." She wished people would quit asking.

As they approached the road that led back to the ranch, Sara noticed several vans parked along the road.

"What's going on up there?" she asked.

"The press has camped out, hoping to be allowed in."

As they drew closer, Sara saw the two county sheriff's cars blocking the road leading up to the ranch. As soon as Rosa switched on her turn signal, the crowd moved toward the car. She slowed down but kept the car at a roll. It took the deputies a moment to move the crowd back.

Rosa eased the window down. "I'm Rosa Saenz. I'm with the historical commission."

"Yes, ma'am," the young woman deputy replied. "I remember you from this morning. You can go on up to the house." She spoke into the mike at her shoulder and one of the cars blocking the road moved out of the way to let them pass.

"When did the press show up?" Sara asked, after they were clear of the crowd.

"I'm not sure. They were here when I got here last night and that was around eleven."

"I really am sorry I unplugged the phone. I never dreamed anything like this would happen so quickly. I assumed the press would at least take time to find some type of evidence to support the story."

"Lost gold is rare so it makes a good headline. If they took time to verify it, some other station might scoop them on the story. Stop worrying about the phones. You've had a lot going on in your life the last few days. You're entitled to a decent night's sleep."

Sara nodded as a series of images formed—James's tears as he came out to her, the sadness in Mandy's voice as she spoke of Bo's death, Taylor's kiss. Merely thinking about it made her body quiver with longing. The car hit a rut and sent her flying toward the roof.

"Sorry, I didn't see that pothole," Rosa said.

Sara braced herself as the car continued to bounce over the washboard surface of the road. At least some things never changed.

When they finally pulled into the driveway, Mandy's old Ford pickup was parked where it normally sat. In addition, there were two county sheriff cars, a new, gray Lexus and a lime-green

Volkswagen van with large red and orange flowers and canary yellow and violet quarter moons painted on it. The van looked like it had dropped right out of the sixties. "What's with the hippie-mobile?" Sara asked.

"That's Tom's van."

Sara's head whipped toward her in surprise. "You're joking."

"Of course I am. The Lexus belongs to Tom. The van belongs to Moon. Arcy told me their whole story last night. Moon and his wife, Flower, live down the road a ways. I'm not sure how far 'a ways' is in country jargon, but it seems to cover a lot of territory. Anyway, Moon and Flower are a couple of harmless old hippies who never left the sixties. When they got married thirty-five years ago, they commingled their names to form a new surname. Now, they are Moon and Flower MoonFlower. They have a son named Red and a daughter named Violet."

Sara stared at Rosa for a moment, to see if she was teasing her still, but she looked completely serious. "Are you pulling my leg again?"

Rosa shook her head. "No, even I couldn't have come up with that one."

Chapter Eighteen

Roscoe and Mandy met them on the front porch. Mandy looked a little pale, but neither she nor Roscoe seemed to be hurt.

"Mandy, are you all right?" Sara asked.

"I'm fine. That EMT overreacted and got Arcy all upset. He was probably afraid I'd kick the bucket in the middle of the night and Arcy would sue the hospital or something."

"Is Arcy all right?"

"Yeah." She nodded toward the house. "She's got a kitchen full of people to feed, so she's happy."

"I'm sorry you couldn't reach me last night."

"Don't worry about it. I told Arcy not to start calling everybody. I can take care of this place just fine."

"Rosa told me what happened. I swear to you, Gracie would never intentionally do anything to hurt anyone and I don't think Jason would either. I can't imagine what possessed him to do such a thing, but I promise you, I'll get to the bottom of this."

Mandy shook her head. "I've already gone over to the jail to talk to those old boys. They're both feeling pretty miserable this morning. I'm not going to press charges."

"That's very generous of you," Sara said, a little surprised. She doubted she could have been so magnanimous if it had happened to her.

"They were drunk. They both offered to come out and repair any damage they'd done."

Sara had a sudden uncharitable thought that they were probably trying to get back out here to look for the gold some more.

"I don't think either one of them will be too eager to go treasure hunting again anytime soon," Mandy said and chuckled. "Rock salt makes a nasty burn."

Before Sara could reply, Tom Wallace came storming out of the house. "Sara, how could you have let this happen?" he demanded. His navy blue Brooks Brothers suit was rumpled and he needed to shave.

"Tom, it wasn't her fault," Rosa insisted.

"Well, I'd like to know whose fault you think it was. Sara was assigned to this project and it was her clerk's husband that they caught out here ransacking Miss Brodie's barn. It doesn't appear to me that Sara has any control over anything."

Sara silently agreed with him. It seemed as though recently her entire life had been turned topsy-turvy.

Rosa stepped in to defend her, but Sara held up a hand. "Tom, I know you're upset, and you have every right to be. If we can just sit down and discuss this, I think we can reach an agreement."

"The only thing I want to discuss is pulling you off the project. As of this moment, you and your department are no longer needed."

"That's fine with me," Rosa replied. "I for one am glad to be out of this mess."

"This 'mess' was caused by your department," he snapped.

"That's not fair, Tom," Sara interrupted.

A sharp whistle from Mandy stopped them all. They turned to

look at her. "Mr. Wallace, your ranting and raving is starting to bother me. I've already run off that first patronizing flunky you sent out here. Do you want to be the next one to leave?"

Tom shifted uncomfortably. "Miss Brodie, I'm only trying to help you."

Mandy made a rude hissing noise. "Bull, you just want to get your hands on that diary, because you think it's going to lead you to a shit pot full of gold."

Tom glared at Sara.

This was going to get ugly, Sara realized.

Mandy stuffed her hands into her pockets and continued as if she hadn't noticed his reaction. "Well, I've got news for you, buddy. It won't. There's not a single word anywhere in the diary that will lead you to any gold."

Tom looked like a kid who had just had his favorite toy yanked away. "Perhaps it needs to be reviewed by a trained—"

"I don't need a degree to read about the daily ins and outs of ranch life, Mr. Wallace. If you're only chasing some wild gold rumor, you won't find any answers in Bo's diary."

Tom recovered quickly. "I assure you, I'm not interested in any rumors of gold. I'm only concerned about your safety and protecting this wonderful old homesite," he said.

It was clear from the expression on Mandy's face that she wasn't buying his story. "Then you'll find a way to help us keep the trespassers off our land, even if there's no gold?"

He fumbled in surprise for a moment. "Most certainly. That's clearly a county law-enforcement issue and something you should discuss with Sheriff Vargas. I'm sure he'll be able to provide you with adequate protection until all this blows over."

"And afterward, what about the land?" Mandy persisted.

He seemed to give the question some thought. "Well, these things take time. It's up to the committee to decide these issues. And as you've said, you weren't very happy with our representative, so perhaps it would be best if Sara remains your contact."

"No." Rosa stepped forward with her hands on her hips. "You're not dropping this bomb on my department."

"Rosa, please." Tom's voice softened, as he turned to the county historic preservation officer. "I'm not dropping anything on you. I'm simply agreeing that the property owner feels better working with Sara. This has absolutely nothing to do with your department. Sara's on special assignment, remember."

Sara had the feeling he was trying to talk around her. It took her a moment to realize that he was telling Rosa that her Bexar County office couldn't be held responsible if anything went wrong. All responsibility was going to fall squarely onto Sara's shoulders.

"I'm not going to let you throw her to the dogs," Rosa started, but Sara reached out and touched her arm.

"Rosa, he's right. Mandy and I have a good working relationship. I'd like stay on and help get everything taken care of."

"That's the attitude, Sara," he said. "Of course, you realize that until the committee makes a decision to accept the property, the state historical commission can't be held responsible for any monetary disbursements."

Sara gave him her sweetest smile. "Trust me, Tom, I'll make sure your office isn't burdened with any monetary issues."

He was practically skipping as he made a hasty exit. The three women stood on the porch watching the Lexus disappear down the road.

When the car was almost out of sight, Mandy turned to Sara. "I hope you know what you're doing."

"I hope I do too," Sara replied.

Rosa looked at her. "*Do* you know what you're doing?"

"No, but I feel better knowing we're in charge rather than Tom."

Mandy gazed out over the front field. "I certainly agree with that."

"What's everyone agreeing to?"

They turned to find Arcy standing behind Mandy.

"That you're the best cook in all of Texas," Mandy said, as she hugged Arcy close.

"I know what you're up to," Arcy said and swatted Mandy's arm. "Well, I made a special batch of blueberry muffins just for you. I just took them out of the oven and there's a fresh pot of coffee, if Moon and the deputies haven't finished it off already. Sara, you and Rosa come on inside and have some."

Rosa made a slight noise of appreciation. "That sounds wonderful. Let's go invade the kitchen."

As they went into the house, Sara touched Rosa's arm. "Are you sure you want to get involved in this? It could prove to be a media field day."

"What I really want to do is find the gold. Then there wouldn't be any reason for anyone to be digging."

Sara rolled her eyes. "You know it's probably a million-to-one chance that it'll ever be found, if he buried it. Why would you want to tackle those odds?"

"Sara, I'm an archaeologist and I've been stuck behind a desk for eight years. Something of this magnitude is like a gift to me." She tilted her head to the side. "Did I ever tell you that when I was a kid I wanted to be a pirate when I grew up?"

"Is that why you became an archaeologist?"

"Yes. I figured if I couldn't live a life of crime, pillaging and plundering the high seas, I might as well join the government where I could pillage and plunder legally and still get paid for it."

Chapter Nineteen

Inside they found two tall, lanky deputies, who could have been formed from the same mold, and the aging hippy sitting at the table enjoying their coffee.

Mandy quickly made the introductions. "Sheriff Vargas left John and Brad here"—she pointed toward the young police officers—"in case we have any more trouble. He also has cars patrolling the property line wherever possible."

Sara studied the men and suspected they were both younger than her own twenty-eight years.

"Actually, he left them here to protect any uninformed trespassers," teased the neighbor, Moon MoonFlower, a short, chubby bald-headed man with sky-blue eyes and a Santa Claus beard.

A tiny stab of disappointment hit Sara. She had expected his dialogue to be filled with words like *groovy* and *sock it to me*, but he sounded like everyone else in the room. The sixties fascinated Sara. The era of free love and a generation's search for peace and harmony. After the socially restricted fifties, the sixties must have filled people with an enormous sense of freedom. She wished she had time to sit and talk to him, to hear his stories.

Moon stood. "I've got to get home. Flower was planning on a busy day gardening. I should go help her."

Sara saw Mandy and Arcy exchange glances. Arcy seemed to be struggling not to laugh as she turned and busied herself with wrapping some of the blueberry muffins. The two deputies seemed to become extremely interested in their coffee cups.

"Take some of these muffins to Flower," Arcy insisted, as she pressed the bundle into his hands. He thanked her, and to Sara's delight, he flashed the room a two-fingered peace sign before he left.

Arcy was making yet another pot of coffee when the deputies' radios began to squawk. A thin layer of tension filled the kitchen. Sara tried to listen, but it sounded as though the speaker had a mouthful of marbles, and the static hurt her ears. Whatever the dispatcher said caused both young men to jump up and grab their hats.

"What's going on," Mandy demanded.

The deputy she had introduced as Brad stopped, but John rushed out of the house. "One of the patrol units has located a section of fence that has been cut and tire tracks leading off across the field. The unit is requesting backup."

"Wait a minute, I'm going with you," Mandy insisted.

"No, you aren't!" Arcy grabbed her arm and turned to the deputy. "Go on, Brad, and do what you have to. I'll keep her here."

"Thanks, Miss Arcy." He tipped his head apologetically to Mandy. "I'd feel better if I knew you were here watching the house since most of the cars will be off chasing these guys," he said before he rushed out.

A moment later, Sara heard the powerful engine of his car roar out of the driveway.

"Okay, he's gone so let go of me," Mandy grumbled.

"I will not. The minute I do, you'll grab that shotgun and take off."

"Well, so what if I do. It's our land after all."

Arcy gently squeezed Mandy's arm, and Sara once again marveled at the enormous amount of love between these two women.

"I could take care of those yahoos," Mandy insisted.

"You always have, dear," Arcy agreed, "but this time we need to let the sheriff handle things. Every time you shoot someone it makes things harder for Sara and Rosa."

Mandy grumbled some more but sat back down at the table.

Everyone's appetite seemed to have disappeared as they sat waiting for word about the intruder. Several times over the next half-hour, Mandy walked to the back door to stare out.

"Poor Flower has probably dug up their whole crop by now," Mandy said.

"What do they grow?" Rosa asked.

"Marijuana."

Rosa and Sara gasped.

"It's only for their own use and I guess maybe a few friends," Arcy said. "I'm sure it must have scared them half to death when that news crew pulled into their yard yesterday."

Mandy chuckled.

"What are you laughing at?" Arcy asked.

"I was just thinking that if we could add up the monetary value of all the pot Moon has grown in the thirty-odd years he and Flower have lived here, it would probably be worth more than the gold that Dudley buried." She returned to her chair and waited.

Everyone jerked when the phone finally rang. Mandy grabbed it before the second ring. The only sound was her occasional murmur of acknowledgment.

Arcy began to towel her already dry hands on her apron as she stared anxiously at Mandy.

Sara realized it was a nervous habit. She listened as Mandy thanked the sheriff before she hung up and came back to the table.

"They caught them. It was five boys from town. One of them told the sheriff that he had heard the story on Channel Twelve last night and decided they'd try to find the gold. They were out there digging at random. Sheriff Vargas was in his Jeep and after they picked up the boys, he made a sweep through the far pasture. Someone has been out at the old line shack digging. Whoever it was tore out what was left of the walls." Her shoulders drooped as she sat down and Arcy moved to stand beside her.

"We've got to find a way to put an end to this." Sara rubbed her forehead. "Mandy, I had to tell Rosa about the gold."

Mandy nodded slowly.

"You have my word that I'll never mention it to anyone else. I've seen enough places destroyed by vandals." Realizing what she had said, Rosa stopped suddenly. "We'll find a way to put an end to this," she promised. "Am I right in assuming that the four of us are the only people who know for certain that the gold really is buried around here somewhere?" she asked.

"I've never told anyone except Arcy and Sara," Mandy said.

"I've never mentioned it to anyone," Arcy assured them.

"I only told Rosa," Sara said. "And I know she hasn't told anyone because I've been with her ever since we spoke."

"As I said, now that I know the situation, I'll not mention it to anyone," Rosa said, as she raised her hand. "I know, I joked around about it before, but I honestly thought the whole thing was a hoax."

"I'm going to play devil's advocate here for a moment," Sara said. "Mandy, are you absolutely sure the gold exists?"

She shook her head and looked away. "No. I've never seen any evidence of it, so I can't say it does with a one-hundred-percent guarantee. All I'm sure of is what my father told me. I know that he believed it, so I'll say that I'm ninety percent certain it's true."

"There's one aspect of the story that bothers me," Sara said. "After Bo died, her brother moved the gold to a spot to where he could see it and Bo's grave at the same time. That seems to me like it would have narrowed down the search location enough that your ancestors could have found it."

Mandy stood and waved them up. "Follow me and let me show you something."

They followed her outside onto the stone porch and then

across the backyard a ways. She stopped and pointed to a hill almost a mile away. "Bo's buried at the top of that hill," she said.

Sara looked at the enormous stretch of land between them and the gravesite. "How far does your land extend in either direction?"

"It goes as far as you can see to the south and to that clump of trees to the north." She pointed out the tree with a tip of her chin. "The lay of the road makes a pretty fair property line to the east, and the west boundary ends a little way beyond the rise."

Sara slowly took in the wide expanse of land that was visible to her. It would take an army of men years to search that much space with nothing but a shovel.

As if reading her thoughts, Rosa said, "There's no way we could possibly search an area that large without some pretty sophisticated equipment, and it certainly couldn't be done without attracting attention."

"Rosa thinks we might be able to stop all this if we could find the gold," Sara said.

"No," Mandy replied quickly. "It has already hurt my family enough. It's better left where it is."

Sara gazed at the distant rise where Bo was buried. "I think we should release a statement to the press and try to stop this madness before it gets any further out of hand."

Arcy looked at her. "How's a press statement going to help? Isn't that just going to feed the frenzy?"

Sara shook her head. "Not if we can convince them that the gold was stolen by the Williams brothers and that there was never a connection between the Brodies and the Williams."

"How do we do that?" Mandy asked, as they started back toward the house.

"It means you won't be able to turn Bo's diary over to anyone until . . ." She hesitated. To say the diary had to remain hidden until after they were both dead and could no longer be affected by the desecration of the ranch was too callous to say aloud.

"We understand," Arcy said.

They returned to the kitchen table and sat down.

"How are we going to convince the press and the general public that the gold doesn't exist?" Rosa asked.

"That's the problem we're going to solve this morning," Sara assured them. "So let's start thinking this through."

Silence filled the room as they tried to think their way out of the problem. Arcy left for a moment and came back with a handful of pencils and pads of paper. "I don't know about anyone else, but I seem to think better with a pencil in my hand." She passed out the supplies.

"I think we should start with what's already public knowledge," Sara began. "We stress the fact that the Williams gang stole the gold—"

"Allegedly," Rosa corrected. "They were never convicted."

"Good point," Sara conceded. She noticed that Arcy was keeping notes. "Then we point out that there was never any physical evidence to indicate the Brodies and Williams even knew each other."

Mandy leaned forward. "What about the muster rolls?"

"What muster rolls?" Rosa asked.

"In her research, Mandy located documents that showed Dudley Brodie and the Williams brothers served in Hood's Texas Brigade," Sara explained.

"Do you think anyone else would even bother to look for those records?" Arcy asked.

Sara shrugged. "There's a chance someone might, but even if they find them, it still doesn't prove the guys knew each other."

"Let's cross that bridge when we get to it," Mandy proposed.

Arcy held up her pencil. "What if we try to shift the focus?"

"In what way?" Sara asked.

"What if while talking to the press someone casually mentions the careless way Channel Twelve handled this situation? After all, they released this story without any facts to back it up."

They all looked at her. "You might be onto something there," Rosa said. "With all the foul-ups that have been happening in the news recently that's a touchy subject for everyone."

"But those guys were here before the story broke," Mandy reminded them.

Sara glanced at Rosa. "What do you think of me giving Gracie a second chance if she makes a public apology and admits that the gold wasn't even mentioned in the folder that she saw?"

Rosa tapped a finger against her chin. "In her defense it's not as if she gave the information to an outside source. I occasionally tell my husband about things I work on at the office. I actually talked to him about this project." She looked at them and shrugged. "He pooh-poohed the idea of buried gold." She hesitated a moment longer. "If you trust her enough to let her work for you again, I guess I could."

"I think her admission and Arcy's idea combined might make an impact," Sara said.

They continued to discuss their options for several more minutes before they decided to go with what they had. Sara took her cell phone out to the front porch and called Gracie.

When Gracie answered the phone, Sara could tell she had been crying. She cried harder when she heard Sara's voice. In between sobs, she tried to apologize.

"Gracie, I need for you to try and tell me what happened," Sara said, as gently as possible.

"It's entirely my fault." She sniffled. "Jason came by to pick me up for lunch. I had called him to tell him . . . to tell . . ." She began to cry again.

Sara realized she should have gone to Gracie's house rather than call her. She waited patiently until the tears slowed. When Gracie didn't pick up right where she left off, Sara left it alone until later.

"I was running late when he got there and he started complaining about having to wait. It was going to be at least fifteen minutes before I could leave so I put him in your office so he could watch your television."

Sara had a small set with a VCR that she occasionally used to watch videotaped overviews of certain projects.

"He'd never admit it, but he's a soap opera junkie," Gracie continued. "Anyway, I left him in there. I'm so sorry. I should have known better. The man is like a damn cat. He's curious about everything. When I went back in to tell him I was ready, he was reading the Brodie folder. I took it away from him and made him promise he wouldn't say anything, but somehow when I wasn't looking he took the sticky note that had the directions to their ranch. I swear to you, I didn't know he took it."

"I believe you," Sara said.

"While we were eating, he started asking me questions about the stuff in the folder. You know, stuff like why was that old ranch important and how was it connected to the newspaper article about the gold." She stopped.

"What did you tell him about the gold?" Sara asked.

"I told him what you told me, that it was a rumor."

"What happened then?"

"He goes back to work, but he can't stop thinking about the gold. After work, he goes over to his fool brother's house and they start drinking. Roger, his brother, has a metal detector and he's always showing off with it. After they'd had a few beers, Roger drags out his *collection*." She dragged out the final word.

"What kind of collection?" Sara asked, hoping to keep Gracie talking.

"It's stuff he found with the metal detector. Most of it's junk, but he keeps it all tucked away in these little boxes. When Roger showed Jason a silver dollar he found, Jason went stupid and started talking about knowing where there's a shitload of gold. Then they have a couple of more beers and he said the next thing he knew they were on their way out to the ranch. They took the metal detector but once they get out there, they realized they didn't have a shovel and they had no clue on where to start digging. They talked it over and decided that if they had that much gold to hide, they would hide it in barn so that they could get to it whenever they needed it. As soon as it got dark they snuck into the barn and started poking around, but I guess they made too much noise and the dog heard them or something."

"Gracie, you really shouldn't have let him into my office."

"I know. I'm really sorry. Jason said the ladies were okay. Are they still okay?"

"Physically, yes, but police cars were needed to block their driveway to keep the media out."

"Please tell them I'm sorry. And so are Jason and Roger. They feel really bad for what they did. Is there anything I can do?"

There was the opening she had been waiting for. "The press vans are already out here. If I made the necessary arrangements to issue a statement in a couple of hours, to try and get this mess straightened out, would you be willing to tell them that all this talk about gold is just a rumor that got started around the office?"

Gracie quickly agreed and Sara promised to call her back as soon as the press conference was scheduled. Sara held off on offering Gracie her job back. To do so now might make it look like she was coercing her to speak to the press.

Chapter Twenty

After a series of calls between the sheriff's office and the deputies who were still guarding the road to the ranch, Mandy was able to verify that all three of the major networks still had vans camped out. At Sara's direction, she relayed a message that a statement would be released before noon.

Sara called Gracie back and gave her the time and directions. She asked her to wait at the road for them. Then the women sat back down and wrote the statement that Sara would read. They agreed that Gracie should speak after Sara had read the statement.

A few minutes before noon, Sara and Rosa climbed into the city-owned car and followed Mandy's truck out to the road. Sara noticed that Rosa was careful to park the car in such a way that the City of San Antonio emblems on the side doors weren't visible from the road.

Camera flashes and shouted questions filled the air as soon as the four women approached the crowd of reporters. When they tried to surge forward the deputies stepped in and moved them back.

The female deputy who had stopped the car when Sara and Rosa arrived that morning came back to greet them. "I'm Deputy Denise Underwood. Which one of you is Sara Stockton?"

"That would be me."

The deputy nodded. "There's a woman, a Grace Lawrey, waiting to see you."

"Let her through, please. She's going to be addressing the press also."

The deputy spoke into the mike on her shoulder before turning back to Sara. "How do you want to handle this?"

Sara spotted a rather large outcropping of rock nearby with a somewhat flat surface. "I'll stand on that rock over there. That should put me high enough for everyone to be able to see me."

The deputy escorted her to the rock and helped her up on it. Sara was thankful that she had worn slacks and shoes with a low heel today. The crowd composed of reporters, camera operators and technicians shifted with them. Sara nodded to the deputy and the reporters were allowed to move closer. Again, there was a tidal wave of questions tossed at her. She gave them a couple of minutes to quiet down before she unfolded the statement in preparation of reading it. The sudden silence threw her for a moment. She glanced at the deputy who was standing to her left and received a second surprise when the young police officer winked at her. With some effort, she pulled her attention back to the crowd of reporters who were looking at her expectantly.

"I'm going to read a statement and then I'll try to answer your questions. A full, written statement will be relayed to you within twenty-four hours." She cleared her throat and began with a brief summary of the robbery and escape of the Williams brothers, being careful not to use the word *gang*. This was followed up with a short timeline of when the Brodies had purchased the property and how they built the ranch. She placed a great deal of emphasis on how hard they had struggled financially over the next several decades. Then she attacked Channel 12. "Less than an hour ago, according to the Atascosa County sheriff's office, five suspects were apprehended after they destroyed a section of fencing to gain access to the Brodie property. These men were caught randomly digging holes in a search for the gold the Williams brothers allegedly stole several hundred miles from here. The boys told the sheriff they decided to look for the gold after one of them saw a story on last night's news." Sara saw the Channel 12 reporter glaring at her. He was the reporter Mandy had run off yesterday. She returned his stare as she continued. "I find the actions of the reporter who ran this story to be irresponsible and incompetent at best. His failure to properly research and validate his claim has resulted in the property owners being forced to take refuge behind a police barricade. This additional output of police man-hours has cost the citizens of Atascosa County a great deal of money and now five of its citizen are behind bars. On behalf of the Texas State Historical Commission and the property owners, I'm requesting that Channel Twelve make a public apology and do whatever is necessary to stop this foolishness. There is not one single shred of evidence to suggest the gold is within three hundred miles of here."

"If there's no gold, why are you out here?" a voice called from the crowd.

"Ms. Brodie understood the historical value of the Brodie Ranch and wanted to ensure its integrity was maintained for future generations."

"How much is the gold worth now?" another voice shouted.

"Nothing. Section 191.002 of the Antiquities Code of Texas prohibits the gold from being touched. Doing so is a misdemeanor, punishable by a fine of not less than fifty dollars or more than a thousand and/or confinement in jail for not more than thirty days."

"That's not much of a deterrent," the reporter replied.

"True," Sara admitted, "but then you come to Section 191.172, which gives the attorney general the right to bring forth action in

128

the name of the State of Texas." She smiled brightly. "Wanna bet who wins that round?"

A ripple of laughter followed. She quickly pointed to a woman who was trying to catch her attention. "I have a source who says there was a disturbance here last night before the television story broke. Can you verify that?"

Sara nodded. Before she could speak a voice from the crowd called out. "I think I can answer that one."

Sara looked up to see the broad-shouldered Jason Lawrey pushing his way to the front of the crowd. She held her breath, not knowing what was about to be said. She had been expecting Gracie, not Jason.

When he broke free of the crowd, he stopped and turned to face them. He cleared his throat several times before beginning. "It was me that broke into the barn last night." He ran a hand over his buzzed head. "My wife works for Ms. Stockton." He tipped his head toward Sara. "Yesterday, I went to my wife's office to pick her up for lunch." He cleared his throat again. "While I was there . . . I . . . um . . . I opened a file on Ms. Stockton's desk and read it."

A murmur ran through the crowd of reporters as they eased closer.

"What was in the folder?"

"Did it tell where the gold was?"

"Did you find the gold?"

Sara could see sweat starting to tickle down the sides of Jason's face. She held up her hands for silence.

He hunched his shoulders and wiped the sweat from the side of his face. "It didn't say anything about gold being out here. There was just a copy of a newspaper article about the gold being stolen and one little note about maybe the Brodies knew these guys who stole it. At first, I just figured it was another one of those stories. You know, like you see on television where they go out looking for those sunken ships and things, but they never find them because it was all a rumor."

"Then why did you break into the barn?"

"After I went back to work—I work over at the Rapid Lube on Bandera—I just kept thinking about how great it would be to find all that money." He glanced up at Sara before turning back to the reporters. "I didn't know I couldn't keep it. Anyway, after work, I went over to my brother's house and we had a couple of beers. He has this metal detector thing and he got to talking about it. We had some more beers while he was showing me all this stuff he'd found. So I asked him if it would find gold." He stopped and gave an embarrassed grin. "I guess we had too much beer, because before you know it, we were out here and that lady"—he nodded toward Mandy—"peppered my behind with a blast of salt rock."

Another round of snickers rippled through the crowd.

"Did your wife's boss ask you to talk to us?" a tall, balding man asked.

"No, sir, she sure didn't. I came out here because I'm ashamed of myself for causing all this trouble for these poor little old ladies."

From the look of annoyance on Mandy's face at being referred to as "a poor little old lady," Sara suspected it was a good thing for Jason that Mandy's shotgun wasn't close at hand.

"Did you read the entire folder?" someone shouted from the back.

"Yeah, it was only a couple of pages. Wasn't much to it at all."

"What was in the barn?" the tall, balding man asked.

"All I saw were some tools and a few bales of hay."

"Do you still think the gold is buried in the barn?" a woman shouted out.

"No, ma'am. As soon as I sobered up, I knew I'd made a complete fool of myself."

Sara quickly spoke up. "If there are no more serious questions, I think we can wrap this up."

"I have a question."

She turned and saw the reporter from Channel 12. "Go ahead."

"If the gold isn't buried here, where do you think it is?"

130

She shrugged. "I have no idea. Anything I'd say would merely be idle speculation."

"What about you, Mr. Lawrey? You read the folder. Where do you think the gold is?"

"Mexico," Jason answered without hesitation.

"Why do you believe it's in Mexico?" the reporter asked, clearly surprised.

"Well, because the United States was at war then. There wasn't much to buy and everybody was shooting each other. If I'd just stole that much money, I'd want to go somewhere where I could spend it and have fun. I'd have run straight to Mexico."

"Ms. Stockton, is there any evidence that might support this theory?"

Sara shrugged. "Who knows? After the robbery, the Williams brothers were never heard from again. So, I suppose it's possible." She quickly wrapped up the conference. Jason disappeared into the crowd before she could speak to him, and the news vans began to vanish as quickly as they had appeared. The deputy helped her off the rock.

"How much longer will you be out here?" Sara asked.

The deputy looked at her and smiled. "Until the sheriff tells us to come back in. But don't worry, we'll keep patrolling the area for a few days. If you like, I could call you." There was the briefest hesitation before she added, "If there's any further trouble."

Sara stared at her. Had the deputy just asked for her phone number? *No*, she told herself. *Why would she ask for my phone number?* Suddenly, Sara found herself looking at her differently. She noticed the soft sensual fullness of her lips, and the swell of her breasts beneath the shirt. *Oh, my God, I'm checking out a woman.* As her gaze flew back to the woman's face, Sara was dumbfounded to find the deputy checking her out as well.

Chapter Twenty-one

"Do you have a pen?" Sara heard herself asking.

The deputy gave her a dazzling smile before reaching into her back pocket and extracting a small notepad and pen.

"Underwood, what are you up to?" Mandy asked, startling Sara so, she had to rewrite her number.

"I asked her to call me, if there's any more trouble," Sara replied quickly.

Mandy looked at the deputy and squinted. "I see. I'm sure that as long as Deputy Underwood is on *duty*"—she seemed to add extra stress to the word—"there won't be any trouble."

The deputy quickly pocketed the pad and pen and replied, "Right, Mandy—I mean, Ms. Brodie." She looked at Sara and shrugged. "I'd better go call in." She scurried off.

Mandy seemed ready to say something more, but Arcy and Rosa joined them and she let it drop. Despite being urged to stay for lunch, Sara and Rosa said their good-byes and started back to San Antonio.

"I'm exhausted," Rosa said, as they pulled onto the interstate.

"Me too," Sara lied. Every nerve in her body was hopping somewhere between terror and nervous anticipation. She couldn't be sure, but she thought she had just given her phone number to a woman. *A woman.* "Oh, my God, what'll I do if she calls?"

"If who calls?" Rosa asked.

Sara's hand flew to her mouth. She had spoken aloud. "Gracie," she said quickly.

"I thought you were going to try to convince her not to resign. I haven't signed off on any of her paperwork yet."

Sara forced her thoughts away from Deputy Underwood. "I should do something to reprimand her. She really shouldn't have let Jason into my office, but I feel partly to blame. I shouldn't have left the folder on my desk. I'm usually so good about remembering to lock stuff up."

"You could put her on a corrective leave of absence for a couple of weeks."

"No. I don't want to be that harsh. They're already struggling financially. It's not like she gave him the folder. She used bad judgment in trusting him. I think I'll give her a week's leave. After this, I'm positive no one else will ever make it past her and into my office when I'm not there."

"Are you ever going to tell Tom about the gold?"

"No. As far as I'm concerned the entire issue is closed." She glanced at Rosa. "What about you?"

"I don't know anything," Rosa assured her. "I hope we've heard the last of all this business."

"Amen to that." Sara leaned her head back against the seat and fell asleep.

The hiss of the tires of an eighteen-wheeler passing them woke Sara. "I can't believe I fell asleep." She glanced around and realized they were only a short distance from the office.

"Don't worry about it. I did too," Rosa teased. "I'm starving. Would you mind if we stop for lunch?"

"No. Not at all." They chose a popular seafood restaurant, since the lunch crowd had already cleared out. There was little conversation between them as they waited to order their food. When the waiter finally arrived, he displayed about as much interest in taking their order as Sara would have to a root canal.

"I can't remember the last time I've been this exhausted," Rosa said, as she rubbed her eyes.

"I promise not to turn my phone off again without having my cell phone close by."

Rosa shook her head. "Don't worry about it. Sometimes I fantasize about dropping all the phones, pagers and computers into the ocean." She leaned back. "I can remember when my grandparents had one black rotary phone and now there's a phone in practically every room of my house. Plus, my husband, my two daughters and I all have cell phones, I have my work pager and, just in case someone can't reach us through any of those methods, there's e-mail." She was warming up to her subject. "You know what really kills me—text messages on cell phones. If you have a phone, does anyone really *need* to send you a text message? Our phone bills are higher than my grandparents' mortgage payment."

Sara started laughing.

"Why are you laughing?"

"You sound like my father. When his firm installed e-mail, he practically blew a gasket. He still refuses to use it to do anything except read the messages. If they need a response he either calls the sender or writes out the reply and has his secretary send it for him."

"Your dad and I are probably close in age. I'm forty-two."

Sara hadn't really thought about it before, but she realized Rosa was right. Rosa just seemed younger than she was because she was always joking around.

It was almost three-thirty by the time Sara made it back to her office. She grimaced when she walked past Gracie's desk and saw the piles of papers that had accumulated there since this morning.

She sometimes wondered if computers had reduced the amount of paper as they were supposed to or whether they simply sped everything up so that more paper could be generated faster. She closed her office door and dialed Gracie's home number.

"Was it all right that Jason spoke instead of me? He wanted to because he felt so bad," Gracie said, as soon as she heard Sara's voice.

"It was fine. In fact, it was probably better that he spoke. How is he?"

"Embarrassed. *As he should be*," she said in a louder voice.

Sara assumed he was probably nearby. "Rosa told me you resigned."

Gracie hesitated. "I tried to call you, but I couldn't get in touch with you. I thought it would be better if I resigned before you fired me."

"I wouldn't have fired you."

"Really?" Gracie sounded genuinely surprised.

"Rosa hasn't processed your separation papers. Do you want to talk about this and see if we can work something out?"

"Would you ever trust me to work for you again? I wouldn't feel comfortable if you didn't trust me. Not that I'd blame you if you didn't."

"I don't think I'll ever have to worry about you letting anyone into my office again."

"You've got that right."

"Are you interested in continuing to work for me?"

"Of course I am. I love my job."

"All right, here's the deal. I thought about putting you on a corrective action leave for two weeks, then I realized I would be punishing myself more than I would be you. Instead, consider this a verbal warning and I'm putting you on one week of corrective action. A letter of reprimand will be placed in your personnel file along with my recommendation that it be removed after a year if there are no further problems. If anything like this ever happens again while you're working for me, I won't give you time to resign. Do you understand what I'm saying?"

"I understand."

"Good. Until this, you have always performed your job with the highest level of skill and professionalism. I'd like to put all this behind us and keep you as a member of this team."

"I'd like that. You have my word it won't happen again."

"I believe you. Then I'll see you in a week, and you'd better get plenty of rest, because your desk is already starting to bow beneath all the paper."

After typing up the statement for Gracie's personnel file, Sara e-mailed it to Rosa for her review before turning her attention to her e-mails. As she clicked on message after message, most of which really didn't amount to anything, she began to think that perhaps Rosa and her father were right. By the time she finished going through the e-mails and phone messages, then typing up the statement for the press, it was after five. Despite the fact that only a couple of things had been marked off her to-do list, she turned everything off and locked her desk.

The drive home was mercifully hassle-free, allowing her to make decent time. As soon as she got home and spent a couple of minutes trying to convince Mr. Tibbs to at least pretend like he was glad to see her, she plugged her phones back in and checked the messages. She deleted the calls from Rosa, Tom and Gracie. Her hand froze when she heard Taylor's voice with its simple message of "call me." A thrill tickled her spine.

Sara punched the button to replay the call twice more, trying to determine Taylor's mood, but the message was too short. She felt foolish doing so; nevertheless, she saved the message. Then she checked the messages on her cell phone and cringed when the automated voice informed her she had seventeen unheard messages. The first four were from Arcy and Rosa. The next one was from Taylor and had come in during the previous night. Again, it was a short request to call her. She raced through another call from Arcy and a series from Tom and Rosa. There was a second call from Taylor. "Sara, it's almost midnight. Please call me."

The final call was from James. "Sara, what's going on? Taylor

136

called me. She was looking for you. She sounded upset but wouldn't tell me what's wrong. Did something happen between you two? Give me a call. I know it's late, but please call me, no matter what time you get this message."

She dialed his number and wasn't surprised when the voice mail clicked on. He would still be at work. "Everything is fine," she said. "I've been really busy with work and was a little lax in checking my messages. I should be home all night. Call me if you have time." She held the phone, trying to summon the courage to call Taylor. What would she say to her? She was still staring at the phone when the doorbell rang. Even before she looked, she knew it was Taylor.

Sara opened the door and tried to calm her pounding heart.

"Since you wouldn't answer my calls, I thought I'd try knocking on your door." A crooked smile softened her words. "Can I come in?"

Sara nodded and stepped back.

Taylor came in but stopped just inside the doorway. She buried her hands deep into the front pockets of her jeans.

Sara closed the door and found herself struggling for something to say. "What's happening to us?" she finally managed to ask. "When did we start having trouble talking to each other?"

"I guess it was when we started thinking about things other than talking," Taylor replied.

A blush crept up Sara's neck. In an attempt to hide it, she motioned for Taylor to sit down.

"Why didn't you call me back?" Taylor asked. She sat on the end of the couch.

Afraid of what she might do if she sat too close, Sara took the chair across from her. "I turned the phones off last night, and all hell broke loose at work today."

"I guess that would be your gold rush."

Sara rolled her eyes. "The gullibility of some people never ceases to amaze me."

Taylor shrugged and looked around the apartment as though

she had never been there before. "It's that get-rich-quick fantasy—marry a millionaire, win the lottery or find a treasure chest full of gold." She laughed. "Do you remember when we were eight or nine and we'd buy those chocolate coins wrapped in gold foil?"

"We'd put them in a shoebox, bury them and then dig them up a few minutes later pretending we'd found a pirate's treasure chest," Sara added.

"And that one time when Shawn Davidson was peeking through the hedgerow and saw us and thought we were burying real treasure."

Sara grabbed her face and snickered. "He snuck over into your yard that night to dig it up, but he got confused in the dark and exhumed your recently departed parakeet instead." For a couple of moments they both laughed, the tension between them temporarily swept aside. When the laughter faded, a deeper silence fell between them.

"Sara, I'm sorry about . . . last night. I shouldn't have said anything. It was wrong of me to do so, with Debbie moving here and all."

It took Sara a moment to push down the pain of Taylor's words. "Don't worry about it. This whole thing with James has me all mixed up." She thought about the way she had looked at the deputy and been looked at in return. She took a deep breath. "Honestly, I don't know what's going on with me."

"I don't think you're a lesbian," Taylor replied quietly.

"You don't?" Sara couldn't keep the surprise out of her voice.

"No. I think you're just confused by James and me. We're all so close. Maybe a part of you is thinking that if we're both gay then you must be too."

Sara wasn't so certain. Besides her reaction to the deputy, she could still recall the feelings that Taylor's kiss had stirred within her. Uncertain and desperate to make things right between them again, she agreed.

Taylor hopped up from the couch. "I have to get going. I'm meeting some people from work for dinner."

Sara walked to the door with her. "Maybe we can all go to dinner this weekend. It's been ages since the three of us have gotten together."

Taylor looked uncomfortable. "I can't. I'll be out of town this weekend."

Sara cursed her stupidity. Taylor would be with Debbie.

"During the week then," Sara said.

"Sure."

After Taylor left, Sara sat on the couch where Taylor had been. The soft leather still held the warmth of Taylor's skin.

"I'm so pathetic." She sighed.

Mr. Tibbs yowled his concurrence from across the room.

Chapter Twenty-two

Sara was trying to balance her checkbook when the doorbell rang a little after eight that same evening. "When it rains, it pours," she said to the cat.

A glance through the blinds revealed James standing beneath her small porch light. When she opened the door, he held up a bag displaying the name of their favorite Chinese restaurant imprinted on the side and a six-pack of Coronas. "I come bearing gifts, but I promise to leave if you're too tired."

"Come on in. You're saving me from my self-imposed torture. I should give up and join the rest of the world with online banking."

"It's the historian in you. It's impossible for you to let go of the antiquated."

"Don't pick on me." She hugged him, relieved to see there was no tension between them. She followed him into the kitchen and grabbed plates while he unloaded the bag.

"I hope you're hungry, because I couldn't make up my mind as to whether I wanted beef or chicken. So I got a little of both. Then I saw the prawns and had to have them too," he said.

"As a matter of fact, I am. I skipped dinner."

"Then dig in."

Sara filled her plate with Kung Pao chicken, beef with broccoli and honey walnut prawns. As they ate in silence, she realized what a relief it was not to have to wonder if he intended to stay the night or not.

"Did you talk to Taylor?" he asked, as he opened each of them a beer.

Sara's appetite started to fade. "She stopped by this afternoon. I told her that I've been busy at work."

"That reminds me. I saw you on the news tonight."

Sara blinked. She had completely forgotten to watch.

He glanced at her. "Are those women going to be all right?"

"I think so. Did I sound convincing on the news?"

"I thought so, but you know if some jerks have already made up their minds that the gold is out there, it'll probably take a lot more to convince them otherwise."

Sara set her chopsticks down. "Then how am I going to stop them?"

He shrugged. "You can't. You know yourself if someone wants something bad enough, they'll find a way to get to it."

Like Debbie had found a way to be with Taylor. Sara pushed the thought away. It wasn't fair to Taylor that Sara should dislike this woman before she ever met her. She wondered if she should talk to James about her feelings for Taylor or if the conversation would end up making her feel uncomfortable around him also.

"What's wrong?" James asked.

"Nothing. I guess I'm not as hungry as I thought I was."

"Sara, you're nibbling your lip. You only do that when you're trying to do something but can't." He pushed back his plate. "So, talk to me."

"I don't know where to start."

"Just start talking."

"Taylor kissed me or maybe I kissed her. I'm not sure."

James's eyes widened. "Wow. You know how to open a conversation."

"She says she . . . that she has been in love with me for years."

He shrugged. "It's about time she told you."

"You knew?"

"I sort of assumed it. She never told me or anything, but there were times when I could see it. As we got older, I realized what was happening."

"How could you tell?"

"The way she looked at you. Eventually, I started seeing that my pain was very similar to hers." He used a chopstick to push a piece of broccoli around on his plate. "I was already trying to convince myself I was in love with you. But every once in a while, some gorgeous guy would come along and I'd fall in love with him. Of course, he'd be straight. I'd float around on my little love cloud for a while before I'd finally admit to myself that he wasn't going to notice me. Then, I'd spiral into these horrible bouts of depression. My parents thought I was being a normal teenager, and maybe I was. Anyway, as I got older I started to notice the same thing happening to Taylor. I came to realize that her feelings for you were the reason."

"Where was I during all this?" Sara rested her forehead in her hand. "I always thought we were all best friends, but now I'm not sure I know anything about you guys."

He chuckled and took her free hand. "Oh, Sara, we are best friends. You can never know everything about another person, and we shouldn't. Everyone holds a little bit of themselves back." He gently jiggled her arm. "I promise you that I only tell you and Taylor my deepest, darkest secrets."

"You do not." She pouted.

"Okay, you're right I don't. What if I told you my most secret of secrets? Would that make you feel better?"

She looked at him, feeling a little nervous. "I'm not sure I want to know it," she replied honestly.

"That's my point. No one should want to know everything about someone. Sure, it's easy to say, 'I want to know all about you,' in those early days of lust, but that's equivalent to meeting a co-worker in the hall and saying, 'How you doing?' I mean honestly, do you really want them to start telling you about their gastrointestinal difficulties?"

"No," she said and giggled.

He patted her hand. "I'd do anything for either you or Taylor. If it's any consolation, you're the only girl I would ever dream of marrying."

Sara pulled her hand free. "Don't make me laugh. I'm trying to be miserable."

"Then tell me more about what happened between you and Taylor."

"Nothing happened and it's not going to. Debbie is moving in with her at the end of the month."

"Ouch." He tapped his finger softly against the table to a silent melody. "Do you love her?"

"I love her in the same way I love you. Except—"

He waited.

She wasn't sure how she could say what she wanted to without hurting his feelings. "When she kissed me, it was different."

He stared at her blankly for a moment before comprehending what she was trying to say. "Are you trying to tell me that Taylor makes you want to do the nasty and I didn't?"

"Something like that," she admitted with a chuckle.

"So what are you going to do about it?"

"What can I do? She's already involved with someone else."

He hesitated. "I'm going to tell you something but I probably shouldn't. I've met Debbie and . . . I think she may be using Taylor."

Sara sat up. "What do you mean?"

"Debbie's ex moved here after they split up, and while we were talking I sort of got the impression that Debbie's moving out here may have been to get closer to the ex, more so than to be with Taylor."

143

"That's silly. She could have simply moved here on her own. Why use Taylor like that?"

He waggled his finger at her. "Maybe she's playing the old green-eyed monster card. Jealousy. If she wants to get the girl-friend's attention, what better way is there than with a new lover?"

Sara shook her head. "That seems like an awful lot of trouble. Poor Taylor. She's going to be devastated."

"No, she won't."

She looked at him in surprise.

"Sara, come on. They're using each other to some extent. Debbie's trying to get the ex's attention and Taylor is trying to forget about—" He stopped and glanced at her. "That's enough speculation. Maybe you should use this time to discover what you really want."

"What if I already know what I want?" she challenged.

He studied her closely. "Do you want my honest opinion?"

"Yes."

"Date someone else first."

Sara suddenly thought about Deputy Denise Underwood.

"Uh-oh, that's a dangerous look."

"What are you talking about?" she asked.

"No, the question is *who* were you thinking about?"

"How do you know I was thinking about anyone?"

"Sara! Please. Give me some credit."

"All right. Today after the press conference the woman deputy asked me for my phone number, or at least I think she did."

James grabbed his head. "How can you still be so innocent?"

"I dated you for ten years."

He looked stunned. "Well, okay. I guess I've been told. Now, tell me exactly what happened with the deputy."

Sara told him what had happened.

Afterward he leaned back in his chair. "You're right. That wasn't much to go on, but I'm betting she calls you."

"What should I do if she does?"

"I'd start by answering the phone."

"I'm trying to be serious here."

"So am I. You talk to her. Have a conversation."

"What if she asks me out?"

"If you like her, go out with her."

"But what if I'm not a lesbian?"

"Sara, stop worrying about what you might or might not be. Be yourself and everything else will fall into place."

She suddenly relaxed. "You're right. Why am I making such a big deal about this?"

"Now you're getting the idea. Go out, have a good time, a little mind-blowing sex—"

"James!" Shocked, Sara looked at him.

"I'm not saying move in with her," he clarified. "I'm simply suggesting that you test the waters, so to speak, to see if you really are a lesbian or if you're just having some kind of weird psychological reaction to your two best friends being gay."

"God, you sound like Taylor. I'm not having a reaction to you guys," she said, and rolled her eyes.

"How do you know? We all grew up together. I swear I had menstrual cramps every time you and Taylor had your periods."

She swatted his arm. "Now you're being silly."

"No, I'm not. When other boys were sneaking their father's Trojans, I was sneaking my mother's Midol."

Chapter Twenty-three

Sara was so dog-tired by Thursday night that even the short distance from her assigned parking spot to her apartment door seemed daunting. For the past two mornings, she had been at her desk by five-thirty and hadn't left until after ten. She glanced at the clock on her dashboard. Tonight was slightly earlier, only nine-thirty. As bad as she felt now, deep down beneath all her exhaustion burned a pleasing sense of satisfaction. Her to-do list had been whittled down to an unprecedented half a page. Tonight she had stayed and gone through most of the mail that had grown to an alarming height on Gracie's desk.

It took every ounce of willpower she possessed to climb out of the truck and walk the few feet to the apartment. As she pushed the door open, her cell phone began to ring. When she saw the name D. Underwood on the screen she started to drop it back into her purse, assuming it was a wrong number. As the name registered, she panicked. Something must have happened at the ranch. She had called Mandy and Arcy each morning since releasing the press statement, and Arcy had told her everything was fine.

"I was about to hang up," Denise said when Sara finally answered.

"Is something wrong at the ranch? Did something else happen?"

"Whoa. Hold on. Everything's fine."

"Are Mandy and Arcy all right?"

"Yeah. I just came off patrol from out there about an hour ago and everything is fine."

Sara took a deep shaky breath.

"Hey, look. I'm sorry I scared you. Maybe this isn't a good time."

"No. It's fine. You caught me off-guard. That's all."

"Are you sure you're okay? You don't sound so hot."

"I'm fine." As the burst of adrenaline faded, Sara slumped to the floor and braced her back against the wall. She didn't have the strength left to make it to the couch. The combination of her exhaustion and her concern for the two women that she had grown very fond of had sapped the last of her energy. As Mr. Tibbs began his daily yowling session, she realized the only thing she had eaten all day was the bagel she had grabbed on the way out the door that morning.

"I know I said I'd only call if something happened out here," Denise said, "but I've been thinking about you. So, I thought I'd give you a call."

Sara sat up straighter as her pulse began to thud a little heavier.

"Please don't be offended if I've misinterpreted the situation." Denise hesitated. "This is the point where you're supposed to either hang up or reassure me that I haven't made a mistake."

Sara found herself smiling. "How can I reassure you, if I don't know what situation you're referring to?"

Denise gave a small groan. "You're not going to make this easy, are you?"

"I don't know. Maybe you should try me." She heard Denise's breath catch slightly.

"I was wondering if you'd like to do something tomorrow night."

"What did you have in mind?" Sara was shocked by her own boldness. It sounded like someone else talking to the cute young deputy.

"How about I pick you up, say, around seven and we go to dinner and then maybe go dancing?"

Sara had absolutely no idea where two lesbians could dance together, but at this moment she didn't care. She would go out with Denise Underwood and settle this *was she or wasn't she a lesbian* issue once and for all. It didn't really bother her that she might be. The upheaval of not knowing distressed her more. "I'd like that," she replied. She gave Denise her address and they agreed to decide where to eat when Denise picked her up.

Feeling rejuvenated, Sara gave Mr. Tibbs a package of his special treats before making herself a salad. After she had eaten, she called James.

She quickly told him about Denise's call. "I don't know what to do. What should I wear? Where should we go eat?"

"Slow down," he said. "Lord, you'd think you had never been on a date before."

"Well, I really haven't except with you and Shawn Davidson back in the seventh grade."

"I forgot to tell you. I saw him a couple of weeks ago. Guess what he's doing now."

"Hello!" She could care less what Shawn was doing; right now she needed help trying to decide what she was going to do.

He ignored her. "He works for the post office. He's a letter carrier or a mailman, whatever they're called, and he was dressed in those horrible shorts they have to wear—"

"Why are we talking about Shawn?"

"Because I had a mega crush on him. I thought I'd die when you told me he kissed you. Oh, I wanted to be you so bad."

"James, he was a horrible kisser. Don't you remember what happened when he tried to french kiss me?" She shuddered at the memory.

148

"Oh, yeah. You hurled, didn't you. Thanks for reminding me. Now there are two great reasons why I should be grateful he didn't show any interest in me."

"Can we get back to Denise?"

"Oh, God, you didn't hurl on her, did you?"

A moment of sheer terror seized her guts. No one had tried to french kiss her since Shawn. James certainly hadn't. What if Denise tried to and she had the same reaction? "You've got to come over right now," she said in a panic.

"Why? What's wrong?"

"I have to see if I hurl every time someone tries to french kiss me or if it was only Shawn."

A moment of shocked silence filled the phone. "Sara, you know how much I care for you," he began slowly. "I have to tell you, though, that I'm a little hesitant to drive across town just to see if you'll hurl on me."

Sara cringed. "I'm sorry. That request was a bit crude, wasn't it?"

"I think it pretty much tops out the chart for me," he agreed.

"I'm sorry," she said again. "I'm so nervous. I don't know what to do."

"What do you want to do?"

A mental image of Denise's full sensual lips formed in her mind. "I don't know." Her response was much too weak.

James began to laugh. "Relax and go with your gut feeling. I'm sure she's a lovely woman, and if she was confident enough to call you the way she did, I'm sure she has been around the block a couple of times. If you start to panic, take your cue from her and what feels right to you." He paused a moment before adding, "Sara, be careful and don't use her."

Stunned that he would suggest such a thing, she started to protest, but he stopped her.

"I know you're a wonderful person and wouldn't deliberately hurt anyone. Sometimes in the need to find answers, it's easy to forget how our actions might affect others. I know, I've been there."

She realized with a sudden clarity what he was trying to say. "If you're feeling guilty about the time you and I shared, please don't. You helped me so much."

"I should have been honest with you a long time ago. You deserved better."

"When I think back, I don't remember ever feeling all goofy and mushy about boys or men. I think my relationship with you provided me with the safety net I needed to get through that time. I saw what Taylor went through before she finally realized she was gay and maybe that scared me, because I certainly didn't want to have to go through it. And even though there wasn't a major backlash from her friends and family when she came out, there were still plenty of people waiting in line to call her names and to try to make her life miserable." She thought of Amber's comments about Taylor. "My relationship with you protected me from that. I should be thanking you."

"I want you to know if I ever did anything to hurt you, I'm sorry."

"Enough to come over and french kiss me?" she teased.

He laughed. "Sorry, you're on your own on that one."

After they hung up, Sara showered and fell into bed. Too exhausted and nervous to sleep, she picked up her book, intending to read. A few moments after she settled into bed, she felt the book slipping from her fingertips. She tried to hold onto it but sleep overtook her.

Chapter Twenty-four

At seven sharp Friday night, Sara's doorbell rang. She tried to chase away the butterflies that kept fluttering around in her stomach as she went to the door. With one last glance at her black jeans and sapphire blue blouse, she smoothed a hand over her hair. *Here goes.* The butterflies vanished as soon as she opened the door to the tall, dark-haired woman dressed in jeans, a crisply ironed white shirt and gleaming black boots. When Denise smiled and Sara's gaze was pulled to her wonderful mouth the last shred of doubt about her sexual preference vanished. At that moment, she had an overwhelming urge to fall into Denise's arms and spend the night letting those lips consume her.

Denise handed her a red rose carefully wrapped in tissue. "I didn't know which color you preferred," she said and smiled again.

Sara invited her in. "It's wonderful, thank you."

"That blouse looks nice on you," Denise said.

Sara felt herself blush. "Thanks. You look different out of uniform."

151

"Oh, no." Denise held up her hands. "Don't tell me you're one of those women who likes uniforms." She started toward the door. "Just give me a minute."

"Where are you going?" Sara asked, confused.

"I picked up my dry cleaning on the way here. I have a clean uniform in the truck." She winked and smiled.

"You're teasing me."

Denise nodded, but suddenly turned serious. "Listen, I know this is awkward to bring up at this point. There's never really a right time so I always try to get this out of the way as quickly as possible."

Sara felt a small tremor of dread. "All right."

"You already know that I'm a cop and I love my job. Being in a small town the way I am, I have to keep my lifestyle sort of low-key. Sheriff Vargas and a couple of the other deputies know, but for the most part, I'm still in the closet."

"I understand."

Denise scratched her jaw. "I like to have a good time. You know what I mean?"

Sara nodded, even though she wasn't sure she did.

"I mean, I want a forever relationship, someday, but not now." She seemed anxious as she tucked her hands into her hip pockets.

Sara frowned. "So when you mentioned you have a truck out-side with clothes in it, you weren't hinting that you were ready to move in tonight."

Denise took a sudden step back. "Good gosh, no!"

Sara couldn't help but laugh at the look of shock on Denise's face.

"Ah, now you're teasing me," Denise said with a smile. "I knew you'd be a feisty one."

"I accept your offer of fun with no strings attached," Sara began, "on two conditions."

Denise stiffened slightly.

"First, wherever we go and whatever we do is Dutch treat, and second, when we stop—having fun—we try to maintain the friendship." She held out her hand.

Denise shook her hand. "I can accept those terms."

"Good. Come on into the kitchen with me while I put this in a vase." Sara held up the rose.

As they started through the house, Mr. Tibbs came running out and went directly to Denise.

"Hey, you have a cat." When Denise leaned over to scratch his ears, he turned into a purring bundle of feline mush.

"I don't believe it." The cat actually rolled over and exposed his tummy to Denise.

Sara found her eyes drawn to Denise's long tapered fingers and neatly manicured nails. Would they feel as wonderful as they looked? She gasped as her body reacted to the thought and left her with a damp reminder that made her squirm.

"Are you okay?" Denise straightened up from playing with the cat.

"Yes. Sure." She fumbled for something to say. "I can't believe that cat. He's usually so arrogant and aloof."

"I always get along well with animals," Denise said. "I guess it comes from growing up in the country."

"Did you grow up around Wilford Springs?"

"No. I was born and raised in Tennessee."

Sara finally located the bud vase she wanted. "What brought you to Texas?"

"The Army." Denise leaned against the counter and watched as Sara filled the vase. "I was an MP at Fort Sam Houston. After my enlistment ended, I managed to get into the police academy here. I liked living out here, but I missed the country. After I graduated from the academy, I started looking for work in small towns around here. I finally lucked into a job with Atascosa County."

"I admit that's beautiful country down that way," Sara said. "I guess I'm too spoiled. I like being able to get to everything I need in less than twenty minutes."

"That's why God made daylight and dark."

"I'm sorry?"

Denise laughed sheepishly. "That's just something my grandma would say. It just means that it's people's differences that make the world what it is."

Sara nodded. "I see."

"Do you like jazz?" Denise asked suddenly.

"Yes, actually I do."

"I know I mentioned dinner and dancing, but on the way in, I heard on the radio that there's a jazz festival going on downtown."

"I think I heard something about that. No. I saw a poster the other day. It's at San Pedro Park."

Denise nodded. "Would you mind if we went to that?"

"Not at all. I'd love it in fact."

"Great. You'd better grab a jacket. It's supposed to start cooling off tonight."

"I'm fine."

Denise looked at her lightweight blouse doubtfully.

"Okay," Sara conceded. "I'll get a jacket."

The temperatures were already starting to cool down when they walked out of the apartment. Sara pulled the jacket on.

"You're right. It is cooler."

"Do you think it'll be too cool to sit out there?"

"No. I'm sure there will be a crowd. We'll just hunker down in the middle of the crowd if we get too cold."

Denise looked at her and smiled. "Yeah, I think we can find some way to stay warm." She winked.

Feeling a little flustered, Sara busied herself with fastening her jacket. The next thing she knew they were standing beside a truck so large it made her small Ranger look like one of those little Matchbox cars. "Good Lord, do you think this thing is big enough?" she asked without thinking.

Denise didn't appear to take offense as she patted the door of the truck affectionately. "She gets me wherever I need to go and can pull stumps all day long."

"Stumps?"

"Yeah, I have a small house with a few acres, but the land is covered in mesquite and huisache trees. I'm trying to clear it a little at a time. Once I've cut a tree down, I use the truck to pull out the stump." She opened the door.

Sara looked at the high step up needed to get into the cab. She wasn't sure she could even get in.

"Need a boost up?" Denise asked with a slight smile.

As bad as Sara hated to admit it, she didn't think she could get in by herself. "I think so."

"Put your left hand there." Denise pointed to the upper part of the door opening. "Your right hand goes over here on the opposite side. The trick is to make sure you start on your left foot. That way when you bring your right foot up, you can use its momentum to swing all the way into the truck. Let me show you." She demonstrated climbing into the truck. She made it look so simple that Sara was certain she could do it. "Are you ready?" Denise asked.

"I think I can do it."

"Okay, I'll leave you alone and let you give it a try."

Sara positioned her hands as she had been shown and planted her left foot just as Denise had. With a deep breath, she pulled herself up. Everything was going pretty good until her right foot came in contact with the truck and her entire body stopped moving.

Denise quickly helped her down. "That's not bad for your first time, but I think I'd better help you for the first few times."

Embarrassed, Sara nodded.

"Ready."

"I think so." She glanced back at Denise. "I don't suppose you could do this with your eyes closed. I hate to think of what I'm going to look like trying to scramble in there."

"Don't worry. You'll do fine. Just put your hands where I showed you."

Sara did as she was told.

"Now put your left foot right here." She reached around and tapped the spot. "Then you'll just use your arms to pull yourself up. Remember to swing your right foot all the way inside the truck."

Sara hoisted herself up and suddenly Denise's hands were molded around her butt and pushing her in. Sara was so surprised she forgot to worry about how high the truck was and practically jumped inside the cab. When she turned around, Denise was standing on the ground, grinning up at her.

"Would you like to practice that part again," she asked, and wiggled her eyebrows suggestively.

Sara rolled her eyes, but had to admit that she liked the feeling of Denise's hands on her butt. "Let's go."

Chapter Twenty-five

At the park, they grabbed a couple of hot dogs and sodas from a vendor and found a place far enough back from the stage that they would still be able to hear each other talk. Denise spread the blanket that she had taken from the truck.

"This isn't exactly the dinner I intended when I asked you out," she apologized as they sat.

"I'm having fun." Sara patted the spot beside her. "Sit here and tell me something about yourself."

Denise sat down and folded her legs Indian style. "Like what?"

"What's your favorite food?"

"Fried chicken," she answered without hesitation.

"Color?"

"Orange."

Sara stopped. "You know, I don't think I've ever known anyone whose favorite color is orange."

"You do now." Denise began to eat her hot dog, so Sara ate her hot dog also.

"What made you want to be a police officer?" she asked, after they finished eating.

"There are days when I ask myself the same question," Denise admitted. "After being an MP it just seemed like going to the police academy was the next logical step."

"Do you ever wish you had done something else?"

"No. I'm not much for looking back and saying *if only*. I don't intend to stay there forever, like some guys do, just long enough to get my place going and to buy some horses."

"Horses?"

"Yeah, some good breeding stock. I want to raise quarter horses. What about you?"

"I like my job. If I could do anything over, it would be to listen more."

Denise tilted her head as though she wasn't quite sure what Sara meant.

"My grandfather used to tell wonderful stories that his father had told him about growing up around the turn of the twentieth century and struggling through the Depression. I wish I had taken time to listen to his story closer, or better yet record them or write them down. Because when my grandfather died so did the stories. Dad and I remember some, but it's not the same. We lose thousands of these stories every single day." She stopped. "Sorry, I can get carried away sometimes."

"I think it's great that you enjoy your job so much. Is that what you do, record living histories?"

She shook her head. "Most of the funding for those projects was eliminated years ago. Predominately, I prepare reports to be used in presentations to the zoning commissions, or the city council. We try to protect as many historically significant structures within San Antonio as we can while still allowing for new growth and technology. Did you know that San Antonio has thirteen hundred landmark properties, a thousand archaeological sites and twenty-one historic districts?"

"I didn't know that," Denise said, as she reached out and casually brushed a lock of hair back from Sara's forehead.

158

Sara's gaze drifted to Denise's lips. They looked so inviting. What would it be like to kiss them?

"Whoa," Denise muttered softly with a slight look of concern.

Sara jerked back when she realized that she had actually started to lean in to kiss Denise. "Sorry. I don't know . . . I don't usually . . ." She let the sentence drift away.

"I want the same thing you do," Denise said in a low voice. "I just have to be a little discreet."

Sara was saved from further embarrassment by a thunderous round of applause as the band came on stage.

It was nearly midnight when Denise parked in front of Sara's apartment.

"Would you like to come in?" Sara asked. She fidgeted with the zipper pull on her jacket.

"I can't. I have to be at work by five in the morning."

Sara struggled to hide her disappointment as Denise hopped out of the truck and came around to help her out.

"I had a good time," Denise said, as they walked up the sidewalk to the apartment. "Can I see you again?"

"Do you want to?" Sara wasn't sure why she felt so hurt that Denise wasn't coming in.

"Most definitely. I have to work until two tomorrow afternoon, but we could do something after that. I still owe you dinner and dancing."

"All right."

They were at the door and Sara realized she didn't know what was expected of her here. Would Denise just leave, or shake her hand? With Denise's need to be circumspect, Sara was certain she wouldn't be getting a kiss on the doorstep. To her surprise, Denise took the keys from her and unlocked the door before handing them back.

"Is this a safe neighborhood?" Denise asked, as she continued to linger.

"Yes. We've never had any problems that I know of, and we have a neighborhood watch program."

Denise nodded. "I didn't know if I should check the house for you before I left."

Sara started to reassure her, but she stopped when Denise stepped closer to her. "Well, if it's not too much trouble. It's always a little uncomfortable going into an empty house alone."

Denise smiled brightly as her fingertips trailed down Sara's arm. "Do you think my uniform will be safe in the truck? Or should I bring it in?"

"I definitely think you should bring it in." Sara's heart was pounding so, she could barely speak.

Denise lost no time in running back to the truck and reappearing with the uniform and a small overnight case. She held it up sheepishly. "I keep my spare toothbrush in here. It's one of those battery-operated ones. I didn't want to take a of chance of leaving it out there."

"That's probably a good idea." She held the door open for Denise.

By the time Sara stepped inside and locked the door the uniform was already draped over the back of the couch and Denise was moving toward her. The realization of what was about to occur froze Sara in place. Something of her fear must have been reflected in her face because Denise stopped short.

"What's wrong?"

Sara licked her dry lips, trying to speak.

"If you've changed your mind, I can leave or I don't have to spend the night."

Sara shook her head. The last thing she wanted was for Denise to leave. "I've never been with a woman before."

Denise took a quick step back, looking much more alarmed than Sara felt. After a long second, Denise ran a hand over her face. "I had no idea. I should go." She grabbed the bag and her uniform from the back of the couch and was gone before Sara could react.

Sara heard the truck's powerful engine roar to life and pull out of the parking spot. She stood by the door listening until it disappeared into the night. Then she slammed the door and stomped her foot in frustration.

Mr. Tibbs raced into the room and looked around.

"She's not here," Sara informed him. "Why didn't someone tell me I needed prior experience? I guess becoming a lesbian is like finding a job. You can't get a laid without prior experience but you can't have prior experience if you've never been laid."

Clearly bored with her petty human problems, Mr. Tibbs began to express his displeasure about his empty food bowl. When it became obvious she wasn't going to relent and feed him another treat, the stately feline stalked out of the room, stopping only long enough to express his anger by hopping onto the coffee table and knocking over the stack of magazines Sara had carefully arranged earlier that afternoon. With a smug look of satisfaction, he stalked away toward the back bedroom.

"Just for that I'm not giving you any more treats for a week," she yelled after him.

Chapter Twenty-six

The following morning, the ringing phone pulled Sara from a deep sleep. She grabbed for the receiver hoping it would be Denise.

"Don't tell me you were still asleep," Eloise said.

"Mom, what time is it?"

"It's already after eight."

Sara fell back onto the bed. She hadn't gone to sleep until after three that morning.

"What are your plans for today?"

"Well, since it's Saturday, I thought I'd sleep late. Then I thought I could get up and have breakfast before I go back to bed and sleep until lunch."

"Sara, honey, are you depressed about the wedding being canceled? I read somewhere that depression makes you feel sleepy."

"I'm not depressed. I'm tired."

"Did you have a rough night? Maybe I should come over."

Sara started laughing and crawled out of bed. "All right, Mom, you win. I'm up. What are we doing today?"

"Since neither of us has eaten yet, why don't we have breakfast and then we could go shopping."

"Breakfast, yes. Shopping, no way."

"Sara, you're as bad as your father."

"You have scores of friends who love to shop with you, so let's do something else."

"Why don't we drive up toward Fredericksburg? The wildflowers are blooming and it's a gorgeous day. Let's go for a drive."

"That sounds like fun."

Two hours later, Sara and her mother were driving through the Hill Country.

"I'm glad you called," Sara said. "It's a beautiful day." The cool front from the previous evening had vanished.

Eloise kept her eyes on the road. "Are you really doing all right?"

"To be honest with you, I'm relieved that the wedding was canceled. If we had gone through with it, I'm afraid our friendship would have been damaged. I need James as a friend much more than I'd ever need him as a husband."

"I saw you on the news last week. I wanted to call, but you know your father. He said you would have called if it was serious. How are those poor women doing?"

"I talked to Mandy yesterday morning and the sheriff's office had caught a couple more kids trying to sneak onto their property. Hopefully, the worst is over."

"Are they sisters?" her mother probed. Since Mandy didn't seem shy about their relationship, Sara didn't think she would mind her telling Eloise the truth.

"No, they're a couple."

Eloise frowned slightly.

"What's wrong? Does that bother you?"

"No. Not really. I mean, I guess I can understand why a woman would turn to another woman."

Sara was eternally grateful she wasn't driving because she would have probably run the car off the road in her surprise. "You understand."

Eloise glanced at her quickly. "Well, not in *that* way, but you know, emotionally. Most men are so emotionally withdrawn. I don't think I could live with someone like that. Do you know that one of the women in my golf league, Marilee Davidson, told us that her husband has never told her that he loves her? Not once." She shook her head. "Why would a woman ever want to marry a man like that?"

"Security maybe, or perhaps she can live with the fact that she senses his love."

"Oh, please. Don't you start believing that crap. If a person loves you, he should tell you and you should tell him." She concentrated on driving for a few seconds before adding, "Marilee Davidson would be better off with a woman."

"Mom!"

Eloise glanced at her again. "Oh, dear. Sara, you can't let James's admission of being gay make you homophobic. You know we raised you to be tolerant of others."

A small bubble of laughter formed in Sara's throat and gradually pushed its way out. As she started to laugh, Eloise chuckled with her, but as Sara's laughter escalated, Eloise began to cast worried glances her way.

Finally, she pulled the car into the parking lot of a small convenience store. "Sara, are you all right? You seem to be a little hysterical."

Sara tried to speak but she couldn't stop laughing, and to her surprise the laughter gave way to tears.

Eloise pushed a handful of tissues at her and tried to talk to her, but Sara couldn't hear anything over her own howling sobs. Eloise hugged her as closely as the console and Sara's seatbelt would allow. When the sobs turned to hiccups, Eloise moved away and pulled a fresh batch of tissues from the console. "Here, dry your eyes and try to take deep breaths."

Sara inhaled a great quivering breath and almost choked when she hiccupped.

"Try again."

Under Eloise's gentle coaxing, Sara began to calm down and started talking. "Mom, I think I'm a lesbian."

"Honey, when I asked you to be more tolerant, I didn't mean for you to become a card-carrying member."

"I'm serious."

Eloise folded her hands in her lap. "Sara, I don't know what to say. One day you and James are getting married. The next day James is gay. A week later you're gay." Eloise's cell phone rang. She waved her hands. "Heck, that's probably your father calling to tell me he's gay." She reached down into her purse and turned the phone off.

"I'm sorry, I didn't mean to tell you this way," Sara said.

Eloise reached over and patted her arm. "Have you told your father?"

"No. This is all sort of new to me too."

Eloise looked at her with a small flicker of hope in her eyes. "You're not sure you're gay."

"I'm sure. I just haven't—"

Eloise held up her hand to stop her. "I understand."

After another short silence, Sara turned to face her mother. "You don't seem very upset."

"Of course I'm upset, but what can I do." She reached over and took Sara's hand. "I want you to be happy. I'm just being selfish. Your father and I were sort of hoping for grandchildren."

"That could still happen. I'm young and it seems as though it's much more common for gay and lesbian couples to be having children."

"That's true." Her interest suddenly seemed to spark. "You know, I always thought James would make an excellent father. You and he could still—"

"I know you're not about to suggest what I think you are." When Eloise continued talking, Sara clamped her hands over her ears and began to hum. "I'm not listening."

After a couple of seconds, Eloise cranked the car. "It's starting to get a little too warm for me. Let's go home. I've suddenly developed a craving for a slice of chocolate cake."

"Andy's Kitchen." Sara chimed, thinking of the small restaurant they had discovered a few years earlier. Their lunch entrées weren't spectacular, but they served the best chocolate cake in town.

After returning to her parents' house, Sara hugged her mom. "When should I tell Dad?"

"Why don't you let me tell him?"

Sara pulled away, concerned. "Do you think he's going to be angry?"

"Not angry, but he might need a little time to adjust."

"Maybe we shouldn't tell him."

"Sara, I've never kept secrets from your father and I don't intend to start now. Give him some credit. He's a good man and he loves you. He just needs to work things out in his own way."

Sara finally agreed.

As she drove home, she remembered she was supposed to have Sunday dinner with Mandy and Arcy. She wondered if Deputy Denise Underwood would be on duty and patrolling the ranch. She regretted not asking for the deputy's number when she had the chance. Mandy seemed to know her, so maybe she would have Denise's number, but how could she explain her interest in it without revealing more than she wanted to at this point?

Chapter Twenty-seven

Sara spotted the top of the gigantic truck as soon as she drove into the apartment complex's parking lot that afternoon. "I am so going to send her packing," she fumed. Her anger melted like sugar in water when she saw Denise sitting on the tailgate, reading a book.

Sara pulled into her assigned slot and took her time getting out. By the time she had gotten her truck doors locked, the dark-haired young deputy, dressed in cargo shorts and a tank top, was already coming around the back of the Ranger.

"I came to apologize," Denise said.

Sara tried to appear nonchalant, but the hard nipples that strained to break through Denise's tank top made it difficult.

"Can we talk?" Denise asked, seemingly unaware of the effect her body was having on Sara.

Sara managed a slight nod. *What's with all the talking lately?* James wanted to talk, Taylor wanted to talk, and now Denise wanted to talk. *What I need is less talk and more action.* A shift in the breeze bathed her in the soft fragrance of Denise's cologne, a subtle rich aroma of vanilla and a whisper of something she couldn't identify. She tried to unlock the door. Her fingers seemed to triple in dimension as she fumbled to separate the house key from the other two keys on the ring.

Denise's hand closed over the keys and gently lifted them from Sara's hand. "Let me," she said in a tone that was better suited for the bedroom than the front steps.

Sara placed her hand on the wall for support as her nerve endings began to run relays through her body. While Denise leaned forward to unlock the door, Sara's gaze caressed every inch of her long muscular back that the tank top accentuated so well. Denise dropped the keys. When she bent over to pick them up the shorts displayed a spectacular show of rippling muscles. Sara grew dizzy. *She's not wearing a bra or underwear.* Sara's lower body tightened as a small gasp of desire slipped through her clenched lips.

Denise glanced back at her before resuming her struggle with the house key.

God, did she hear me? Sara struggled to get control of her body and emotions. She shifted uncomfortably and prayed that the spreading evidence of her excitement wouldn't soak through her khaki shorts. *Stop looking at her and think about something else.* She tried reciting the alphabet backward, and when that wasn't enough, she made herself take a step back from Denise. She quickly realized it was a mistake. From the new vantage point, she had a view of all of Denise. She closed her eyes. What was wrong with the damn door lock? Why wouldn't it open?

A cool breath of air rushed over her as the apartment door swung open. Denise stepped back to allow Sara to enter.

Sara did not intend to try to slip around that minefield. The area was too tight. If she attempted to squeeze by, bodily contact was a certainty. "Go on in," she urged. She kept her distance as she followed her inside.

Closing the door created such a strong intimate feeling within the room that she was tempted to open it back up.

168

They stood in awkward silence until Sara remembered she had a guest. "Please, sit down." She waited until Denise was perched on the edge of the couch before she took the chair across from her. The heavy natural wood coffee table sitting between them suddenly didn't seem substantial enough to block the sexual energy buzzing between them.

"About last night," Denise began. "I freaked a little when you said . . . what you did." She leaned forward and rested her arms on her knees.

"You don't have to explain," Sara mumbled, wishing Denise would sit farther back on the couch so the legs of her shorts wouldn't pull so snugly between her legs.

"I'd like to." She stood so suddenly that Sara leaned back in surprise.

Denise moved to the end of the couch and paced in the small open space. "I told you I'm not looking for a serious relationship, and the idea of getting involved with someone who was testing the water scared me." She wiped a trickle of sweat from her face.

It was then that Sara realized Denise was as nervous as she was. That small sign of vulnerability was the sedative that her jangling nerves needed. As her body grew calmer, her voice and rationality returned. "I apologize if I gave you the impression I was 'testing the water.' I'm certain I'm gay. I simply haven't taken that final step, yet."

Sara's newfound calmness seemed to have a settling affect on Denise also. She went back to the couch and thankfully sat farther back. "How can you be so sure you're gay, if you've never been with a woman?"

"I just know." Sara hedged as she recalled the feelings Taylor had evoked when she kissed her. *Not to mention the orgy I almost had with the inseam of my shorts ten minutes ago.* She glanced up to find Denise studying her closely.

"Is she straight or involved?"

Sara considered playing dumb, but there didn't seem to be any point to it. "She's involved."

"Does she know how you feel?"

169

"No." *How could she when I don't even know?* she wanted to shout. She knew she loved Taylor as she loved James. She had definitely lusted after Taylor, but she was doing the same thing with the woman sitting across the room from her now, so she couldn't be in love with Taylor. Denise seemed to be waiting for her to expound on her denial. "It would have been wrong of me to tell her," Sara added.

Denise nodded slightly. "What are you going to do now?"

"What can I do? I'm going to get on with my life."

Denise got up from the couch. "I should get going. I just wanted to come by and apologize."

Sara stood. As she stepped past the coffee table, she saw a blur shoot between her feet. She gave a small squeal of fright as she tried to leap out of the way of whatever it was. The toe of her sandal caught the area rug just enough to send her toppling forward into Denise's arms. Sara's momentum sent Denise crashing back to the couch. As they struggled to disengage their tangled arms and legs, Sara found her face hovering directly over Denise's luscious lips. To hell with waiting for her to make the first move, Sara thought as she lowered her head and softly kissed Denise. As the kiss lingered, their bodies began to relax and unfold themselves naturally. Sara's hands found their way into Denise's short, glossy hair. Bodies slowly shifted until the women stretched full-length on the couch. As the kisses and touches grew more intense, Sara experienced a moment of doubt in her ability to do the right thing. That was, until Denise eased her hand beneath Sara's shirt and began to caress her bare skin. Everything except the feel of Denise's kisses and touches ceased to exist. She wasn't even aware of the clasp being released on her bra until a warm hand covered her breast. As her nipple was teased between a thumb and forefinger, a line of desire blossomed in her breast and made its way to her groin. Never had she felt such exquisite pleasure or such burning need for more. Her blouse and bra were gone and Denise's lips were against her skin—kissing her neck, her collarbone, her shoulder and then, her breast. Pleasure so sharp it bordered on pain

170

radiated from her nipple to every inch of her body. Their positions on the couch were swapped without Denise's mouth ever leaving her breast. Fingertips teased her other breast before dancing across her stomach, causing her abdominal muscles to contract and her hips to elevate slightly. Her breathing became increasingly ragged as the fingers made their way steadily closer. The soft rasp of a zipper being lowered had never sounded so delicious, so sensual. When the zipper stopped, the edge of Denise's hand rested over the apex of the V formed by Sara's legs. Sara's hips rose higher, straining to push the hand lower. A low whisper of protest formed on her lips as the hand eased back up to cover her stomach.

Denise kissed her again. Long passionate kisses that escalated as the searching gentleness was replaced by an insistent hunger. Wrapping her arms around Denise, she tried to pull her closer, but her efforts were useless. Denise was not going to be rushed. When the hand started back down her stomach, there was a new determination, a new destination. Shorts and panties were pushed aside as the hand pushed between her legs and slipped into her wetness. Sara's hips began to move on their own as fingers stroked her. A whimper of pleasure began in her throat when the fingers eased inside her, and a thumb took up the steady stroking. The hand's movement synchronized its strokes to match Sara's thrusting hips. Her whimper grew to a low moan as Denise's body moved more directly over her. The shift in her weight drove the fingers deeper. Control slipped away. Sara wrapped her legs around Denise as her body took over and sent her soaring to heights of pleasure she had never dreamed existed.

Chapter Twenty-eight

A hand on Sara's shoulder shook her awake. She rolled over, stretched luxuriously and smiled at the sight of Denise's face hovering over her. "Good morning."

"Good morning to you," Denise said. "Someone's at the door."

"It's probably one of the kids in the complex, selling something for school. If we ignore them, they'll go away." Sara knew her parents would call before they came over, and Taylor and James were both out of town.

"I don't think so. They seem pretty insistent." As if to emphasize her point, a loud pounding on the door erupted.

"I guess I should go see who it is."

"That's probably a good idea," Denise urged when Sara didn't move.

Sara looked at the clock. It was only a little after nine. "It's Sunday," she complained. "Doesn't anyone sleep late anymore?" After getting out of bed, she glanced around, searching for her clothes, then realized that neither she nor Denise had been wearing any by the time they had finally made it to the bedroom. She stepped into the bathroom to get her robe. When she returned she found Denise sitting up in bed with a sheet pulled around her and a pale, shaken-looking Taylor standing in the bedroom doorway staring. From Sara's viewpoint, it would have been difficult to determine which woman was more shocked.

When they both turned to her, Sara wished desperately to be anywhere but where she was. She did the only thing that came to mind. She introduced them.

Denise tucked the sheet tighter around her and extended her hand. "I'm sure you'll forgive me if I don't stand up."

Taylor slowly stepped forward and shook her hand before turning to Sara. "I'm sorry. Your truck was out front and when you didn't answer I was worried that—" She stopped. "I'm going to go home now. I'm really sorry about this," she murmured as she backed out of the room.

Sara started after Taylor. "Give me a minute to talk to her."

Denise shrugged as she glanced down at the sheet covering her. "I'm not going anywhere," she replied.

Sara pulled the bedroom door closed as she ran to catch up with Taylor. "Wait," she called as Taylor opened the door.

Taylor stopped but didn't turn around. "I'm sorry I barged in on you. You'd think, after the last time, I would have learned a lesson. I'll call from now on before I come over." She took off before Sara could say anything.

Sara stood staring after her.

"Is the coast clear?"

She turned to find a sheet-enshrouded Denise peeking out the bedroom door. "Yes. She's gone." She began to gather up the discarded clothing from the previous night. It was a wonder Taylor hadn't noticed them. She froze as she picked up Denise's tank top from the floor. Had Taylor seen the clothes and come in anyway? Taylor knew Sara well enough to know that she would never leave clothing lying around her living room. Taylor would have had to walk around the tank top at least. Why hadn't she called out when she came in?

"How many people have keys to your apartment?" Denise asked, as she took the tank top from her and pulled it on.

"Three or four."

"You might want to install a security chain to prevent this from ever happening again."

Mr. Tibbs chose that moment to announce his desire for breakfast.

Denise looked around in surprise. "That's one loud cat."

"He's upset that he hasn't been fed yet."

Denise put her arms around Sara and kissed her softly. "You should give him an extra treat this morning."

"Why?"

"If he hadn't darted out from beneath the coffee table and tripped you last night, I would have spent a long lonely night at home."

Until that moment, she hadn't realized what had caused her to fall, but she did remember seeing a blur. *I'll give him two packages of treats today*, Sara thought as Denise's hands slipped beneath the robe.

They stumbled back to the bedroom and made love again. Sara was drifting off to sleep when she remembered she was supposed to have Sunday dinner with Mandy and Arcy. Her eyes flew open. Had it really been less than a week since Mandy invited her to join them for dinner? She glanced at the clock and sighed. It was already after eleven.

"What's wrong?" Denise asked, as she snuggled closer.

"I'm supposed to have dinner with Mandy and Arcy today."

"Lucky you. Arcy's a great cook."

"*Sunday* dinner," Sara emphasized.

Denise slowly sat up and squinted at the clock. "You're going to be late."

Sara kept procrastinating. She didn't want to get out of bed. "Why do we refer to meals as breakfast, lunch and dinner, but Sunday dinner and Christmas dinner are served at noon?"

174

"You're stalling."

"I know, but I want to lie here a little while longer."

Denise kissed her shoulder. "Go shower. There will be plenty of other mornings when you can sleep late."

Sara didn't say anything as she trudged off to shower, but there would never be another morning like this one. She knew this as surely as she knew she would never be the same. The woman who had sat in her mother's car yesterday and cried because she might be a lesbian was gone. Today she knew she was a lesbian and there were no regrets and no turning back. She couldn't wait until she could touch Taylor again. She stopped short as the water pounded down on her. *Denise*. She meant she couldn't wait to touch *Denise* again.

The gentle sway of the rocker and the sumptuous meal slowly lulled the three women into a comfortable silence. It had rained in the area the night before and lowered the temperatures considerably from the previous day's heat. A cool breeze ruffled Sara's hair. She closed her eyes and thought about Denise. When they parted earlier that morning, neither of them had mentioned getting together again. Sara tried to decide whether she wanted to go out with Denise again or not. They'd had fun and the sex was great, but something wasn't quite right. She tried to figure out what it was. As her body continued to relax into a light doze, thoughts of Taylor began to sneak in. She didn't try to stop them. Would making love to Taylor be as exciting as it had been with Denise? Or was the power of the experience with Denise heightened by the fact that she was the first? Would a second time with Denise be as powerful?

The phone inside the house rang, jarring Sara awake.

"There are times when I wonder if that thing is really necessary." Mandy sighed, as she pulled herself from the rocker.

Sara prepared to settle back into her comfortable dozing state.

"Anyone want to join me for a ride?" Mandy asked. "That was Moon calling to let us know Houdini's out again." She glanced at

Sara. "Houdini is a cow. It's almost impossible to keep her inside a fence, hence the name."

Sara stood and stretched. "A ride sounds good to me. If I don't get up and move around some, I'm going to fall asleep."

"I think Roscoe and I will stay here and keep the chairs company," Arcy said with her eyes still closed.

Sara smiled at the woman and sleeping dog. They looked as comfortable as she had felt before the phone rang.

They piled into Mandy's truck and drove toward the main road. They went less than a mile before turning back onto an unpaved road that appeared to run parallel to the side of the house. To Sara the road seemed to be little more than a path composed of stretches of caliche, with its cement-like hardness, intermixed with short stretches of sandy soil. The rain had turned the sandy areas into small mud pits. Mandy didn't seem to notice the spine-numbing bouncing that occurred every time the tires hit a washed-out section in the caliche. Sara wondered if living out here all these years had numbed her butt to the jarring pain. They hadn't traveled far down the lane when Mandy spotted the cow contently grazing on a patch of new grass.

"There she is," Mandy said. When she honked the horn, Houdini took a few last bites before turning and trotting toward them.

Sara watched in amazement as the cow made her way along the fence before stepping back between the wires. "How did she do that?"

Mandy killed the engine and stepped out of the truck. "She finds a loose spot in the wire. In the old days, cowboys would spend hours riding the fence line checking for breaks or loose spots. Houdini saves me the trouble. I simply move her from pasture to pasture and it doesn't take her long to find any trouble spots." She removed a toolbox and a pair of gloves from behind the seat.

"Can I help?" Sara asked.

"You can come and keep me company, if you like."

Sara followed her to the fence post on the left side of the sec-

176

tion Houdini had walked through. She was surprised that the fence was nothing more than two strands of barbed wire.

Mandy pulled on each strand of wire. "It's this top one," she muttered.

"How will you fix it?"

"It's probably just a missing staple." They made their way to the next post. "See right here. That's the problem."

Sara looked at the area where Mandy was pointing, but nothing seemed wrong to her, except the wire did seem to be just sitting against the post without anything securing it.

"The staple has rusted out."

The image of the staple Sara imagined was quite different from the large U-shaped fastener Mandy took from the toolbox. Sara watched as the wire was caught inside the staple, which was then driven into the post. Mandy grabbed the wire and tugged on it again. There was a noticeable difference in its tautness.

"That one little fastener made a big difference," Sara said.

Mandy rested a gloved hand on the top of the post and watched as Houdini found a new patch of grass to munch on. "I'm getting too old to take care of everything. The little things are starting to get away from me."

"From what I've seen, the place still looks well cared for."

"It will for a while, but out here it won't take long for the little problems to develop into big ones. You have to stay on top of everything."

Sara didn't know what to say. She had no idea what kind of effort it took to maintain a ranch as large as this one.

She followed Mandy back to the truck. Rather than turning around and going back the way they came, they continued driving between the pastures. Sara soon lost track of the number of twists and turns they made. She gradually realized they were climbing. When Mandy stopped the truck, they were looking down at the pastures.

"Are you up to a short climb?" Mandy asked. "It's a pretty smooth path."

"All right." Sara was glad she had worn sneakers rather than sandals.

As Mandy had promised, the trail was easy to navigate. When they reached the top, Sara caught her breath at the beautiful landscape. From this height, the grass looked much greener and she was better able to appreciate the wide spans of pastureland. She turned and was surprised to see the house.

"That's your house, right?"

"That's the back of the house." Mandy propped her foot up on a good-sized boulder and stared down at the house.

Sara glanced around again. "Then this is the hill behind the house, the one where Bo was buried?"

Mandy nodded. "Come on. I'll show you." They picked their way over a few small boulders and came out onto a small pathway. "Whenever I come up here, I usually walk across the back pasture and up this side," she explained. "The gravesite is a lot easier to get to from that direction."

When they finally arrived at the site, Sara was surprised by how well maintained it was. The grave was located in a niche that had been hollowed from the hillside by millions of years of the wind and rain. White stones about twice the size of Sara's fist lined the grave. At the head sat a simple stone marker with crudely chiseled letters that read:

Bo Brodie
Born: 1830
Died: 1865

Behind the headstone, an enormous rosebush heavy with small red roses occupied a large area of ground and filled the air with a heady fragrance.

"I don't think I've ever seen a rosebush so large," Sara said in awe.

"It's old. I really don't know who planted it, but it has been gigantic for as long as I can remember." Mandy pointed to one of the canes. "Look at that cane. It's nearly as big around as my wrist." She held up her wrist as a comparison, then began to pull away a few small weeds that were beginning to pop out.

Sara sat down on a large boulder at the foot of the grave and found herself staring down at the back of the house. She hadn't noticed before that the back of the house didn't run straight across. One room protruded out from the rest. "Is that room the original cabin?" she asked and pointed to it.

Mandy glanced over. "Yes. When Dudley added the rest of the house on, he built toward the front and side." She walked over to join Sara. "I think he did it because the old well used to be somewhere along where the back porch is now. That well went dry sometime after Dudley had finished the additions. He filled it in and added the porch."

Sara studied the porch for a moment. Something about it was distracting. Finally, it hit her. "The back porch is made from stones, isn't it?"

"Yeah," Mandy replied slowly. "It's the only part of the house, except for the fireplace, made from stone."

"Why do you think he used stones?"

Mandy was slow in answering. "Maybe times were hard then and he couldn't afford to buy lumber. Lord knows, there are plenty of rocks around here."

Sara nodded but couldn't help but think that it was strange, since he had been so meticulous with the rest of the house.

Chapter Twenty-nine

Sara moved over so that there was room for Mandy to join her on the boulder. Neither of them seemed to be in a hurry to leave the peaceful spot.

They sat in silence for a long while before Mandy spoke. "How are things going with you?" she asked.

Sara tensed. Was something about her different? *Stop being silly,* she told herself. "I'm fine. Why do you ask?"

Mandy shrugged. "I'm just being a nosy old woman. I couldn't help but notice the last time you were out here, you weren't wearing your engagement ring. You still aren't today."

Sara glanced down at her hand. She rarely thought about the engagement. It embarrassed her slightly that she had forgotten it so easily. "We decided to call off the wedding." She paused a moment. When she spoke again, she changed the subject. "How long have you and Arcy been together?"

Mandy grunted slightly. "I met her in nineteen sixty. She was fresh out of college and had gotten her first teaching job in

Wilford Springs. The town has a Fall Festival each year in late September and a parade kicked off the festivities. Back then, the school was still small enough that each class would make a little float, out of a wagon or some such, and march along beside it. That's when I first noticed her. Right away, I knew she was something special. I followed her around for an hour or so, trying to pretend like I hadn't noticed her. Finally, she walked right up to me and told me that if I had something on my mind I ought to spit it out." Mandy laughed. "I was scared to death. Back then, it was harder for gays. But something about her gave me enough confidence to ask her if she would like to join me for a plate of barbecue." She stopped and gazed down at the house.

"What happened?" Sara asked, eager to hear the rest the story.

Mandy glanced at her and grinned. "We've been eating barbecue ever since."

Sara picked up a small stick from the ground and began to twirl it between her thumb and forefinger. "When did you know you were gay?"

"Uh-oh," Mandy said softly as she gazed at Sara. "That's one of those questions that makes me ask a question in return."

"What?"

"When did *you* start thinking you might be gay?"

Sara stared at the stick. She wasn't sure how much she should tell Mandy. After all, Denise had stressed her need to be discreet.

"Does this have anything to do with Denise Underwood?" When Sara shot a surprised glance her way, Mandy nodded. "I noticed you two talking the other day after the press conference. When I saw you give her a piece of paper, I wondered."

"You already knew about Denise?"

Mandy snorted. "Hell, everyone in town knows about that girl. She keeps pretending that most people don't know, but she's living in her own little dream world."

"She seems to be worried about how people will relate to her, but no one seems to bother you and you're in an open relationship."

"I discovered a long time ago that most people treat you the

181

way you act. If you hide like you're ashamed of what you're doing, then that's how others perceive you." Mandy held up her hand. "Having said that, I'll counter it with the acknowledgment that there are still plenty of assholes out there who think their way is the only way, but thankfully those people have been few and far between in my own experience."

"Do you think it helps that you've lived here your entire life and most people know you?"

"Definitely. It also helps that Arcy and I have made ourselves a valued part of this community. We don't broadcast our relationship with public displays, but we don't hide it either. No one faints anymore if we slip an arm around each other or hold hands. Hell, we even dance together at the community dances. Most people don't care."

"I envy your and Arcy's relationship," Sara said.

Mandy seemed to consider her next comment. "I know it's none of my business and we haven't known each other very long, but I like you and wouldn't want to see you get hurt."

"Denise warned me she wasn't looking for a long-term relationship," Sara said, suspecting where the conversation was headed.

Mandy seemed surprised. "Maybe she's not as irresponsible as I thought. I apologize if I butted in where I shouldn't have."

"No, I think it was sweet—you were trying to protect me." She leaned over and gave Mandy a quick kiss on the cheek. "It's nice."

Mandy blushed and turned away quickly, but not fast enough to hide the small smile. "What are you looking for?"

Passionate kisses. Knowing she couldn't admit that aloud, Sara took a deep breath. "I'm not sure I know. So much has been happening to me recently. It sometimes feels like my life is changing faster than I can catch up." She told Mandy about growing up with James and Taylor, about dating James, and then recently realizing she had strong feelings for Taylor. She told her all that had occurred in the last two weeks before ending her story with the scene where Taylor had walked in and caught her with Denise. When she finished she tossed away the stick she had practically shredded.

"Talk about bad timing," Mandy said with a low whistle. "Your friend Taylor seems to be having more than her share."

"I love Taylor, and there's something about her that—" She stopped as her face grew hot.

"It sounds to me like you're not sure whether you're falling in love or in lust," Mandy said.

Sara's face grew warmer. "I guess that's it exactly."

"And now that this woman, Debbie, is in the picture you're not going to be able to find out." Mandy shook her head. "That's not going to be easy. I've found that most of the time, the thing you want most is the thing you can't have. Then once you get it, you sometimes find it was a lot better as a fantasy."

"Do you think that's what I'm doing with Taylor?"

Mandy shrugged. "I can't answer that. I don't know you well enough to make that assumption. I'm just telling you what I've come to notice."

Sara picked up a rock and rolled it around in her hand for a moment. "How am I going to know? What if Taylor and I were meant to be together and bad timing keeps us apart?"

"If you're really meant to be together, bad timing won't keep you apart."

"But if we act on our feelings and it's a mistake, what happens then?"

Mandy took the rock from Sara's hand and threw it at a slightly larger rock of the side on the hill.

Sara listened as the larger rock broke loose and caused a miniature avalanche.

"Everything has a consequence," Mandy reminded her. "All you can do is to try and do what's right. Then pray you made the right decision."

"Where do I start?" Sara hadn't intended to ask the question aloud.

"Start by facing the problem," Mandy said, as she stood and waved toward the house.

Sara looked down to see Arcy standing on the back porch waving up at them. She tucked Mandy's advice away to think about later when she was alone. She waved back. "I didn't think she would be able to see us up here, because the grave sits back in the niche."

Mandy was silent for a long moment. "Because of the way the walls here come around"—she pointed to either side of the grave—"that spot where Arcy is standing is the only place in the house where you can actually see the gravesite."

A bell of recognition sounded in Sara's head. Why was that important? It took her a moment, but her memory slowly dredged up the fact. "Dudley buried the gold in a spot where he could see it and the grave at the same time," she whispered. She turned to Mandy. "Do you realize—"

"We'd best be heading back," Mandy interrupted as she turned and headed back toward the truck.

As they rode back to the ranch, Mandy kept up a steady dialogue on the history of how barbed wire changed ranching, but Sara missed most of it. She was trying to develop a mental picture of the view available from the spot where Arcy had been waving from and whether that view had changed any since Dudley died.

Chapter Thirty

Sara spent the drive back to San Antonio thinking about Taylor. Was she falling in love with Taylor? Or was Mandy right—she simply wanted what she couldn't have. She pulled off the road and dialed Taylor's number. She needed to do this now, before she had time to change her mind. Taylor answered on the second ring.

"I think we should talk," Sara said without preamble. When Taylor didn't respond, Sara pushed harder. "I'd like to come over now, if you're alone."

"I don't see where any good can come from this."

"I can be there in about twenty minutes."

Taylor sighed. "All right, but—"

"I'll see you in twenty minutes," Sara said and hung up before Taylor could try to talk her out of it. The drive seemed to take forever, but the clock reassured Sara that she was on time. As she walked up the driveway, she saw Taylor standing by the front window as though she had been watching for her. As she made her way up the sidewalk, Sara's steps seemed to grow smaller. What if Taylor was right and this was a mistake? She couldn't bear the thought of losing Taylor's friendship. The thought made her stop just short of the door.

Taylor stood in the open doorway. "You've made it this far. Don't you think it's sort of late to chicken out now?"

Sara swallowed and stepped into the house. When Taylor closed the door behind them and turned back to face her, Sara reached for her. *This is a mistake*, she told herself, but she seemed unable to stop herself. Taylor tried to pull back, but Sara kissed her before she could speak. She felt a moment of panic when at first there was no response from Taylor. Sara kissed her with more intensity as she pulled Taylor deeper into her arms.

Taylor's apparent resolve melted away and she began to return her kisses.

"Why do you keep torturing me?" Taylor asked, as she left a trail of kisses along Sara's neck.

"I thought we should talk," Sara answered eagerly.

"It's too late for talking," Taylor argued, before kissing her again.

Sara gave up all pretense of talking as Taylor's kisses became more passionate. She pulled Taylor closer and returned her kisses with a matching fervor that left her breathless and dizzy. When Taylor's tongue began its pressing demands, she welcomed it and pulled Taylor closer. As she swirled into a delicious vortex of pleasure, a small spot of reason returned. Taylor was with Debbie. Reluctantly, Sara pulled away and stepped back. Her voice trembled so, her words were barely audible. "I'm sorry. I didn't come here meaning to do that. I only meant to talk to you."

Taylor took several deep breaths before stepping away and crossing her arms across her chest. "What is there left to talk about? We've spent the last twenty-something years talking and where has it gotten us?" She turned and went to the sofa and sat down.

Sara followed her and sat beside her. "There are others we have to consider now."

Taylor sighed. "Oh, yes. You have a woman in your life now.

How could I have forgotten?" She turned away, but Sara saw the glint of tears in her eyes.

Sara didn't know how to explain that what had happened between her and Denise wasn't serious. "And you have Debbie," she countered.

Taylor leaned forward and scrubbed both hands over her face. "Then what is there to talk about?"

A flicker of irritation shot through Sara. She considered walking out but common sense told her to stay put and get this matter settled before it did destroy their friendship. "I don't want this to ruin our friendship."

The horrified look that Taylor gave her clearly showed she hadn't considered that possibility. "Do you think I'd ever let anything or anyone come between us?"

"Taylor, recently, all we do is storm in and out of each other's lives. When was the last time we had dinner together or just sat and talked to each other? This . . . this . . . whatever it is between us keeps getting in the way. We have to work this out."

Taylor looked at the floor. "I can't bear to think of you with another woman. It was hard enough when it was James, but I can't stand by . . . not with another woman."

She placed her hand on Taylor's arm.

"Please, don't," Taylor whispered harshly as she moved away.

Stunned by the rejection, Sara could only stare for a long moment. *It was too late.* She was already losing Taylor. "I don't want this to happen," she said. Tears burned her eyes. "I don't love Denise. It was nothing like that. What happened between us was just a . . . a . . . hell, I don't know what it was, but it's nowhere near what you and I have always had together."

"What have we had?"

"You and James are my dearest friends. We were the Three Musketeers."

"So, that's it? We were childhood friends."

"No. It was more than that."

"Was it?" Taylor stared at her with such intensity Sara was forced to look away.

The room filled with a silence so powerful it hurt Sara's ears. Mandy was right. The pebble had been bumped and now it seemed as though a full-scale slide was imminent.

"I don't think I can do this," Taylor said at last.

"Please, don't say that."

Taylor looked away.

"Taylor, for God's sake, don't close me out. We can work through this. I'll do whatever you want. Things can go back to the way they were before."

"How can you think that? It'll never be the same again."

Tears began to roll down Sara's face. The look of anguish that reflected in Taylor's face twisted Sara's heart. She had to do something to stop this from happening.

"I need time," Taylor said softly.

"What does that mean?" Sara asked, as her fear was suddenly replaced by anger.

"It means I need a few days to think about—"

"What? You need time for *you* to decide if we remain friends. Who gave you the right to make that decision? Do I have any say in this or am I just supposed to slink away and wait around for your call?"

"That's one thing you can never be accused of," Taylor said bitterly.

"What are you talking about?"

"I'm talking about how as soon as I announced I was gay, you and James grabbed onto each other as if you were each other's lifeline."

"That's not true."

"Really? When did you two start dating?"

Sara thought for a moment. "It was just before Christmas, our freshman year."

"I came out to my parents that same year during the Thanksgiving break."

Sara recalled how she and James had started dating. She remembered the date because the first time James kissed her had been in Foley's department store. He had gone with her to help her pick out a Christmas gift for Taylor. "The timing was a fluke. It had nothing to do with you coming out."

"Of course it didn't. I guess it's just a fluke that now we're all suddenly gay. It's also just a fluke that the moment I mention I've met someone who may mean something to me, you suddenly decide you're gay and that now you may be interested in me."

Sara stared at her in stunned silence. How could Taylor think that? She didn't have answers to refute her claims, and worse, everything Taylor was saying had the ring of truth to it. "I should go. We can talk about this later, when we've both cooled down some." She stood and started for the door.

"Sara, wait. I'm not—"

"Please, let's not argue anymore. Can I call you in a week or so? Maybe we could have dinner or something."

Taylor's shoulders dropped. "Why don't we wait and see how it goes?"

Sara managed to hold herself together as she walked out the door. Heavier than normal traffic kept her occupied as she drove home. It was only once she reached the apartment that she allowed herself to fall apart. As she lay across the bed sobbing uncontrollably, Mr. Tibbs hopped up on the bed and pushed his way under her arm. He spent the night huddled beside her, not once protesting against the tears that stained his glossy fur.

Chapter Thirty-one

Sara opened her eyes to darkness and a pounding headache. When she started to unfold her cramping body, a slight murmur of protest made her freeze. She wasn't alone. It took her exhausted brain a moment to identify the sound as coming from the warm, silky feline curled up against her.

"Thank you," she whispered to the cat and brushed her hand along his back.

Mr. Tibbs stretched and hopped off the bed, seemingly aware that his work here was complete.

Sara turned on the bedside lamp before making her way to the bathroom to wash her swollen, tear-streaked face. "You are so pathetic," she said to the image in the mirror. Since she had realized she was gay, she had been unhappy. Her relationship with James might not have been as passionate as her affair with Denise, but at least she hadn't been miserable. Mandy was probably right. She and Taylor were going to end up destroying their friendship over some silly fantasy. There were things going on in her professional life that she couldn't control directly, but her personal life was different. It was up to her to make the decisions that affected it. Denise had shown her what a woman's love could be like. Sara couldn't deny she was gay, but she could stop making stupid mistakes. Throwing herself at Taylor was inexcusable. From now on, her relationship with Taylor would be nothing more than friendship. Sex wasn't that important. Taylor was trying to make a life with Debbie and she needed to honor and respect that relationship. No matter how much it hurt her to do so. Sara looked into the mirror and squared her shoulders. "From now on, Taylor is a friend and nothing more." Her voice sounded unsure and flat. She kept repeating the phrase until it sounded like she meant it.

When she went back into the bedroom, the clock read 12:02. She dialed Taylor's number and wasn't surprised when she answered on the second ring. Her heart clenched when she realized Taylor sounded as miserable as she felt.

"I've called to apologize for the way I acted this afternoon," Sara said. Taylor started to speak, but Sara stopped her. "Please, let me finish. You were right. I think I was jealous of your relationship with Debbie. A lot has been happening recently and I think I turned to you as I always do, but because of what happened between me and James, then me and Denise, somehow in my mind everything got jumbled around and interconnected." She stopped and released a long sigh. "Your friendship is the most important thing to me. If you'll give me another chance, I promise you I'll never again act the way I did this afternoon. I want us to be friends."

"Is that all you want?" Taylor asked in a voice that sounded strained to Sara.

"Yes." Saying the simple word was much harder than she had thought it would be, but she had made herself and Taylor a promise that she intended to keep. No matter how badly it hurt. "Can we please try and put this behind us?" The pause that followed grew so long that a light sheen of sweat began to break out along Sara's hairline.

"I'd like to try," Taylor said at last.

Sara had a gut feeling that if she didn't push, the relationship would die. "Can I call you during the week?"

"It might be better if you waited until next week. I think I need a little more time."

She wanted to protest that she couldn't wait two weeks before she talked to her again, but she forced herself to swallow her disappointment and agreed.

During the days that followed, all Sara could think about was Taylor—even work couldn't distract her. She had called James so many times, he was threatening to change his phone number.

There had been no further contact from Denise. In moments of rational thought, Sara knew she should probably be upset about not hearing from her, but she wasn't. The time they spent together had been fun and the sex had been great, but overall, something was missing. She didn't take time to analyze what it was. She was too busy missing Taylor. She continued to talk to either Mandy or Arcy almost daily. The calls were no longer business. She had developed a genuine liking for the two women. Another trespasser had been caught digging on their property, but for the most part, the gold madness seemed to have settled down.

By eight o'clock Thursday night, Sara was on the verge of ignoring all of her well-meaning resolutions. Since arriving home from work, she had picked up the phone half a dozen times to call Taylor. She was so anxious and grumpy that Mr. Tibbs stopped begging for treats. He seemed to prefer the peace and quiet of the back bedroom to the emotional storm raging around Sara.

Too anxious to read, she tried to watch a movie. When the phone rang, she practically threw herself over the end of the couch to get to it.

"Oh, hi, James," she said when she heard his voice.

"Well, don't drown me with enthusiasm," he said in response to her lackluster greeting.

"Sorry, I was just—"

"Trust me. I know what you were doing. The real question is what are you doing tomorrow night?"

"Nothing."

"Good. I'm fixing dinner. Be here at eight."

"I don't know."

"It'll be a nice dinner, so come looking elegant and at least try to pretend like you're trying to have a good time. Remember, eight sharp and park in the front. I'm having some repairs made on the garage." He hung up before she could protest.

As she went back to the television, she realized what he was trying to do. Tomorrow was Friday and Taylor would be going to see Debbie. He was giving up his poker game to ensure she wouldn't be alone. Tears burned her eyes and she longed for the earlier days of the Three Musketeers, before words like *love* and *sex* ruined everything.

When Sara parked in front of James's house the following evening at eight sharp, she reminded herself that he had gone to a lot of effort to prepare dinner for her. She glanced at the stately home and smiled. She rarely saw the front of the house because the garages to the homes along this street were located in the back and were accessed by a private entrance. She stepped from the truck and smoothed the dove gray linen jacket and matching slacks. The blouse was one of her favorites, a royal blue silk with tiny black vertical stripes. As she strolled up the sidewalk, she glanced at the large front yard of the house. A lawn care service kept it in immaculate condition. The roses along the side of the house were in full bloom and their heady fragrance drifted out to tease her. The house was a large two-story Victorian located in the venerable Monte Vista district. She rang the doorbell, no longer feeling comfortable simply walking in unannounced. When a short, heavy-set man dressed in white opened the door, Sara took a step back, momentarily confused. James hadn't mentioned inviting anyone else.

The man stepped back and bowed. "I am Andre. Please come in."

Sara tried not to smile as she stepped inside. It looked like James was going a little overboard tonight. "Is James here?" Sara asked.

"Mr. Edwards asked that I give you this," the man said, as he pulled a small envelope from his pocket. "If you would follow me please, dinner is being served on the sun porch."

Sara tore open the envelope as she followed him. Inside was a note written in James's sprawling script. *Patience, dear Sara, is sometimes more than a virtue—Love, James.*

She frowned at the note until she stepped out onto the patio and saw Taylor sitting by the small indoor koi pond. When Taylor saw her, it was obvious from the look on her face that she wasn't expecting Sara.

Andre pressed a glass of champagne into Sara's hand. "Dinner will be ready in fifteen minutes." He disappeared back into the house.

Taylor looked stunning in black flowing pants and short jacket over a ruby-red camisole, from which the smallest hint of cleavage was visible. Sara gulped half the champagne before approaching the pond. "I think James has pulled a fast one on us. He told me to park out front because his garage was being repaired. He didn't want either of us to see the other one's car." She was surprised but pleased to hear her voice sound so steady.

"He probably thought we'd leave," Taylor said, as she tossed a note card on the table. "Well, at least I know what this means now."

Sara handed over her note before picking up the other one from the table. The message on it read, *Honesty really is the best policy—Love, James.*

They both laughed at the same time. "I guess he was tired of listening to me whining and crying night after night," Taylor said.

Sara sat down on the chair next to Taylor and smiled. "Poor guy, we were both bombarding him. He threatened to change his number if I didn't stop calling so often."

"He threatened to block my calls."

An awkward silence fell between them and then suddenly they both started talking at once. "You first," Sara insisted. When Taylor leaned forward slightly and inadvertently gave Sara a better view of what lay beneath the camisole, Sara forced her gaze to the koi pond.

"I've been an ass to you—"

"No. It was me," Sara interrupted.

Taylor held up her hand. "There's something I need to tell you. I should have told you the other day, but I guess I was too embarrassed or scared. I don't know." She sipped from her almost empty glass of champagne. "Debbie . . . I'm not seeing Debbie anymore."

Sara felt sick. "Oh, my God, Taylor, if I'm the reason—"

Again, Taylor stopped her. "Debbie and her ex got back together. I knew they still saw each other occasionally. I just didn't know how involved they still were."

Sara placed a hand on her friend's arm. "I'm so sorry. Are you all right?"

She shrugged. "You mean, other than feeling like a fool. I always seem to pick the wrong one." Tears glistened in her eyes.

"Do you want to talk about it?"

"No. Not really. I think the worst is over."

"When did this happen?" Sara asked, feeling a little confused.

"She called me right after I came home two weeks ago and told me she and her ex had been talking and they wanted to try and work things out. She had been trying to tell me while I was there but couldn't."

"It's her loss. You're a good, decent person."

Taylor squeezed Sara's hand. "Thank you. I'm sorry I took some of my pain and anger out on you. I was so scared. I really care for you, but I've always screwed up every relationship I've had. I didn't . . . don't want to become romantically involved with you."

Sara swallowed the pain the words caused and nodded. Friendship was better than never seeing Taylor. "I agree. We were meant to be friends, not lovers."

"It's strange, isn't it? You would think great friends would make great lovers."

"Maybe it has to work in the other direction," Sara suggested. "Maybe great lovers eventually become great friends."

Taylor nodded. "Like you?"

A spark of desire shot through Sara. Taylor quickly doused it.

"You and Denise were right to become lovers first. You can become friends later."

"I told you whatever happened between me and Denise was one of those spur-of-the-moment, probably once-in-a-lifetime things."

"You mean you haven't seen her again?"

"No. She never called after that night. I guess it wasn't very memorable for her."

"I find that hard to believe."

Sara squirmed. "Where is James anyway?"

"I don't know for sure. I suspect he's in Dallas with Clint."

"How's that going? Did you know he's talking about moving to Dallas?"

"Yes, he mentioned it to me. I tried to talk him out of moving, but he seems pretty determined." Taylor drained her glass and set it aside. "It'll be strange not to have him nearby."

A sense of loss stung Sara. Until recently, it had never occurred to her that James and Taylor might not be in her life forever. She stole a glimpse at the woman beside her and bit her tongue to keep from telling her of the feelings that seemed to grow stronger with each passing day.

Chapter Thirty-two

Sara, Taylor and James once again began spending the majority of their free time together. It was as though their personal adversities had drawn them back together to help each other heal. The city elections rolled around and when David Brock, the candidate James had endorsed, won there was another brief flurry of the media rehashing James's decision to withdraw. The attention didn't last long. Other local, juicier news came along and sent the reporters and public curiosity scurrying after it.

On Mother's Day, Sara went to church with her parents before taking them to brunch. Sara bought her mom the Prada handbag that Eloise had been dropping less than subtle hints about, but it dimmed in comparison to the gold-and-onyx bracelet her father gave his wife.

After brunch, they went back to her parents' house and while her mother was off changing out of the dress she had worn, Sara's father called her into his office. She had been waiting for this summons, but she hadn't expected him to do it today.

When they were seated in the modern home office of stainless steel and glass, he leaned back in his chair and slowly crossed his legs. Sara knew he was waiting for her to start talking, but he had taught her well. She forced her mind away from what was happening in the room and concentrated on remembering every single file waiting for her attention at work. When she made it through those, she worked at recalling all the ones she had completed in the last week. She was working on the second week when he finally spoke.

"I've heard some rather disturbing news from your mother," he began.

Sara continued to wait.

"I understand that you now believe you're gay."

"No, I know I'm a lesbian."

He flinched at the word. "How can you possible know such a thing?"

Sara swallowed the most obvious response that dealt with Denise and tried one she hoped was more tactful. "I'm not attracted to men, in that way."

He sat forward, folded his hands on his desk and peered at her as if she were a witness he was about to interrogate. "Am I to assume that you are attracted to women sexually?"

She cringed as she felt her face grow warm. Maybe it wasn't him she had been trying to protect with her tact. "Yes," she replied.

"Are you certain this isn't simply some sort of anomaly that was brought on when James broke off your engagement, or perhaps from the fact that your two closest friends are homosexuals?"

"First, I don't think being gay is an anomaly and second, James wasn't alone in calling off the engagement. We told you, we both thought it was the right decision." She looked him in the eye. "Dad, I'm gay and have been since high school. It may have been those unconscious feelings that drew the three of us together all those years ago. That whole birds-of-a-feather thing, but it certainly wasn't the cause of my being gay."

"Are you happy?"

His question threw her for a moment. "Yes and no. Overall, I am, but there are issues that I'm trying to deal with."

"Is Taylor one those issues?"

Again, she stared at him, surprised. "Yes, she is."

He nodded and leaned back in his chair. "I truly expected us to have this conversation several years ago."

"You knew I was gay?"

"Let's say I had a strong suspicion. There was always a closeness between you and Taylor that extended beyond the normal young girl friendships."

"Why didn't you say anything?"

"I knew you would find your way by yourself."

"Are you angry?"

"No. I won't say I'm happy. I have concerns that this will make your life harder, but if it's what you truly want, I believe you'll be happier in the long run."

"Thank you, Dad."

The sound of her mother's footsteps walking through the living room toward the kitchen reached them. "Your mother bought ice cream. That's probably where she's headed." He stood. As he came around the desk he draped his arm around her shoulder and hugged her to him. "This problem you're having with Taylor, is there anything I can do to help?"

"No. It's something I have to deal with on my own, but thanks."

He kissed the top of her head. "You know your mother and I are here if you need us."

"Who wants ice cream?" Eloise called from the kitchen.

When James began to spend more time in Dallas than in San Antonio, Sara and Taylor filled the void his absence made by spending more time together, shopping and goofing off as they used to. The tension between them gradually melted away. It was only in unguarded moments that Sara would look into Taylor's eyes and be hit with an almost overwhelming sense of need. When those moments occurred, she learned to get through them by reminding herself what it would be like to lose Taylor's friendship.

In was nearing the end of May when Tom Wallace called Sara. In what must have been a record turnaround time, he was calling to let her know that the state historical commission wasn't interested in acquiring the Brodie Ranch. He blamed it on an already abundant source of data about ranch life in Atascosa County during the period the Brodies lived there. When Sara didn't accept that reason, he gave her a song and dance about the drastic decreases in the commission's budget. If Mandy wished to donate the land with the stipulation the state could use it as it deemed necessary, they would be most appreciative of the donation. Bo's diary would be accepted by the state library, if Mandy still wished to donate it.

Sara went to Rosa's office to tell her the news.

"It sounds like Tom lost interest after learning the diary wasn't going to lead him to his fabled gold," Rosa said.

"That's what I thought too. I feel bad for Mandy. She really loves the place and doesn't want to leave it to chance that the next owner will care for the place as she has."

"Sometimes we have to let go."

Sara had a sudden image of Taylor. "Sometimes that simply doesn't work."

Rosa looked at her and Sara realized too late that her boss probably thought she was talking about James. She relaxed when Rosa let it slide. "It's too bad—" She stopped and glanced toward the outer office. True to her word, Rosa hadn't mentioned the gold again. "I wish there was some way we could rub Tom's nose in all this. That sanctimonious ass would have been all over this if there had been something in it for him."

"I'm going to drive out to the ranch after work and tell them. I'd rather not give them bad news over the phone."

"You've really gotten close to them, haven't you?"

Sara smiled and nodded. "It's costing me too. I've gained four pounds from Arcy's cooking."

"Listen, feel free to bring any leftovers you don't want right on over here," Rosa teased. "How's it working with Gracie?" she asked, as Sara stood.

"Fine. It was a little awkward when she first came back, but she seems to have settled down. She's trying hard. She hasn't been late or left early a single day since she's been back."

"Good." She stood. "Give my best to the ladies and remind them that they might want to think about approaching the commission again in a couple of years."

Sara didn't say anything, but she knew Rosa was suggesting they wait until after Tom left the commission.

Chapter Thirty-three

Sara went back to her office and closed the door. She didn't want anyone accidentally wandering into her office and overhearing her conversation. The sooner everyone forgot about the Brodie file the better. As she sat down, her phone rang. It was Taylor.

"Do you have plans for tonight?" Taylor asked.

"I may drive out toward Wilford Springs."

"Oh." There was a touch of disappointment in her voice. "What are you doing?"

"Nothing," Taylor replied. "I thought you might want to go to dinner or something. It's Wednesday, so there will be a jazz band playing at The Curve."

Sara liked going to The Curve, a small burger joint that used its large outdoor patio to showcase local bands on certain nights. "I'm going to see Mandy Brodie. The state historical commission decided not to accept her offer and I'd like to tell her in person. Why don't you come with me? I won't be long."

"No. I wouldn't want to intrude."

"You won't be. If they can see me today, what I have to do won't take long. We can go to dinner afterward."

Taylor hesitated.

"It's a beautiful drive."

"Are you sure they won't mind?"

"I'm sure, but if it'll make you feel better. I'll ask when I call them."

"Okay."

"I'll give you a call back." Sara hung up and dialed Mandy's number. As she suspected, Mandy assured her Taylor was welcome to come with her.

Taylor was able to leave the office a little early. It was only a little after four when the pair headed out of town from Sara's apartment.

"I've never been to Wilford Springs," Taylor admitted. "What's it like?"

Sara turned up the fan on the air conditioner to combat the late-afternoon heat. "I don't know what the town is like. I've only been to the ranch. The people all seem like good, hardworking folks."

"How did you meet them?"

Sara started telling her the story.

"These are the women with the gold?" Taylor interrupted.

"Rumored gold," Sara reminded her. She wanted to tell Taylor the entire story but didn't think she had a right to do so. Telling Rosa, her boss, was one thing, but repeating it to someone outside the project seemed unethical.

"Can you imagine what it would be like to find that much gold?" Taylor asked.

"I wouldn't want to."

"Get outta here. You can't mean it." She shook her head. "I don't believe that. You spend all that time working your butt off to save those old buildings and things that everyone else is ready to give up on, but you don't think hunting Confederate gold would be exciting?"

"It has already caused too much trouble. Sometimes things are better left alone."

"I suppose so," Taylor replied, and turned to look out the window.

"You should see the stars out here at night," Sara said, trying to draw Taylor back.

"They're probably pretty clear so far out away from the city lights. The stars are the only reason I'd ever want to live in the country. Well, that and being able to have a horse."

Sara chuckled. "I'd forgotten how badly you wanted a horse."

"I asked for one each year for Christmas and my birthday from the time I turned nine until I went to college." She turned back toward Sara. "Do you remember the time Dad took me, you, and James to that old riding stable over near Brackenridge Park?"

"God, those were the laziest horses on earth." Sara groaned. "The one that James got stuck with stopped every two feet to munch on the grass."

"Yeah, but they knew exactly when the thirty-minute ride was over because they practically galloped back to the stable."

"I remember my butt was sore for a week from bouncing around in that saddle."

"Mine too, but I was in pig heaven for a while."

"Why don't you buy yourself a horse now? You could board it in a stable."

Taylor looked at her and frowned. "Now, why didn't that ever occur to me? Here I've been whining and crying for years because my parents wouldn't buy me a horse, when I could have bought my own after I started working." She tapped her fingers on her knee. "I wonder how much a horse costs."

"I don't know. I know a Mustang will run you about twenty thousand."

Taylor gasped. "Twenty thousand! No way." She stopped when she saw Sara smiling.

"Oh, ha ha, you're very funny, Ms. Stockton. I'll keep that in mind the next time I'm car shopping."

They talked about horses until Sara slowed down to turn onto the road leading back to the ranch. "You may want to hold on," Sara informed her. "This road is a little rough." The truck did its normal dancing routine before she could find the section of roadway with the fewest potholes. "Sorry about that."

Taylor shifted under the continued barrage of bumps. "They must have cast-iron butts to be able to go back and forth over this road."

Sara laughed. "Believe it or not, you get used to it. The first time I came out here my reaction was about the same as yours was, but it doesn't really bother me now."

Taylor suddenly smiled. "Hey, I just had a great idea. I'm going to open an office out here. If all the roads are like this, everyone out here needs physical therapy. Think of all the compressed spines and—ouch!"

Sara had been so engrossed in watching Taylor, she had failed to see a deep pothole. Luckily, she wasn't going very fast.

"You did that on purpose," Taylor accused.

"I did not. It was your fault. You were being goofy and distracted me." She eased off the road and onto the driveway leading up to the house.

"They have horses," Taylor said, and pointed toward the pasture where five or six horses were grazing.

Roscoe came tearing toward them.

"What the heck is that?"

"That's their dog, Roscoe. He's friendly enough once you get to know him."

"Who the heck would wait around for an invitation," Taylor muttered.

Mandy was standing on the porch with her hands in her pockets. She was wearing her usual wardrobe of faded jeans, a white shirt with the sleeves rolled halfway to her elbows and boots.

"Um, was there something you forgot to tell me about Mandy?"

Sara frowned. "What do you mean?" She waved as Arcy came out to stand by Mandy.

"Like, they're lesbians."

"Oh, yeah. I guess I forgot."

Taylor started laughing.

"Now, what?"

"Sara, you're priceless."

A warm feeling of pleasure flowed through Sara and she smiled. For the briefest instant, she saw something she couldn't quite define in Taylor's eyes. She pondered on it as they climbed out of the truck and approached the house. *It was a look of longing.* The thought shocked her so, she stubbed her toe on the bottom step and would have fallen if Taylor hadn't been there to catch her.

Chapter Thirty-four

Mandy and Arcy took the news of their offer being declined without any outward show of surprise or disappointment. "I think you should try again in a couple of years. Things change. Hopefully, by then someone will come to their senses and realize we need increased funding if our historic treasures are to be preserved for future generations."

"Who knows," Mandy began, "we may be able to find our own solution before we both kick the bucket and not have to worry about the state."

Sara peered at her. Was she hinting about the gold? She suddenly recalled them standing by Bo's grave and looking down at the rock porch. Could the gold be buried beneath the porch? If so, why use rocks? Had he not used wood because he was afraid someone would find the gold when the wood eventually rotted and needed to be replaced?

Arcy offered them tea and Taylor went to help her.

"Mandy, you're not thinking about looking for . . . you know." Sara spoke low, so that her voice wouldn't accidentally carry out to the kitchen.

"Hell, no. That stuff has caused my family enough grief. I wish to God Dudley had taken that secret with him. Arcy and I have been talking about selling off all the land except for a few acres right around the house and putting the proceeds into some kind of trust for the maintenance of the house. Land prices are high now. I think we could get a pretty good chunk of change for it."

Damn that Tom Wallace, Sara fumed silently. She hated to see homesteads broken up. There were so few of them remaining. This one had already been chipped away at until it was down from its original six thousand acres to eighteen hundred. "I wish there was another way." She suddenly remembered Denise Underwood's dream of breeding horses. She repeated it to Mandy.

"That girl couldn't afford to buy this place. She's barely making ends meet on that little old spot she has. Besides, I'm not going to be selling anytime soon. We're just trying to come up with other options."

"I understand and can appreciate your desire to protect the place. I really admire your loyalty to your homestead."

Mandy blushed and changed the subject. "With Debbie and Denise out of the picture, it appears you and Taylor have worked through your problems."

After the long talk she and Mandy had shared that afternoon by Bo's grave, Mandy would occasionally inquire about the situation whenever they spoke on the phone. Sara glanced down at the arm of the couch and began to trace the faint pattern in the material with her thumb. "We've decided to keep things as they were before. Our friendship is too important to jeopardize it with any-thing else."

"You think you can't be friends and lovers?" Mandy asked bluntly.

"It didn't seem to work for us."

Arcy and Taylor came in with the iced tea before further comments could be made.

"You have a beautiful place," Taylor said, as she handed a glass to Sara before sitting on the other end of the couch. "I noticed you have several horses."

"Do you ride?" Mandy asked.

"Not really. I always wanted to, but somehow I just never seem to get around to learning."

"Well, there's no time like the present." Mandy started to stand.

"Mandy, sit down and let the girls finish their tea," Arcy scolded.

"She wants to learn to ride a horse."

"I know, dear, and there will be plenty of time for that after we have our tea."

Sara watched the couple and smiled. She wanted the kind of relationship they had. Why couldn't she have it with Taylor? Why couldn't they be lovers and still maintain their friendship? She glanced at Taylor and found her staring at her. At that moment, Sara knew without a doubt that Taylor was having the same thoughts. The look of longing returned to Taylor's eyes.

"Where do you work, Taylor?" Arcy asked, unknowingly breaking the spell.

Sara took a large gulp of the ice-cold tea and was rewarded with a blinding pain of brain-freeze. Lost in thought, she only half-heartedly listened to the conversation flowing around the room. It wasn't until her ears picked up the word *camping* that her attention returned. Mandy and Arcy were telling them about a camping trip they were getting ready to go on.

"It's nothing elaborate," Arcy explained. "There's a large patch of woods over by the river on the far south end of the property. Every year around Memorial Day, we load our supplies on a pack mule and ride the horses over. It's just for the weekend. We fish a little, but it's mostly an excuse to get away from everything for a while."

"That sounds wonderful," Sara said.

"You and Taylor should go with us," Mandy said. "It'll give Taylor a chance to practice her horsemanship, and you both look like you could stand a few days away from the city."

Sara blinked in surprise. "I didn't mean for it to sound like I was angling for an invitation."

"Yeah, we wouldn't want to intrude on your weekend," Taylor added.

"You wouldn't be intruding," Arcy insisted. "It would be fun to have company."

Sara looked at Taylor and saw she was interested. "When are you leaving?"

"We'll leave out of here early Friday morning."

Arcy held up her hand. "I'll warn you. Her idea of early is before daybreak."

"We've only been on a horse once," Sara reminded Taylor.

"Mandy said we could learn as we go."

Sara turned to Arcy, who looked a little concerned. "Can we really learn as we go?" she asked.

Arcy gave a small smile. "Yes," she said hesitantly, "I suppose you could, but if you're not used to riding, you're going to be—"

"Fine," Mandy interrupted. "They will be fine. These two need to get away and relax." She looked pointedly at Arcy and some invisible signal seemed to pass between them.

Arcy frowned slightly and glanced back at the two of them on the couch. Suddenly the frown gave way to a smile. "Of course," she said. "You should come. We'll have fun. All you two need to do is show up here Friday morning with your stuff. Don't worry about food or anything. I'll have that covered."

"Just remember to pack light," Mandy said. "We'll be using a mule and the horses to pack everything in. I don't like to overload them."

"Can you take Friday off?" Sara asked Taylor.

"Sure, I can get someone to cover for me. I try to keep a light schedule on Fridays anyway."

A twinge of pain pricked Sara. Taylor had started keeping light Friday schedules because of Debbie.

The four spent the next several minutes planning their trip. It was six-thirty when Sara discreetly caught Taylor's attention and tapped her watch.

Sara and Taylor stopped at a burger joint on the way back to San Antonio. It wasn't The Curve, but the place looked as though it had been a bar at one time, with the neon beer lights and metal signs still hanging on the walls. The floor was made from unpainted boards that had been worn smooth by years of use. A young woman in jeans and a blindingly white tank top led them to a rustic wood table in the back. They each ordered a Corona and began to study the menu.

"The printing is the only thing on this menu that's not fried," Taylor joked.

"When did you become so health-conscious?"

"Since I ended up with two stroke patients who are both under thirty-six."

"That's scary." Sara looked back at the menu. "Do you want to split a burger?"

Taylor glanced from the menu and then back to Sara. "Not really. I'm hungry."

Sara began to laugh. "You're impossible."

"I want to be good and eat healthy, but it's hard. I'll compensate by riding my bike to work tomorrow."

"You have a ten-mile commute."

"Oh, yeah." Taylor puzzled the problem for a moment before smiling brightly. "I'm going horseback riding this weekend. That's bound to be enough activity to negate a hamburger tonight."

Sara simply nodded. She had a feeling that their adventure in horseback riding was going to be more than enough.

Chapter Thirty-five

They had been riding for almost an hour by the time the eastern sky came alive with a brilliant display of color. The four women stopped their horses to watch the landscape slip out of the darkness and slowly reveal its hidden beauty. Nearby was a patch of Indian blankets that were still hanging on to a vestige of their vibrant red, orange, and yellow petals. Scattered clumps of prickly pear cactus with their normal yellow blooms occasionally gave way to various shades of orange and red. Pink primrose, yellow buttercups, winecups, and white prickly poppies were sprinkled throughout the area. In the distance, the trees began to take on individual shapes along the bottom of a hill.

"That's where we're headed," Mandy said, pointing toward the hill.

With the brief magical spell of the sunrise broken, Sara was again aware of her aching thighs. If Taylor was hurting, she showed no signs of her misery.

"I'm starting to feel this saddle," Arcy announced suddenly. "Let's get down and walk for a while."

Sara saw Mandy's look of surprise and suspected the rest was meant for her and Taylor. She felt a moment of sadistic pleasure when she saw Taylor wince slightly as she stepped down from the horse. At least Sara wasn't the only one hurting. They spread out side by side and continued toward their destination. Mandy led her horse and the pack mule. At first, Sara wasn't sure her trembling legs were going to allow her to walk far. It took a few minutes before she started to feel better. By the time they remounted, she felt like she could make it a while longer.

When they rode among the trees, Sara realized how hot it had already gotten. She had been so busy concentrating on maintaining her seat on the horse and worrying about her aching thighs, she hadn't noticed the heat until they entered the much cooler woods. Looking around, she recognized some of the trees as being live oaks, persimmon, and pecan.

"What a difference in temperatures," Taylor remarked.

"It'll be even cooler alongside the water," Mandy assured them. "A campfire will feel good tonight."

A few minutes later, they rode into a beautiful glade. A river bordered with towering cypress trees ran through the glade. It took Sara a moment to realize they were at the base of the hill she had seen earlier.

They continued riding toward the river until Mandy finally stopped and stepped out of the saddle. "We're home, ladies."

Sara climbed off the horse and clung to the saddle until the trembling in her legs eased. Slowly her ears became accustomed to the sounds of birds. At first it sounded like one big clamor, but as she listened, individual tones and calls began to separate themselves. It took her a moment, but she eventually located the scarlet hue of a male cardinal. A female cardinal joined him for a moment before they both flew deeper into the tree's canopy. She heard Taylor emit a muffled moan as she stepped down from her horse. A moment later, she made her way over to Sara. Her movements were slow and measured.

"That was fun," she said, and tried to smile as she rubbed her lower back.

"I'm glad we came," Sara said and meant it.

Mandy began to unpack the mule.

"What can we do?" Sara asked, as she hobbled toward her.

Mandy looked at her and chuckled knowingly. "There's an old stone ring firepit over there." She nodded toward the river. "You can clean it out and then firewood will need to be gathered."

"I can help with the firewood," Taylor said, as she turned to go with Sara.

"Taylor, why don't you hang around? I'll show you how to unsaddle the horses and rub them down," Mandy called.

"Sara, I'm headed in your direction," Arcy said, as she grabbed up a large duffle. "If you can take this other bag here, it'll save me a trip."

Sara picked up the bag and grunted in surprise at its weight. She had to hustle to keep up with the older woman. As they approached the river, Sara was able to see that the opposite bank consisted of little more than a rock wall.

"The river is fed by a natural spring," Arcy said, as they walked along. "The water stays cold year round. We used to come up here and swim during the summer, but my old bones don't appreciate the cold so much anymore."

"How long have you two been coming up here?" Sara asked when they finally reached the firepit.

Arcy dug around in the duffle and pulled out a small shovel with a handle that folded over. "You can use this to dig the center of the pit out some."

"How deep?" Sara asked.

"Just enough to keep the fire contained."

Sara leaned over the circle of stones. Old ash indicated the presence of previous fires.

"We've been coming here since our third date," Arcy finally said. "I guess by then she had decided I was a keeper."

"What about you? When did you decide she was a keeper?"

Sara asked, as she scooped a shovelful of ash and carried it several feet away before scattering it over the grass.

"Oh, I knew the moment I saw her. I was at the Fall Festival, helping my school kids with their float, when I noticed this tall handsome woman. Everywhere I went I'd look around and there she'd be. She was wearing a white western shirt with the sleeves rolled up just enough to show off those wonderful muscular arms of hers." Arcy shivered. "She had a classy chassis."

"A what?" Sara stopped scooping.

"You know, a great body." Arcy looked over to where Mandy and Taylor were unsaddling the horses. "A lot like your Taylor, except Mandy was taller and broader through the shoulders. It came from all that hard work on the ranch."

Sara looked at the two of them. Mandy was a little taller and her waist a little thicker than Taylor's was, but other than that they did have very similar body shapes.

Mandy caught them staring. "If you two don't have anything better to do than ogle us while we work—"

"Oh, hush up," Arcy called. "I was just wondering where you had strayed off to. I couldn't distinguish you from the other horses' butts over there."

Mandy laughed loudly as Arcy went back to work unpacking the coffeepot along with utensils, cookware, tin plates and cups and four brightly colored metallic glasses.

As Sara continued cleaning the firepit, she wondered how Taylor would react to being told she had a classy chassis. She knelt down to reposition a couple of the stones and looked up to find Taylor and Mandy walking toward them. They were similarly clad in jeans and boots, and both carried a saddlebag over each shoulder and a bedroll in each hand. As Sara watched them, she had the uncanny feeling that they had stepped back through time. She felt certain that if she were to turn, she would find Bo and Dudley Brodie riding toward them. Taylor laughed at something Mandy said and the lock around Sara's heart broke open. There was no more kidding herself. She was in love with Taylor. Turning away before Taylor could see the truth that Sara was certain showed on her face, she found Arcy watching her. The kindness reflected in her eyes was almost more than Sara could take.

Arcy stood suddenly and took Sara's hand. "We're going to gather some firewood," she called to the others. "You two can finish setting up the camp." They walked out a ways before she said, "Have you told her how you feel?"

Not yet trusting her voice, Sara nodded.

"The first year Mandy and I were together was rough. To be honest with you, I didn't think we would make it to the second year."

Sara looked at her, surprised. "That's hard for me to imagine. You're so close now."

"My mother used to tell me that nothing worth having was easy. When I look back now, she may have been right. Mandy and I were living on the ranch in a little trailer out near the road. The trailer had originally been put there for ranch hands, so you can imagine the condition it was in, but we didn't care. We were young and told ourselves it would be fun to fix up. I was teaching and Mandy worked the ranch with her father. Being a teacher, I had to be careful about how people perceived me. We told everyone I lived in the trailer, and officially, Mandy was still living at the ranch, even though she spent most nights at the trailer. When I think back about those times, it seems to me that most people knew Mandy was different; they simply never put a label on it. I grew up in San Antonio and was still trying to adapt to small town life. I wasn't used to everyone knowing my business. Sometimes, it's still hard. I swear there are days when people know what I'm going to do ten minutes before I do it."

Sara laughed and picked up some more limbs.

"Anyway, we fell into these roles, I guess you'd call them. When we did, we stopped talking to each other. Then one Saturday morning we had a horrible fight. As soon as she left to go to work, I packed my bags and left. I didn't know where I was going, so I ended up at my parents' house. I didn't say anything to them. They

216

just thought I was there for a visit. Of course, by the time it started getting dark, I had calmed down and was ready to go home. We didn't have a phone in the trailer, so I couldn't call her."

Sara could see Arcy was getting tired and took some of the wood from her. They were almost back at the campsite and she was concerned Arcy wouldn't have time to finish the story. She was grateful when Arcy picked up where she had left off.

"It was while I was driving home that I realized that it was fear that was tearing us apart. I was afraid the school board was going to discover I was living in a lesbian relationship and fire me. I didn't think I was being a good *wife* to Mandy. I was worried about my parents learning the truth about me. When I pulled into the driveway that night, Mandy was sitting on the steps of the trailer. Sara, you probably won't understand the significance of this, but she was crying. I've only seen her cry twice since and that was at her parents' funerals."

"I think I can understand," Sara replied.

"We spent the rest of the night talking, and we made a promise to each other that we would never stop talking to each other again. That's also when we realized we couldn't spend our lives living a lie. We learned the difference between living discreetly and living a lie." She looked into Sara's eyes. "There comes a point when you have to face your fears or they'll devour you."

Chapter Thirty-six

As soon as the campsite was set up, Mandy pulled a pair of binoculars from her saddlebag and announced that she and Arcy were going bird-watching and would return in a couple of hours.

"Do you think they're really going bird-watching?" Taylor asked, as soon as the couple was out of sight.

"Why wouldn't they be?"

"I don't know. It seems kind of strange to ride all the way out here just to bird-watch when they could watch the same birds from their living-room window."

Sara was sitting on a rock she had rolled up from over by the river. "Did you know that this is where they came for their third date?"

Taylor flopped down on the ground beside her and grimaced as she grabbed her inner thigh.

Sara pretended not to notice. She was sore too, but the walk she and Arcy had taken searching for wood seemed to have helped.

"Mandy told me this is where they first made love."

"She told you that?" Sara asked, surprised.

"More or less, but I knew what she was talking about." She twisted around as if she were having trouble getting comfortable.

Sara rolled her eyes. "I'll bet you did. I suppose you told her about the time you and that swimmer were nearly caught in the pool while you were in college."

"No, I didn't tell her any of that stuff." She slowly got up. "Do you want to go for a walk? I'm getting so stiff and sore I can hardly move."

"Sure, we can gather some more wood while we're at it." As they walked, Sara considered telling Taylor what Arcy had told her about fear, but she wasn't sure how to bring it up. The last time they had attempted to talk hadn't gone very well. It would be horrible to have a fight out here and have to spend the rest of the weekend pretending that nothing was wrong.

"What are you thinking about?" Taylor asked suddenly.

"Us," she answered without thinking.

"You know I care for you, but I have a crappy track record with relationships. I can't take that chance with you."

Sara picked a stick up but dropped it. "Have you ever gone into a store and had to try on five or six pairs of shoes before you found the ones that fit perfectly?"

Taylor glanced at her. "Do you think you are those shoes?"

"I don't know. You haven't tried them on yet." She stopped.

Taylor looked back at her. "Why did you stop?"

Sara took a deep breath and slowly released it. "I want you to kiss me."

"Here?"

"Here or there, I don't care where you're standing when you do it, just kiss me."

Taylor ran a hand over the back of her neck and backed away. "Sara, we agreed."

"I'm breaking that agreement. Don't you see? I'm falling in love with you. I'm tired of just being your friend. Oh, the hell with it. If I keep waiting on you, I'll be too damn old to kiss you." Sara grabbed Taylor and kissed her. Taylor's initial feeble protests quickly melted away as Sara slid her arms around her waist. When Sara felt her kisses being returned, she made up her mind. If this relationship was ever going to get started it would be up to her to make it happen. As their kisses grew more passionate, Sara slipped her hands up Taylor's sides, allowing her thumbs to linger on the sides of her breasts. Taylor tensed slightly and Sara moved her hands to Taylor's back. She took a chance and began to kiss Taylor's neck, moving slowly but deliberately toward the opening in her shirt. When she pressed her lips to the bare skin just above the bra, Sara forced herself to move slowly. She kissed her way back up to Taylor's lips, gently using her tongue to gain more access, as her fingers released the top two buttons of Taylor's shirt.

When Taylor made a weak attempt to pull away, Sara stopped but kept her hand between their bodies. She knew from years of trying on clothes together in department store dressing rooms that Taylor preferred bras that fastened in front. With a slight brush of her thumb, she checked for the hooks and almost shouted when she found them. She took her time in arranging her fingers into position. When she was ready, she popped the hooks opened and pushed the material away in one quick move. Before Taylor could protest, Sara had the nipple in her mouth, and from that point on, there was no turning back.

Taylor's hands clasped Sara's head. "That was a dirty trick," she murmured. She pulled Sara's head up and kissed her before pushing her to the grass. "You asked for this, so I'll leave it up to you to explain the grass stains all over your butt."

Taylor kissed her with a new intensity that left Sara struggling to breathe. When Taylor unbuttoned Sara's blouse she didn't stop at two buttons and she didn't stop with the blouse, the pants, underwear or even the sneakers. By the time she was finished, Sara was naked and her clothes were beneath her.

"That's better," Taylor whispered as she leaned over, teasing Sara's collarbone with her tongue. "I've dreamed of this so many times." She licked her way to first one breast and then the other, slowly circling the nipples until they grew rigid and so sensitive that Sara quivered with each touch. She shifted slightly and opened Sara's legs.

Sara gasped as the cool breeze hit her throbbing center. That sensation was nothing compared to the one that occurred when Taylor lowered her head and ran her tongue along the inside of her thighs. She tried to grab Taylor's head to pull her closer, but this time Taylor was having her own way. With slow deliberation, she kept moving toward her goal until Sara was practically begging. She used her hands to part Sara's swollen lips, then started a slow lapping motion. When she began a subtle combination of sucking and stroking, Sara felt herself losing control. She tried to hold on, but Taylor simply went after her harder. The treetops seemed to swirl out of control as the orgasm sent Sara spiraling into a whirlpool of pleasure. Slowly she made her way back, but Taylor wasn't ready to relinquish her prize.

"I want to touch you," Sara murmured.

Taylor ignored her and continued her feast. It didn't take long for Taylor's magic to have Sara teetering on the brink again. Only after Sara came the second time did Taylor finally give up her spot and lie down beside her.

Sara didn't give her time to get comfortable before she unfastened Taylor's jeans and slid a hand inside. She smiled as her fingers slipped through the creamy evidence of Taylor's passion. Sara pulled a nipple into her mouth and began a slow rhythmic stroke with her fingers. It wasn't long before Taylor was frantically struggling to push her jeans down to her ankles, where the stubborn boots refused to release them. When the first wave of pleasure hit Taylor, Sara twisted around until her head was by Taylor's hips and replaced her fingers with her tongue. As the second orgasm hit, Sara buried her face deeper between Taylor's legs.

She was surprised when Taylor grabbed her by the legs, slid between them and pulled her down to her mouth. Sara had heard of this position, but she had never before tried it. She found herself wavering between giving and receiving pleasure. When their motions synchronized and their bodies seemed to merge into one, Sara let her body take over as it was pleasured from both ends.

Afterward they lay in an exhausted huddle. "Do you realize what we're going to have to do now?" Taylor asked.

"Get dressed and go back to camp."

"They'll smell us ten minutes before we get there."

Sara sat up, confused. As she did so, the musky scent of sex tickled her nostrils. "What are we going to do?"

"Go swimming."

"Are you crazy? Arcy said that river was fed from a natural spring. The water is freezing."

"I'm open to other suggestions," Taylor said, as she kissed Sara's nose. "We need to get back. We've been gone for a while. They might start worrying about us."

Sara sighed and began to pull her blouse, pants and shoes back on. "We didn't plan this very well," she said, as she gathered her underwear.

They scurried through the trees, keeping a sharp eye out for Mandy or Arcy. When they reached the water, Taylor started stripping. "Jump in fast and it'll be just like the pool was when we were kids."

"As I recall the water at the pool was cold," Sara said and undressed.

"Give me your hand. We'll jump on three."

Sara took Taylor's hand and nodded. "We jump when you say three, right?"

"That's right."

"Are you ready?"

"Yes."

Taylor began to count. "One . . . two . . ." Without warning, she pushed Sara in and jumped in behind her.

The water was colder than Sara could have possibly imagined. She was amazed that Taylor was trying to pull her toward the center of the river, but the water was too cold. Sara wanted out.

She quickly realized that trying to fight Taylor was useless. She was much too strong. As they neared the center of the river, the water did seem to get a little warmer. Sara realized it was because they were now out from beneath the trees and in the sun. Even with the sun, her teeth were still chattering. She rinsed off as quickly as possible and scurried back to the bank.

"There's a big rock over to the left that's in the sun. We can sit on it until we dry off," Taylor said, as she continued to swim.

Sara snatched up their clothes and picked her way over to it. "How can you stand to stay in there?"

"It feels good once you get used to it."

"You're crazy." She pulled her clothes on quickly before lying back on the rock and letting her skin soak up its warmth. "Ah. Now this feels better." Sara enjoyed the warmth of the rock while watching Taylor swim to the opposite bank that was only about ten feet away. Taylor made several more laps before stepping out of the water. Sara's breath caught as she watched her walk over to the rock. "Arcy's right. You do have a classy chassis."

Taylor looked at her and laughed when Sara explained.

"Your chassis isn't so bad either," Taylor said before kissing her. "Are you dry already?" she asked, as she stepped back and tried to shake some of the water from her hair.

"I was until a moment ago."

Taylor looked at her and smiled. "I never knew you were such a naughty girl."

"There's a lot about me you don't know."

"Maybe it's time I found out a little more." She started toward Sara.

"Don't you even think about doing anything, if you intend to make me jump back into that river," Sara warned.

"Damn. I've heard of lesbian bed death, but I've never heard of a case happening so soon."

Sara hopped off the rock and kissed her. "As soon as we get back to civilization, I'm positive the bed can be revived. Let's hope you can be too, once I'm finished with you."

Chapter Thirty-seven

On the way back to the campsite, Sara and Taylor picked up as many dead limbs as they could carry. They were surprised to find that Mandy and Arcy had not yet returned to camp.

"I hope they're all right." Sara dropped her armload of wood down beside the firepit and brushed bits of dead bark off her arms.

"I'm sure they are," Taylor said, adding her wood to the pile.

"How long have they been gone?"

Taylor looked at her watch. "It's a little after one now. So they've been gone about three hours." She sat on her rolled-up sleeping bag. "I hope they get back soon. I'm starting to get hungry."

"I meant to ask you, did you notice any food when you and Mandy were unpacking the mule?"

Taylor looked at her thoughtfully. "No, I didn't actually. There were two smaller bags that held the ground cover and another tarp we can use in case it starts to rain. Then there were the two bags that you and Arcy took."

"One of those was pots and pans, and the other was their clothes, a small radio and some other little miscellaneous things like that. I didn't see any food."

"They must have forgotten to put it on the mule," Taylor said.

Sara felt a moment of dread. Someone was going to have to ride all the way back for it. That meant they wouldn't be eating for at least four hours.

"Are you two still sitting around here?" Mandy called out from behind them.

Sara and Taylor jumped, startled by her sudden appearance.

Sara couldn't help but notice that both women had a definite glow about them. Somehow, she didn't think it had anything to do with the walk or bird-watching. "We've been working hard at gathering firewood," Sara protested.

Mandy looked at the small pile of wood and grunted.

"I don't know about anyone else, but all this fresh air has given me an appetite," Arcy declared. "How about a sandwich?"

"Sounds good to me," Mandy said. "You two come and give me a hand."

Sara and Taylor exchanged glances before following Mandy down to the river.

"Grab ahold of that rope up there," Mandy said and pointed to a rope that was tied off around a young cypress tree. Once they both had a hand on it, Mandy nodded. "Okay, pull her up."

Sara followed the rope up to where it was fed through a pulley that was firmly attached to a cypress limb that was thicker than her waist. A large knot had been tied in the free end of the rope to keep it from accidentally slipping out of the pulley. Together she and Taylor hauled a four-foot-by-three-foot metal box out of the water.

Mandy reached out and grabbed the box. "Okay, let it down slow."

"It's like a cistern," Sara said, and laughed.

Taylor looked at her.

"Years ago, before iceboxes," Sara began, "people would keep their milk cool by sealing it inside a jar or cream can and lowering

225

it into their cisterns or, sometimes, wells. The water was cold enough to keep the milk from spoiling."

"This baby works better than the refrigerator at home," Mandy said, tapping the box. We store everything in plastic, just in case the box should spring a leak, but so far we've never had a problem." She removed three square plastic boxes and another gallon-sized plastic container of tea. "We also have beer, sodas, and bottled water." They all agreed to tea. Mandy closed the metal box before it was lowered back into the river.

By the time they made it back to the campsite, Arcy had spread out a large tablecloth on the grass and stacked the plates, glasses and a roll of paper towels in the center.

Sara couldn't help but marvel as Arcy took the boxes from Mandy. One box held several slices of bread, the second box had a variety of luncheon meats and a package of sliced cheese, and the third box was a virtual smorgasbord of condiments in those small plastic packets.

"How did you get all of this up here?" Taylor asked, as she built herself a hefty sandwich.

"We brought it up in the truck last night."

"Truck?" Taylor asked. "How did you get a truck in here?"

Mandy chuckled as she passed around glasses of tea. "There's a road right over there." She pointed in the direction in which Sara and Taylor had gone earlier that day.

Sara choked on the sip of tea she had just taken. How close had they been to the road when they were making love? She was positive no one had driven by while they were out there.

"It's a field road," Mandy said.

Sara wasn't certain, but she thought she saw Mandy wink at Arcy. Could they have been walking along that road? Her face flushed. She glanced over and saw Taylor staring at her.

Later that night, as the four of them lay in their sleeping bags around the campfire that had burned down to glowing embers,

Taylor gave a sigh of contentment. "Have you ever seen anything as beautiful as that sky?" she said to the group.

"You and Sara will have to come back in August during the meteor showers," Arcy said. "We've seen some wonderful showers."

"We'd like that, thank you."

Sara smiled. She liked the sound of that *we*.

Silence settled over the little group and it wasn't long before she heard the steady breathing that told her Mandy and Arcy were asleep. Taylor's hand reached through the darkness and gently closed over hers. A sense of peace descended over her as she hugged Taylor's hand to her and fell asleep.

Epilogue
Eleven Months Later

"Do you think they'll ever pave this road?" Taylor asked.

"I doubt it. It doesn't handle enough traffic." Sara eased the truck over to miss a rough spot and hit a hole. "I've sort of gotten used to it."

Taylor grabbed onto the door. "I still say I should open a practice out here."

"It was nice of Mandy and Arcy to invite us out today," Sara said, as she slowed to pull into the driveway. "Here comes Roscoe."

"Mandy won't be far behind."

True to Taylor's prediction, Mandy stepped out onto the porch.

"It's the Island Girls," Mandy called out as they started toward the porch.

"Three days until liftoff," Sara said, waving her arms over her head in celebration. She and Taylor were going to Maui for two weeks for a slightly early celebration of their first anniversary.

Arcy joined Mandy on the porch and began an exaggerated hula. Taylor was quick to join in. Within seconds, their antics had Roscoe racing around the yard barking.

"You two are scaring the dog," Mandy said and waved them inside.

Taylor threw an arm over the shoulders of the older women. "Arcy, you should leave this old homebody here and come with us," she teased. "We'll spend all day on the beach watching girls and soaking up the warm sunshine."

"I wouldn't even make it to Dallas before I missed her so bad I'd have to turn around and come home," Arcy admitted.

"Mandy, you're a lucky woman," Taylor said, as she kissed Arcy's cheek.

"Don't I know it." Mandy chuckled.

As soon as they were seated in the living room, with large glasses of sweet tea to quench their thirst, Mandy glanced at Arcy with a questioning look.

Sara saw the exchange and wondered what was going on.

"Go ahead, dear," Arcy said. "You know you won't be able to keep still until after dinner."

"What's going on?" Sara asked.

"We're starting a new business," Mandy announced. "Sara, I finally took your advice."

Sara looked at her, confused. "You took my advice?"

"Yes. We've talked to Denise Underwood and we're going to form a partnership and raise quarter horses."

"That's wonderful," Taylor and Sara exclaimed at once.

"If things work out the way we hope, we won't have to sell off any land and the place will be in good hands, after we're gone," Mandy explained.

"Denise loves this area of the country and she seems to know horses," Arcy said. "That little spot of land she has is nowhere big enough for raising horses. She's going to quit her job and work on the ranch."

"We get a full-time ranch hand and she gets to start her dream job ten years earlier than she had hoped to," Mandy added.

"It sounds like a win-win situation," Taylor said.

Sara had a moment of trepidation. She and Taylor loved their visits with Mandy and Arcy. She wondered if Denise being around would make Taylor feel uncomfortable. Sara hadn't seen or talked to Denise since that one night they had together and that was fine. She tried to imagine what it would be like to see her again and felt nothing but a distant, warm glow. The two stipulations she had given Denise that night came back to her—no ties and whatever friendship developed would remain intact.

Taylor took Sara's hand. "For what it's worth, I think it's a great idea."

Sara looked at her and smiled. Taylor would be fine and so would she. "Me too," she agreed.

Mandy continued to regale them with plans for the ranch's future. Arcy would occasionally slip out of the room to check on dinner.

After enjoying a sumptuous meal of barbecued chicken with sautéed squash, the group drifted to the front porch where they sat laughing and talking until almost midnight.

When they were preparing to leave, Mandy motioned for Sara to follow her inside. Mandy took a small white jeweler's box from the fireplace mantel. "We wanted to give you this as a kind of thank-you gift."

"For what?" Sara asked.

"Well, it was your idea that got us to thinking about Denise. We really believe she'll come to love this place as much as we do."

"Thank you, but I didn't do anything."

"You've done more than you'll ever know," Arcy said from behind her.

Sara turned and saw that the other two had joined them. She opened the box. Inside was a gleaming gold double eagle, dated

1865. It was encased in a rather oddly shaped, yet beautiful gold case with clear inserts that provided protection and yet allowed the coin's features to shine through. Her breath caught when she saw what it was. She looked at Mandy and then to Arcy. "It's beautiful, thank you."

"It can be made into a necklace by running a chain through here," Mandy explained, as she pointed out the unusual opening at the top.

Sara felt torn. The gift was obviously expensive. She felt compelled to protest it was too much, but she didn't want to hurt their feelings. *Take it in good grace*, she told herself. "Where did you ever find such a gorgeous—" She gasped as she realized that the case was made to resemble an old well bucket. "You found—"

Mandy placed a finger over Sara's lips. "Some things are better left unsaid," she replied. The historian in Sara began to twitch, but she forced her curiosity down and hugged Mandy and then Arcy tightly. "I'll always treasure it," she whispered, as she fought back tears.

"Look at it anytime you find yourself forgetting what the real treasures in life are," Mandy said in a voice thick with emotion.

"I will," she promised. "I'll always cherish this, but it's you and Arcy who have already shown me the importance of following my heart without being afraid."

Mandy blushed and looked at Arcy with eyes brimming with love.

After another round of hugs and warm wishes, Sara and Taylor left. As they drove out of the driveway, Sara glanced into her rearview mirror to see the silhouette of the couple standing on the porch arm in arm. She smiled as she pulled out onto the bumpy road with Taylor beside her.

Publications from
BELLA BOOKS, INC.
The best in contemporary lesbian fiction

P.O. Box 10543, Tallahassee, FL 32302
Phone: 800-729-4992
www.bellabooks.com

THE KILLING ROOM by Gerri Hill. 392 pp. How can two women forget and go their separate ways?   1-59493-050-3 $12.95

PASSIONATE KISSES by Megan Carter. 240 pp. Will two old friends run from love?
     1-59493-051-1 $12.95

ALWAYS AND FOREVER by Lyn Denison. 224 pp. The girl next door turns Shannon's world upside down.   1-59493-049-X $12.95

BACK TALK by Saxon Bennett. 200 pp. Can a talk show host find love after heartbreak?
     1-59493-028-7 $12.95

THE PERFECT VALENTINE: EROTIC LESBIAN VALENTINE STORIES edited by Barbara Johnson and Therese Szymanski—from Bella After Dark. 328 pp. Stories from the hottest writers around.   1-59493-061-9 $14.95

MURDER AT RANDOM by Claire McNab. 200 pp. The Sixth Denise Cleever Thriller. Denise realizes the fate of thousands is in her hands.   1-59493-047-3 $12.95

THE TIDES OF PASSION by Diana Tremain Braund. 240 pp. Will Susan be able to hold it all together and find the one woman who touches her soul?   1-59493-048-1 $12.95

JUST LIKE THAT by Karin Kallmaker. 240 pp. Disliking each other—and everything they stand for—even before they meet, Toni and Syrah find feelings can change, just like that.
1-59493-025-2 $12.95

WHEN FIRST WE PRACTICE by Therese Szymanski. 200 pp. Brett and Allie are once again caught in the middle of murder and intrigue.   1-59493-045-7 $12.95

REUNION by Jane Frances. 240 pp. Cathy Braithwaite seems to have it all: good looks, money and a thriving accounting practice . . .   1-59493-046-5 $12.95

BELL, BOOK & DYKE: NEW EXPLOITS OF MAGICAL LESBIANS by Kallmaker, Watts, Johnson and Szymanski. 360 pp. Reluctant witches, tempting spells and skyclad beauties—delve into the mysteries of love, lust and power in this quartet of novellas.
     1-59493-023-6 $14.95

ARTIST'S DREAM by Gerri Hill. 320 pp.When Cassie meets Luke Winston, she can no longer deny her attraction to women . . .   1-59493-042-2 $12.95

NO EVIDENCE by Nancy Sanra. 240 pp. Private Investigator Tally McGinnis once again returns to the horror-filled world of a serial killer.   1-59493-043-04 $12.95

WHEN LOVE FINDS A HOME by Megan Carter. 280 pp. What will it take for Anna and Rona to find their way back to each other again?   1-59493-041-4 $12.95

MEMORIES TO DIE FOR by Adrian Gold. 240 pp. Rachel attempts to avoid her attraction to the charms of Anna Sigurdson . . .   1-59493-038-4 $12.95

SILENT HEART by Claire McNab. 280 pp. Exotic lesbian romance.

1-59493-044-9 $12.95

MIDNIGHT RAIN by Peggy J. Herring. 240 pp. Bridget McBee is determined to find the woman who saved her life.   1-59493-021-X $12.95

THE MISSING PAGE A Brenda Strange Mystery by Patty G. Henderson. 240 pp. Brenda investigates her client's murder . . .   1-59493-004-X $12.95

WHISPERS ON THE WIND by Frankie J. Jones. 240 pp. Dixon thinks she and her best friend, Elizabeth Colter, would make the perfect couple . . .   1-59493-037-6 $12.95

CALL OF THE DARK: EROTIC LESBIAN TALES OF THE SUPERNATURAL edited by Therese Szymanski—from Bella After Dark. 320 pp.   1-59493-040-6 $14.95

A TIME TO CAST AWAY A Helen Black Mystery by Pat Welch. 240 pp. Helen stops by Alice's apartment—only to find the woman dead . . .   1-59493-036-8 $12.95

DESERT OF THE HEART by Jane Rule. 224 pp. The book that launched the most popular lesbian movie of all time is back.   1-1-59493-035-X $12.95

THE NEXT WORLD by Ursula Steck. 240 pp. Anna's friend Mido is threatened and eventually disappears . . .   1-59493-024-4 $12.95

CALL SHOTGUN by Jaime Clevenger. 240 pp. Kelly gets pulled back into the world of private investigation . . .   1-59493-016-3 $12.95

52 PICKUP by Bonnie J. Morris and E.B. Casey. 240 pp. 52 hot, romantic tales—one for every Saturday night of the year.   1-59493-026-0 $12.95

GOLD FEVER by Lyn Denison. 240 pp. Kate's first love, Ashley, returns to their home town, where Kate now lives . . .   1-1-59493-039-2 $12.95

RISKY INVESTMENT by Beth Moore. 240 pp. Lynn's best friend and roommate needs her to pretend Chris is his fiancé. But nothing is ever easy.   1-59493-019-8 $12.95

HUNTER'S WAY by Gerri Hill. 240 pp. Homicide detective Tori Hunter is forced to team up with the hot-tempered Samantha Kennedy.   1-59493-018-X $12.95

CAR POOL by Karin Kallmaker. 240 pp. Soft shoulders, merging traffic and slippery when wet . . . Anthea and Shay find love in the car pool.   1-59493-013-9 $12.95

NO SISTER OF MINE by Jeanne G'Fellers. 240 pp. Telepathic women fight to coexist with a patriarchal society that wishes their eradication.   ISBN 1-59493-017-1 $12.95

ON THE WINGS OF LOVE by Megan Carter. 240 pp. Stacie's reporting career is on the rocks. She has to interview bestselling author Cheryl, or else!   ISBN 1-59493-027-9 $12.95

WICKED GOOD TIME by Diana Tremain Braund. 224 pp. Does Christina need Miki as a protector . . . or want her as a lover?   ISBN 1-59493-031-7 $12.95

THOSE WHO WAIT by Peggy J. Herring. 240 pp. Two brilliant sisters—in love with the same woman!   ISBN 1-59493-032-5 $12.95

ABBY'S PASSION by Jackie Calhoun. 240 pp. Abby's bipolar sister helps turn her world upside down, so she must decide what's most important.   ISBN 1-59493-014-7 $12.95

PICTURE PERFECT by Jane Vollbrecht. 240 pp. Kate is reintroduced to Casey, the daughter of an old friend. Can they withstand Kate's career?   ISBN 1-59493-015-5 $12.95

PAPERBACK ROMANCE by Karin Kallmaker. 240 pp. Carolyn falls for tall, dark and . . . female . . . in this classic lesbian romance.   ISBN 1-59493-033-3 $12.95

DAWN OF CHANGE by Gerri Hill. 240 pp. Susan ran away to find peace in remote Kings Canyon—then she met Shawn . . .   ISBN 1-59493-011-2 $12.95

DOWN THE RABBIT HOLE by Lynne Jamneck. 240 pp. Is a killer holding a grudge against FBI Agent Samantha Skellar?   ISBN 1-59493-012-0 $12.95

SEASONS OF THE HEART by Jackie Calhoun. 240 pp. Overwhelmed, Sara saw only one way out—leaving . . .   ISBN 1-59493-030-9 $12.95

TURNING THE TABLES by Jessica Thomas. 240 pp. The 2nd Alex Peres Mystery. *From ghosties and ghoulies and long leggity beasties* . . .   ISBN 1-59493-009-0 $12.95

FOR EVERY SEASON by Frankie Jones. 240 pp. Andi, who is investigating a 65-year-old murder, meets Janice, a charming district attorney . . .   ISBN 1-59493-010-4 $12.95

LOVE ON THE LINE by Laura DeHart Young. 240 pp. Kay leaves a younger woman behind to go on a mission to Alaska . . . will she regret it?   ISBN 1-59493-008-2 $12.95

UNDER THE SOUTHERN CROSS by Claire McNab. 200 pp. Lee, an American travel agent, goes down under and meets Australian Alex, and the sparks fly under the Southern Cross.   ISBN 1-59493-029-5 $12.95

SUGAR by Karin Kallmaker. 240 pp. Three women want sugar from Sugar, who can't make up her mind.   ISBN 1-59493-001-5 $12.95

FALL GUY by Claire McNab. 200 pp. 16th Detective Inspector Carol Ashton Mystery.   ISBN 1-59493-000-7 $12.95

ONE SUMMER NIGHT by Gerri Hill. 232 pp. Johanna swore to never fall in love again—but then she met the charming Kelly . . .   ISBN 1-59493-007-4 $12.95

TALK OF THE TOWN TOO by Saxon Bennett. 181 pp. Second in the series about wild and fun loving friends.   ISBN 1-931513-77-5 $12.95

LOVE SPEAKS HER NAME by Laura DeHart Young. 170 pp. Love and friendship, desire and intrigue, spark this exciting sequel to *Forever and the Night*.   ISBN 1-59493-002-3 $12.95

TO HAVE AND TO HOLD by Peggy J. Herring. 184 pp. By finally letting down her defenses, will Dorian be opening herself to a devastating betrayal?   ISBN 1-59493-005-8 $12.95

WILD THINGS by Karin Kallmaker. 228 pp. Dutiful daughter Faith has met the perfect man. There's just one problem: she's in love with his sister.   ISBN 1-931513-64-3 $12.95

SHARED WINDS by Kenna White. 216 pp. Can Emma rebuild more than just Lanny's marina?   ISBN 1-59493-006-6 $12.95

THE UNKNOWN MILE by Jaime Clevenger. 253 pp. Kelly's world is getting more and more complicated every moment.   ISBN 1-931513-57-0 $12.95

TREASURED PAST by Linda Hill. 189 pp. A shared passion for antiques leads to love.   ISBN 1-59493-003-1 $12.95

SIERRA CITY by Gerri Hill. 284 pp. Chris and Jesse cannot deny their growing attraction . . .   ISBN 1-931513-98-8 $12.95